Why did the in a thousand miles end up in his camp?

He hadn't seen a white woman for three years. And he hadn't see one cry since Elizabeth. Delia had made him remember. Damn her for coming to the mountains.

He glanced up at the cedars swaying in the wind. There was no one to help him. Here a man did it alone or did without. He straightened as a rustling sound intruded.

"Mr. Nash?" Her voice was soft, like a kiss.

He couldn't look into those sad brown eyes again. They were the same color as fine whiskey and he could get drunk just looking at them.

He faced her and was instantly sorry. "What?"

"I can only imagine your shock at my arrival. I do not wish to be a nuisance—"

His smile was humorless. "Lady, mosquitoes are a nuisance. You're a full-blown catastrophe."

* * *

Winter Woman
Harlequin Historical #671—September 2003

**Harlequin Historicals is proud
to present new author**

JENNA KERNAN

**DON'T MISS THESE OTHER
TITLES AVAILABLE NOW:**

Jenna Kernan

Winter Woman

HARLEQUIN®

TORONTO • NEW YORK • LONDON
AMSTERDAM • PARIS • SYDNEY • HAMBURG
STOCKHOLM • ATHENS • TOKYO • MILAN • MADRID
PRAGUE • WARSAW • BUDAPEST • AUCKLAND

ISBN 0-373-29271-6

WINTER WOMAN

Copyright © 2003 by Jeannette H. Monaco

This edition published by arrangement with Harlequin Books S.A.

® and TM are trademarks of the publisher. Trademarks indicated with ® are registered in the United States Patent and Trademark Office, the Canadian Trade Marks Office and in other countries.

Visit us at www.eHarlequin.com

Printed in U.S.A.

Please address questions and book requests to:
Harlequin Reader Service
U.S.: 3010 Walden Ave., P.O. Box 1325, Buffalo, NY 14269
Canadian: P.O. Box 609, Fort Erie, Ont. L2A 5X3

My deepest appreciation to my first readers:
Terry and Margaret, the Hudson River
Romance Writers of America and my husband, Jim.

Many thanks to my editors, Ann Leslie Tuttle and
Jessica Regante, for their extraordinary work with this story.

And finally to those readers who enjoy
a sweeping adventure, I dedicate this story.

Chapter One

Rocky Mountains, April 1835

The instant he saw movement, Thomas Nash reached for his Hawkins rifle. He stood knee-deep in the stream with the rifle sighted on the center of the Indian's chest.

The man raised his open hand in greeting. *Flathead,* Nash thought and lowered his gun. He raised his hand as well. *Damn, I hope they didn't rob my traps.*

"Howdy," he said, and then he repeated his welcome in the man's dialect.

The man spoke in Flathead. "You are Nash?"

"Yes."

"We have been looking for you."

Nash glanced around but saw no other Indians. His attention focused on the man before him. "Why?"

"We have something that belongs with you. Come."

Nash's mind briefly flicked back to the six traps

he'd dropped into the river when the Blackfoot Indians attacked him two weeks ago.

He sloshed out of the stream and headed back up the hill. Most Indians he knew traded with or stole from trappers. He never knew one to give anything away.

Nash led the way to camp.

On the log beside his wigwam sat a woman wrapped in a dirty quilt.

"What the hell?"

At his appearance she stood. He stared at the baggy brown dress, which appeared to belong to someone larger. Her skin was sallow and she was as skinny as a wolf in February. He'd seen stray cats with more meat on them. Lordy, it hurt just to look at her.

"We found this white woman. You are the only white man here. We brought her to you."

Nash shot a glance at the man, then pinned his gaze on the waif before him. "To me! I don't want her."

"Do all white women have this yellow hair?"

He glanced at her pale blond locks. "Damn few— rare as ermine pelts."

"This woman has no man. She has no horse. Yet she survived the winter, alone."

"Impossible."

"Yes. Still this one survived. We do not know how. She has great powers, so she will bring you luck."

"Women don't bring luck. I can't take her."

"Hunts Buffalo and I think she belongs with her people. Such a special woman deserves to go home. We would take her, only we are going to war with the Blackfoot now. Perhaps later."

Nash flapped an arm in frustration. "Well, what am I supposed to do with her?"

"Feed her. She is very hungry."

The trapper turned his hard gaze upon her. "Where's your people?"

Cordelia Channing's jaw dropped open. English. How long had it been since she'd heard English? John's voice rose in her mind. *Don't fret Cordelia. I'll bag an elk and be back by nightfall. I just don't fancy going up the pass without a full larder. Snows come early in the mountains.* And oh, how they had come. The whole world had turned gray and she'd been buried alive in a cold white blanket.

"What's wrong? You addled?" His voice snapped her back to attention. "What're you doing up here alone?" He scowled, looking strong as a buffalo and just as dangerous.

"Our wagon train was headed west. My husband meant to minister to the savages."

"Where's he at?"

A vivid image of the last time she'd seen John flashed in her mind. Would the memory never leave her? Tears burned the back of her throat and brimmed in her eyes. Her lip trembled as she kept the cries buried deep in her throat. She shook her head.

"Gone."

"Gone left or gone dead?"

She stared at his scowling face a moment in shock. "I found his remains last October."

Nash leaned forward. "Not Indians, or they'd have you, too." He scratched his chin and regarded her. "Grizzly?"

Fifteen days after his disappearance she'd found John's body. Scavengers had eaten at his corpse. She shuddered. "I don't know."

"I'm real sorry for your loss," said the trapper, his frown unwavering.

Her voice sounded brittle as autumn leaves blown across bedrock. "What will happen to me now?"

"You'll stay with me."

"Will you take me East?"

He shook his head. "Not until fall."

Her eyes flew to her rescuers. "Will they?"

"They're going to war with the Blackfoot. You can't go."

The Indian she knew as Hawk Feathers squatted before her and patted her cheek. His sad eyes spoke to her. She smiled.

"Thank you," she said.

"Gordeela," he said, and lifted a hand in farewell. The other man nodded his goodbye. She watched them grip the horses' manes and leap astride. In a moment they were gone, melted into the evergreens. How differently she felt seeing them go. Five days earlier, when they'd appeared in her meadow, hope and horror mingled. They were the first human beings she'd seen in seven months. Her food was nearly gone. Yet, she feared capture. In the end she recognized them as her last chance. Without immediate help, she'd die beside her roofless hut and mired wagon, so she'd crossed the meadow to meet her fate. And they'd rescued her.

The trapper pushed his wide-brimmed leather hat back on his head. She studied his eyes. They were clear blue, like a glass medicine bottle. The small lines near the corners were the only part of his face not tanned. A close-trimmed beard covered his square jaw. She guessed he was not yet thirty. His muscular body was clad entirely in soft brown buckskin. Both shirt and britches were trimmed in a long fringe. About his shoulders a powder horn and shoulder bag crisscrossed. A leather belt cinched his narrow waist and held a variety of objects including a long knife and smaller pouches. *My word, he is the tallest man I've ever seen.*

"How'd ya know them two was Flathead?" he asked.

Cordelia puzzled a moment, lifting a finger to her chin. "Flat heads?"

"Good Lord Almighty—you didn't know if they was Flathead or Blackfoot?"

She shook her head and watched his face redden.

"Don't you know that Blackfoot hate whites and would have as likely scalped ya as helped ya?"

She lowered her head. "No one else came. You have only to look at me to know I would not have lasted long alone. I feel this deep within myself and so you see, it did not matter if they planned to kill me. I have made my peace with God."

He dragged the hat from his head and choked it in both hands. "You're either the bravest or the stupidest woman I ever met. There're worse things than dying, ya know."

She gave him a hard stare as an image of her husband's body, mauled by beasts flashed in her mind. She remembered the snows that covered the canvas roof of her rude cabin and stovepipe, leaving her in darkness. She knew about fates worse than death.

He scratched his beard in silence, waiting, and then turned away. As he arranged wood for a fire, she studied him. His mink-colored hair hung down to his shoulder blades. She tried to see his face. Between the beard and shaggy mane, she could distinguish very little.

What kind of man was this?

"What's your name?" he asked.

"Channing. Mrs. Cordelia Channing."

She stood and extended her hand. He stared at it for a moment as if he expected her to perform some magic trick, then grasped it. She watched her hand disappear in his. The heat from his body radiated up her arm and she thought of John. Her husband's hands were fine and gentle, not rough like this trapper's. She released her grip and he did the same.

"I'm Nash."

"Mr. Nash—"

"No mister. Just Nash."

"I see. Well Nash, what will happen now?" She stood still before him, tugging repeatedly at the frayed sleeve of her dress.

"Those fellas think you got no kin. You got people back East?"

She felt as if a hand squeezed her windpipe. The tears welled up. John's image swam before her. They'd married prior to their departure to minister to the savages. A good match he'd said, he an orphan and she an only child. No one at home to miss them. Hot droplets of pain washed her cheeks.

"Damn. Now stop that." Nash backed away as if her tears were contagious.

''I am sorry,'' she said. ''The Indians were correct. I have no kin.''

He stood several paces away with his arms folded before him like a shield. He rocked slightly as his fingers scratched his beard. He kept his distance, like a lone wolf at the edge of a camp, until she cried herself out.

Her husband had been the funniest, warmest man in the world. She glanced at the trapper. Nash—the sound of teeth grinding together. The name suited him.

Why did the only white woman in a thousand miles end up in his camp? Nash hadn't seen a white woman for three years. And he hadn't seen one cry since Elizabeth. He splashed the running water onto his face with one hand, and then sank down beside the stream to think. Elizabeth hadn't cried in the street when the carriage ran her down, gashing her thigh. No, tears came later in the hospital when she realized they'd taken her leg.

He pounded his fist down in the gurgling water. Droplets flew in all directions.

Cordelia Channing had made him remember. Damn her for coming to the mountains.

He glanced up at the cedars swaying in the wind. There was no one to help him. Here, a man did it alone or did without. He straightened as a rustling sound intruded, the sound of long skirts brushing tall grass.

''Mr. Nash?'' Her voice was soft, like a kiss.

He stood and thumped his hat against his knee in frustration. He couldn't look in those sad brown eyes again. They were the same color as fine whiskey and he could get drunk just looking at them.

He faced her and was instantly sorry. "What?"

Her smile was sweet like April rain. "I'd like to apologize for my hysterics."

He scooped up his gun. "It's understandable."

She stood a few feet away, waiting. He rubbed his nose. "Now what?"

"I can imagine your shock at my arrival. I do not wish to be a nuisance but—"

"Lady, mosquitoes are a nuisance. You're a full-blown catastrophe."

He stepped closer and watched her straighten. Her head reached only to his shoulder. Still, straight as a stick, not a curve in sight, she stood her ground.

"How old are you?" he asked.

"Twenty-five."

His gaze met hers. Liquid eyes studied him. A squeezing ache grabbed hold of his gut.

She cleared her throat. "As I was saying, I realize my presence is an intrusion. I do assure you that I will be glad to part company, if you will just escort me to the nearest trading post or fort."

He snorted and shook his head.

He leaned forward. A wisp of hair had slipped from her braid. The color reminded him of corn silk. His fingers grasped the lock, sliding along the downy surface. Then he tucked the hair behind her ear and stepped back. She blinked and said nothing.

"Nearest fort is five hundred miles."

"We could make it before fall," she said.

"Delia, what do you think I'm doing here? I'm a trapper. I can't spend two months of the season dragging you back to the Missouri.'' She straightened her shoulders and glanced toward the horses. ''Get that thought out of your head. You might have cheated the mountains once, never twice. You'll stay with me until fall.''

She blinked her whiskey eyes and his gaze drifted back to her golden hair sitting upon the body of a boy.

''When the season is done, I'll take you to the Rendezvous.''

''The what?''

''The Rendezvous. All the trappers will be at the gathering to sell their furs and get drunk. You'll probably be the only white woman there. That gives you power. I'd imagine you'd have no trouble finding a way back East, even if you do look like a boy.''

She stared down at herself, her expression a mixture of horror and embarrassment. The tops of her ears turned pink. The color spread across her cheeks and down her thin neck.

''Delia, I—''

''Stop calling me that. My name is Cordelia, you wretched man!'' With that she whirled about and dashed up the hill toward his camp.

Wretched? Was that her idea of name-calling?

He checked his traplines, recovering four beavers, and decided he'd been too hard on her. He should have explained the situation better, gone slow. She'd lost her man and had no family. He was all she had.

''Well, I'm not a nursemaid.'' For the first time since Elizabeth had died, he was afraid. Four years last January, he realized. Could it be so long? Now another woman depended on him.

He glanced skyward and noticed the clouds in the west turning pink. Soon it would be dark.

He stopped before entering his camp to look at her. That dress was pure impractical. The tattered hem dragged on the ground while she tended the fire. He'd seen better-looking feed sacks. She'd need buckskin. Tomorrow he'd look for deer.

He hadn't noticed before that her chin pointed and her nose turned up at the end. The squeezing sensation returned to his gut. This time it traveled all the way to his groin. The firelight gilded her hair.

He thumped the beaver against his leg, so the clatter of the trap chains would get her attention. Her head swiveled toward the sound as he expected. He strode into camp and laid his catch on the grass.

"Too early for a fire," he said.

"I beg your pardon?"

"Sky's still light. This is Blackfoot country. That smoke could draw them from miles."

"I'm sorry. I was cold."

"'Cause there's no meat on you. Next time stomp around. That'll warm you." There were other ways, too. He growled at the thought. She stared at him with huge eyes and he felt as trapped as a leg-locked beaver. He inhaled deeply to catch her scent. He met her cautious gaze with a smile, which felt rusty and unnatural. "You hungry?"

"Yes."

He formed coals into a pile at the fire's edge. Then he cut off all four beaver's tails and skewered them on a green stick and set them to roast.

Her lips pinched together. "Is that what we are eating?"

"I'm fresh out of fat cow."

Her face blanched. "I've had enough beef for a lifetime."

He stared at her a moment. "You don't like beef or beaver? No wonder you're as thin as a pike."

The tails simmered. Blood and fat hissed on the coals.

"Where were you bound?" he asked.

"My husband was a man of the church. He and five other ministers were traveling to Oregon to bring the word of God to the savages."

"Five families in wagons?"

"The men were all single, except for my John."

"Where are they at now?"

"Our wheel broke. We could already see snow on the mountains. A decision was made—"

"To leave you behind."

"To blaze a trail. We were to follow after our wheel was repaired."

"There is no trail through them mountains, least-wise none fit for wagons. Who's your captain?"

"Reverend Harcort led us."

"He been across them mountains?"

"No, but he had a vision. He said we were to establish an outpost and teach the heathens of the coming of our Lord."

"Then he still ain't."

"What?"

"He still ain't been over them mountains. He's dead."

"You have no faith."

"Yes, I do. I believe in my Hawkins rifle and the power of them mountains. I got no time for idiots."

He drew the tails off the coals and set them on the stones to cool.

"I didn't ask to come here," she said.

"Well, I didn't invite you, neither."

He slit the tails down the middle, flaying them into two pieces and handed her half. She held it in two hands.

"Well, go on," he said.

But she didn't do as he said. She put the tail back on a flat rock and clasped her hands. Then she lowered her head and said grace. He groaned.

"Amen," she said. "Do you have a knife and fork?"

"I left it in my pack with the good china."

She stood and walked silently to her blanket pack and rummaged a moment. She returned with two tin plates and silverware. She offered him a plate. He shook his head and took a huge bite from the tail. When the hot juice ran down his beard, she looked away.

Despite her fancy manners, the woman polished off two and a half tails and was eyeing his other half. The Flatheads weren't lying. She was hungry.

"Go on," he said.

"Oh, thank you. This really is delicious."

"You're welcome, Delia."

She gazed at him a moment. "What is your Christian name?"

"Thomas."

"Perhaps, I could call you by that and you could call me Cordelia."

He shook his head. "Delia."

She glanced away.

"Did you have enough to eat?"

"More than my share, I fear."

"You've got some catching up to do."

He kicked dirt on the fire and listened to the hiss. She pulled the shabby quilt tightly about her bony shoulders and shivered.

He turned from her shuddering frame and added more wood to the fire. Under cover of darkness, the rising smoke posed no threat. Then he drew back the leather hide that covered his wigwam.

"Won't the Blackfoot see the flames?" she asked.

"I'm up against a cliff here in a little holler. They'd have to be right on top of us to see the fire."

"My Indians found you," she pointed out.

"That was different. They'd passed by a while back and knew where to look."

"Oh, I see."

This next part would be tricky. He'd be damned if he'd sleep outside. *When had he last lain beside Elizabeth? He wouldn't think about it.* His blood pounded in his ears. His whole body stung. Damn Cordelia for this.

"Women belong at home," he said. "What kind of man drags his woman into such a wilderness?"

"My husband's actions are none of your affair, Mr. Nash." She yawned.

"Let's go to bed," he said.

She looked wide-awake now.

"You shall not touch me, Mr. Nash. I am in mourning."

"Didn't intend to."

He crawled into the tent with his rifle and threw back the buffalo robes. Then he put his butchering knife and pistol beside his head and thrust his legs between the furs.

"You wear your boots to bed?" She sounded shocked. A smile crossed his face. She really was green.

He pointed to the rock before him. "Hell yes! Once I shot a bear that sat on that very ledge. Grizzly was after an elk I took. But he weren't particular. He figured I'd do. Here, a man has got to be ready, always."

She peered over her shoulder into the darkness, then crawled quickly into the wigwam and scooted beneath the furs coming to rest beside him. He chuckled.

"And they ain't boots," he said. "These here are moccasins."

The robe was now up to her nose and her words were muffled. "I see."

"Night, Delia," he said.

"Good night, Mr. Nash."

He growled.

The buffalo robe sagged, forming a kind of divider between them. But he could smell her now. The fragrance of sweet grass, like the hayfield in early summer, surrounded her. He fought the urge to drag her little body to his. He didn't want to bother her; he just craved her scent.

Chapter Two

The next morning Cordelia awoke to the aroma of brewing coffee. She tipped back her head to better inhale the aroma. Then she sat up, feeling stiff from sleeping with nothing but the buffalo skin beneath her. Her neck hurt. She must make a pillow of some kind.

Sorrow descended upon her. John was gone. She swallowed back the bile in her throat.

She stared at the buckskin tent above her and remembered the trapper. Nash was a gentleman. He had not touched her in the night.

Hunger brought her out of bed. She knelt beside the fire for a closer look. When she straightened, she found Nash grinning at her.

"I cooked you something special—johnnycakes, coffee and beaver again."

"It smells wonderful."

She left the fire long enough to find a private place behind the rocks to relieve herself. She returned to her blanket roll of belongings and drew out her tortoiseshell comb. Her fingers loosened her braid.

Slowly she combed her hair beginning at the tips. When the tangles were out, she rapidly divided her hair into three parts and made one thick braid down her back.

She wrinkled her nose.

"Thomas—the cakes are burning!"

His gaze left her and he frowned at the skillet. "Damnation." He flipped one blackened cake out of the pan with his knife. "I'll eat that one." He poked at the remaining cake. "This one's just brown."

"I'd be glad to cook your breakfast from now on," she said.

His tone was angry again. "I cook my own meals. I said I'd eat that one. I like 'em that way."

She stared at the smoking biscuit, then lifted her gaze to meet his. His eyes dared her to say otherwise.

"Is the coffee ready?" she asked.

Nash poured the brew into a strange cup. She held the handle and studied the black and brown surface. It looked like stone, but was light.

"What is this cup made from?"

"Buffalo horn."

She made no comment as he scraped the black exterior from his johnnycake. She held out her tin plate and received a huge portion of meat and one small cake the size of her fist. She craved flour. Her body longed for it, and greens. Her stomach gurgled in anticipation. Nash eyed her rumbling middle and smiled.

He ate his breakfast straight from the skillet, using only his knife. She bowed her head and prayed for patience. He knew she had a second plate and for some reason refused to use it.

"I generally have cakes once a week. Have to make them every other week, now, if the flour is to last."

She chewed slower. It would be a long while before she had another.

"Do you drink coffee every day?"

He laughed but didn't answer.

She finished her meal in silence and hollowness left her. How long until she regained her strength? How long would it take to recover from those months of want?

"That was a wonderful breakfast. Thank you."

"Yup," he said.

"I will clean the skillet."

"No, you'll rub all the seasoning out of it. I got it just right."

"Very well then. I'll just wash my plate."

She took her leave of him, walking to the brook. There she scoured her plate and utensils with sand. Then she washed her face and neck with a torn handkerchief. When she opened her eyes, he was kneeling beside her. She jerked her hand to her throat. "You gave me a start," she said.

His voice sounded defensive. "I came from downwind."

"Are you suggesting I can smell you?"

"You can't?"

"Well, no. I mean you don't smell badly."

"I can smell you."

A tingle vibrated up her spine, lifting the hairs on her neck. What did he mean? And why had his voice dropped to nearly a whisper?

"I have not acquired the knack."

He scrubbed his skillet quickly with sand and dipped it briefly in the water. "I don't know what you're saying half the time." Then he dried the iron thoroughly with a soft bit of leather. "The grease keeps things from sticking. Too much washing or heat and you have to start again. I've got to go hunt. You stay put."

A rippling wave of panic broke in her belly. John had gone hunting, too. He never came back.

"I'll come along."

"I says 'stay put.'"

Her hands grew moist. What if he didn't return? What if a bear or wildcat found him or he fell. She sprang to her feet.

"No, Mr. Nash, I will not."

He pointed a finger at her.

"You can't come. You'll slow me down and scare the elk. If I can smell you, so can they. You're staying."

"No."

"I ain't asking, you little bit of nothing. I'm telling you."

He stalked off. Cordelia followed him to camp. She bridled the other horse as he placed the saddle on his own.

"Give me that!" He jerked the bridle off the horse and stuffed it into his saddlebag. "I'll be back by dark."

He swung into the saddle and rode off. She doubled as if kicked by his horse. Her knees drove into the soft earth and she fell on all fours.

He'd left her.

John's words echoed through her mind. *Don't fret, Cordelia. I'll be back by nightfall. Don't fret.*

She ran for her blanket and snatched up the hatchet the Indians had packed for her. Nash had disappeared.

She turned to the remaining horse and stroked his head. Could she control the creature with only a halter? She had to try.

She led the animal to a log and jumped onto his back. With effort she managed to get her head and shoulders over his withers. The beast walked after his comrade as she struggled to throw her leg over the horse's rump.

Seated at last on the horse's bare back, she raised her chin high and gripped the halter lead.

"I'll not be left alone again."

In spite of her brave resolve, panic immediately choked her as she sat motionless on the horse, listening. Nash had told her this was Blackfoot country. If she could see him, she'd know he was safe. She nudged her heels into the animal's furry sides. The bay's winter coat acted like a saddle blanket beneath her.

If he'd give her a chance, she could help. She knew how to shoot, if only she had a gun. Her hand clutched the hatchet. She had enough practice with this and her long ax to qualify as an expert. Her heart hammered as she crossed a patch of rock. The horse's hooves rang as loud as a skillet struck with a wooden spoon. Her head swiveled about looking for Indians.

She couldn't survive up here without him. She knew it. Neither could she travel to Fort Hall alone. Nash was her only hope. Without him, she'd die in this wilderness. Better to go quick, she decided, than slowly starve to death over another long dark winter. She wouldn't do it again, did not have the strength for it. Only her faith in God and sure knowledge that she would not see John in heaven if she took her own life kept her alive. Helpless, she'd prayed for death a dozen times. She thought the Indians were her answer for a swift end. Instead they brought her to Nash.

She lost his trail. Uncertainty gnawed at her insides as she stopped the horse. Should she go forward with no trail and risk losing her way or go back alone? Her frantic gaze swept the ground and her heartbeat slammed inside her ears like a war drum.

Which way?

The ground was too rocky to leave an imprint of his horse's hooves.

She stroked the thick fur of the beast's powerful neck. "Find your friend."

The horse pivoted one ear to listen to her, then stepped forward into the cottonwood grove. Each stride seemed to take her farther from him and farther from camp. She swiveled around to look behind her. Could she find her way back again? The horse stopped as if comprehending her uncertainty.

She kicked him forward. Soon afterward she heard a nicker. Before she could grab her horse's nose, it returned the call. Too late, she thought. *Please let the horse belong to Nash and not an Indian.* She clutched the hatchet. Her heels pressed the horse's sides and they were off.

She recognized his horse, black with three white feet and a blaze down his face. A long breath of air escaped her. She was close. His animal was tied to a tree. A prickling started on the back of her neck.

What had happened to his master?

She dismounted and slid to the ground. She stomped her numb feet to bring the blood back to them as she tied her horse beside his.

A rifle shot reached her ears. The bubble of panic burst within her. Blindly she ran toward the sound as another round echoed in her ears. He was under attack. Her dress snagged on the brush. She yanked at the fabric and heard it tear. Her legs now pounded along the uneven ground. Her lungs burned. She had no wind. The winter had taken her strength. She ran through briars, the thorns grabbing her dress and piercing her skin. She fell into the clearing.

"What the hell!" Nash stood before her, his rifle in one hand, a cocked pistol in the other and both aimed at her. "Idiot woman. I coulda shot you!"

"I thought you were in trouble."

"Only since you showed up." He lowered his pistol, released the hammer, then reloaded his rifle. She watched him pop a ball and cover from the wooden pallet, which hung from his waist. He used a small horn cup to measure the load, then rammed it home.

The cork from his powder horn, which he held in his teeth, muddled his words.

"Thought I told you to stay put."

"I'm sorry."

"You surely are that."

"But I heard shots." She leaned forward now, pinching her side with one hand as she tried to relieve the burning cramp that seized her.

He corked his horn.

"You knew I was hunting. How'd you expect me to bring down an elk?"

"I thought you needed help."

"From you?" He laughed. "That'll be the day." His gaze traveled down her body. "What a mess."

She looked at her dress. The torn waistband gaped, revealing her white petticoat. She clutched the tattered fabric. Blood beaded in a line along the scratch on her hand.

"My skirt caught on the brush."

"So did your hair and your face." He stepped forward. His finger brushed her cheek. He held his hand before her, revealing the blood. "Come on. Damn, you waste more of my day."

"I'm sorry." She bowed her head to hide her burning cheeks.

"That all you can say?"

"I'm glad you are uninjured."

He sighed loudly, then grasped her wrist and pulled her toward a beaver pond. He wet a soft bit of deer hide and washed her arms and face. She sat on the bank and enjoyed the cool water on her hot cheek.

"Are your legs bleeding?" She pulled the hem of her dress over her feet. He batted her hand away and yanked up her dress. He shook his head. Her black woolen stockings showed several new holes. The places she'd darned were obvious. Her cheeks burned as he studied her state of disrepair. "What kind of shoes is that to wear? No wonder you can't run worth a damn."

He dropped the skirt back in place and handed her the scrap of soft buckskin.

"Keep that on your cheek. It's still bleeding. You thirsty?"

She nodded.

He dropped a water skin beside her and pointed to the ground.

"Now stay there. I have to skin them critters."

The water made her teeth tingle it was so cold. She drank as he strode angrily away. Obviously, he hated her. Her cheek stung when she pressed the moist leather to her face. The scratch on her hand turned dark as a scab began to form. Thankfully he had some shred of human decency left or he'd surely leave her here.

The thought brought her to her feet. Her gaze scanned the empty meadow. Where was he? She ran along the pond searching the clearing. Then she raced back to the horses. They both raised their heads in question at her frantic approach. Relief broke in her belly and swept through her. He was still here—somewhere. She petted the bay's velvety nose.

"It's all right. We're safe," she cooed.

She offered each animal a large hank of grass before going to search for Nash.

She found him up to his elbows in blood, skinning a large buck. A second deer without antlers lay a few yards from the first.

"Can't you stay put?"

"I thought I might help."

"You know how to skin a deer?"

"Well, no—"

"I thought not," he said. The disdain in his voice needled her.

"But I skinned an ox once."

His eyes lifted from the task to meet hers.

"An ox?"

She nodded.

"Now, people don't generally skin oxen."

"Well, I did."

He stood and extended the bloody knife. She swallowed back the memories of the last time she'd done this. She'd wept as she slit the beast's throat. There was no gun. The ox looked at her as the blood poured from the gaping wound. Tears rolled down her cheeks and into the blood all about her. They had carried her across the prairies in good faith, and she had slaughtered them.

"Well?" he asked.

She grasped the knife and knelt beside the buck. She would give him no reason to abandon her. Somehow she couldn't stop herself from glancing at the animal's face. His eyes were already glazed in death, and the large pink tongue lolled from his mouth. Her shoulders straightened and her fingers coiled about the knife with determination. She inserted the blade between the hide and muscle, cut the thick yellow membrane that held the skin and drew it back.

A long breath escaped her. She felt Nash judging her from two paces back. She labored until the ribs and back were free of the hide, then moved to the flank. She shuddered as warm blood coated her hands.

"I'll start the other," he said. She'd passed this test.

After removing the hide, she let Nash do the butchering. He took the flanks, ribs, liver and brain of each beast and wrapped them in the hides.

"With any luck that will hold you for dinner," he said.

She frowned at the barb. Then saw his smile. Was he teasing her? He threw the hides over his shoulder and headed back to the horses. He tied the bloody bundle on her mount. "Wash up, then we'll head back."

She reached the pond first. Leaning over, she caught a glimpse of her reflection in still waters. Her hair was in wild disarray, falling about her shoulders and tangled in knots. Her face showed the red line of the briar thorn. She looked like a crazy woman. Her hand splashed down in the center of her image. The ripples distorted her reflection. She was careful not to loosen the new scabs as she washed away evidence of the deer. Her clothing was streaked with blood from the skinning. She had only her Sunday dress left.

Nash finished washing as she struggled with her hair. Without her comb, the job was impossible.

"Come on," he said.

She drew her tresses into an unruly mess at her neck with a bit of fabric from her hem.

He offered her a hand from the back of the black horse.

"Can't I ride the bay?" she asked.

"If you'd rather ride with the meat," he said.

She looked back at the bloody hides and wrinkled her nose. Then she accepted his hand as he pulled her up behind him.

She let her hands rest loosely at his hips. He sat the horse as if the animal were a part of him, while she shifted and squirmed, trying to find a comfortable seat on the lip of his saddle.

"Quit wiggling," he ordered.

She stilled instantly. His proximity was unsettling. After so much solitude, his nearness made her body unnaturally sensitive to touch. The heat from his broad back radiated warmth into the cool afternoon. She allowed herself to move closer. Heat warmed her chest, belly and thighs. She was grateful. But now his scent disturbed her. The smell of smoked leather filled her nostrils. His hair tickled her face. She blew a strand from her nose and heard him laugh. She didn't care. The rocking of the horse and the warmth of the man's broad back lulled her. She let her eyes drop closed.

When the horse stopped her eyes popped open.

"You awake?"

"Yes."

"Good," he said. "Slide off." He held her arm and pulled her from her place. She shivered and glanced up at the first stars cutting through the darkening sky. They were back at camp. "Unpack the horse. I got to run my traps."

"I'll come, too."

"I said, 'unpack the horse.'" He was angry again. He wheeled his mount about and headed off.

She stood motionless, torn from within.

"He'll be right back," she whispered to the night. Blood rushed past her ears in a deafening roar. No, he'd never be back. She ran after him, her feet echoing the pounding of her heart.

Chapter Three

Nash returned later with his catch, three more beavers. One was nearly the size of a grown pig.

The fire gleamed through the tree cover. Damn, the woman made it bright enough to see from a hundred yards. She was making it near impossible for him to protect her.

She couldn't shoot him without a weapon, but he didn't want to frighten her. So he called to her.

"Delia."

He received no answer, nor did he to the next call or the next. In a moment he galloped into the camp looking for tracks.

Fool of a woman, where was she? He slid off the horse and tossed his catch toward the fire. His heart raced with his feet. What if she'd followed him and gotten lost in the forest? She'd be alone in the dark.

"Delia!" he shouted. Anyone in the area would hear him. He didn't care. He had to find her.

He ran from one side of the camp to the next, sweeping his gaze along the ground for tracks.

"Here I am," she called.

He whirled to see her standing beside the fire. Her wet hair curled about her scratched face. Worry crystallized into anger as he ran the few feet separating them and grabbed her by the shoulders. Surprise registered in her face as he held her much too tight.

"Where were you?" he shouted.

"I was by the stream. What did I do wrong?"

"Didn't you hear me calling?"

"I came when I did."

He released her then. If he didn't, he was afraid he'd shake her. She stumbled a moment before regaining her footing.

"Do you have any idea…" He stopped and ran a hand through his hair. "You don't leave camp in the dark—understand? What the hell do you think you are doing?"

"I was washing up before dinner. I'm cooking ribs," she said proudly. At the same moment, the skewer branch burned through and their dinner plummeted into the fire.

She lunged for the ribs, but his hand flashed out and stopped her.

"Sit down, you idiot." He used two branches to fish the food from the ash. "Didn't you use green wood?"

"Green wood?" she echoed. He rolled his eyes.

He doused the meat in water and skewered it on a branch he cut from a tree. "Green wood," he said.

She lowered her head. At last she raised her gaze to meet his. He could see the sorrow reflected in the tears that slid down her thin face. His anger slipped away.

"I don't understand why you are always angry with me. But I am sorry."

"Just don't wander off after dark. It's dangerous."

She nodded.

He set the skillet over some coals and added grease. He cut the liver into steaks and fried it.

"Do you ever eat vegetables?" she asked.

"I don't have time to collect any."

"If you'll show me what is edible, I'll collect them."

"All right."

He lay the cooked liver on her tin plate, then added some ribs. They were too large and hung over the sides. She tried for a time to cut the ribs with her knife and fork as Nash held his like an ear of corn.

"Like this, ya idiot."

He heard her stomach growl and chuckled when hunger won out over table manners. She grabbed a rib in her hands.

She picked clean seven ribs and ate all the liver he'd given her.

"That was delicious, Nash, thank you. I am still unaccustomed to outdoor cooking and prefer my woodstove. I would like to learn to cook on a fire. I'm accustomed to a stove."

"You know," he said, "the only time you're quiet is when you're eating."

"I'm sorry my conversation disturbs you."

"Well, I ain't finished yet."

She sat in silence for a time. "Do you enjoy stories, Nash? I could read to you."

"You got a book?"

"I have the Bible."

He groaned. "No, thanks. I like quiet."

"Perhaps you'd prefer to read it to yourself."

He considered telling her that the only time he'd asked God for something he'd been turned down flat. Since He'd taken Elizabeth, they were not on speaking terms. Instead he said, "I can't read."

"Oh, I am sorry," she said.

Momentarily guilt jabbed at him.

"I can read a trail and read the land and read an expression well enough. No reason to be sorry."

"Of course." Why did she have to be so understanding? If she wasn't apologizing, she was being understanding. It was damn irritating.

"Well, if you change your mind. I will be glad to read to you."

"You got any other books?"

"No, I'm sorry."

"You're sorry about most everything."

"I'm—yes."

"I got work to do."

She watched as he skinned his beaver very quickly. She admired his skill. He held up the hide. "Good plew!"

"Plew?"

"Beaver skin is called plew."

She nodded her understanding.

He turned and threw one hide over a felled log. She watched in astonishment as he lifted the large trunk easily and set it in a notched tree. Then he sat behind the skin and began to scrape the bits of flesh from the leather.

"Can I help you?"

"No." He never glanced up.

She sighed and returned to the fire.

When the hides were all scraped, he retrieved an awl from the bag hanging at his waist and punched holes about the edges of one pelt. She watched him thread leather through the holes and stretch the hide onto round frames of green wood using rawhide.

"I think I could make those holes," she said.

He handed her the awl. So he stretched and she used his metal punch for the holes. When they finished, he took the remaining deer meat and hung it away from camp, high in a tree.

When Nash returned, he retrieved his pipe from another bag dangling from his leather belt. This signaled to her the end of his work.

She retrieved her journal from her skirt pocket and dug about in the fabric lining for the stub of a pencil. The worn leather book fit easily in her hand. She noted the small scratches as she lifted the cover and smiled at the elaborate signature she'd penned many months and many miles ago. Turning to a blank page, she began to write. The wood in the fire popped as the graphite scraped rhythmically across the blank page. She recorded her thoughts and feelings of the day. She wrote about her terror of being left alone again and her pride at skinning the deer. She was just recording her humiliation at the ribs falling into the fire when he spoke.

"What's that?"

He rarely spoke except to answer a question or give an order. She smiled at his interest.

"My most precious possession. This is my journal." There was no need to hide it. He could not read, after all.

"What you writing?"

"I write my thoughts and experiences."

He nodded.

"How long you been at it?"

"I began this journal when we started our journey west. I thought it would be a grand adventure." The journal faithfully recorded terrible things she could never have dreamed. The book held her sorrows and hopes, all on neatly lined pages.

He pointed with his chin, his clay pipe clamped between his teeth. "Read that."

She placed a protective hand over the page. "No, this is private. Perhaps something from Ecclesiastes?"

"What?"

"The Bible?" He shook his head and lowered his eyes to the fire.

He was gone before Cordelia woke. The man made her feel lazy as an indoor cat. The sun wasn't even up, but he was gone. She'd fallen asleep to the soft sound of him scraping hides. He'd been to bed. She remembered him telling her to shove over, which she had. But a cold wind had brought her to his side of the buffalo robe during the night, and she'd been huddled in a ball against him dressed only in her petticoat. He did not tell her to move again.

She crawled out from beneath the heavy hides and stretched. Sunshine warmed her face. She discovered the horses were still hobbled in the field. He wasn't far. For a moment she felt torn between the need to search for him and the desire to take a few moments to repair her clothing. She'd battled the same demons last night when he'd run his traps and stayed behind only because she'd known she could not follow in the darkness. *He'll be back.* She quickly changed into her Sunday dress. Her brown dress was covered with dried blood. She scrubbed the fabric with sand from the river, then retrieved her needle and white thread from her sewing kit.

She clucked as she assessed the damage. The waist-band was torn in three places. The hem had ripped. She didn't dare look at her stockings. She repaired the waist first. The length was now uneven by several inches. She hung the dress on a branch and tore out the rest of the hem. How she longed for her pins. The Indians had left those behind.

At last the task was complete and she turned her attention to her stockings. The heel was worn through again and several new holes gapped as a result of her dash through the briar patch. She rubbed fingers over the deep scratches on her ankles. She winced and considered the results of her last attempt to find him. The urge to follow tugged at her again, this time even stronger.

Beaver was scarce. Soon Nash would need to move again. First, he'd smoke the deer hides and make her a proper set of clothes. Homespun was not sturdy enough for the mountains.

He came upon the camp silently, as was his custom. Would she still be in bed? The gray morning had given way to brilliant sunshine. His eyes relayed an unfamiliar splash of blue. He darted behind a tree and peeked around the trunk to find Delia wearing a dark blue dress. The color made her hair look more

startling in contrast as it hung loose down her back.
She sat on the ground, bare feet and white leg showing against an indigo background. She ran her fingers
over her skin. His mouth went dry. *What the devil?*
he thought. *Is she trying to drive me mad?* He crept
closer. She was studying her scratches, running her
hand over the red welts. He remembered those fingers
lifting his arm as she weaseled against him last night.
She was warm as a Franklin stove, except her feet.
He smiled in memory. She insisted on taking off her
shoes and dress. Her toes were the same temperature
as ice water.

Fingernails poked at bruised flesh.

"Don't pick at that," he said. She jumped at the
sound of his voice and yanked the skirt over her long
legs. "The scab won't heal if you pick at it."

"I didn't hear you."

"You never will," he said, and threw the beaver
skin down by the cold fire pit. He set to work stretching his plew. *That damn dress.* She looked like an
angel. Why didn't she put her hair up? Delia's mane
rippled in thick waves down her back. Soft as mink,
he recalled.

"Going to a party?"

She smiled at his gibe. He watched the corners of
her lips turn up and felt a tugging ache in his rib.

"I'm repairing my other dress."

"Neither one's worth fixing." Although that blue
suited her.

"Well, they're all I have."

"I'll make you some buckskin."

She shifted from one bare foot to the next. Her toes
peaked out from beneath her hem.

"These will do," she said.

"No, they won't. They catch and tear. You make a fine target in that color."

"Still, you needn't bother."

"Delia, you put me at risk."

She stilled, her face suddenly serious. "Oh, I see. Whatever you say, then."

He nodded and filled his clay pipe. Warm smoke filled his lungs as he punctured the beaver hide. When he finished, he called her over and made her stand on a piece of rawhide.

"About time you had proper footwear," he said. He traced her feet using a bit of charcoal. Her skin was pale as porcelain. He found her gaze on his powder horn.

"Did you do that scrimshaw?" she asked.

"Yup."

"May I see it?" He looked up at her, then glanced about the clearing to be sure he would not need his powder. His rifle leaned against a tree beside him and he had a second shot in his pistol. He handed her the horn.

She studied the little scene he had scratched into the surface last winter. He had drawn his precious mountains as the background of the battle between the grizzly bear and himself. You could see the fire coming out of his gun as the bear reared up to attack.

"Thomas, this is beautiful! You're an artist. The trapper looks just like you. And the bear, did you really face him like this? You're lucky to be alive. He must be ten feet tall."

He didn't answer her. There seemed no need. If he

waited, she'd be on to the next thought that entered her head without any help from him.

"Step off," he said. She moved to the side and handed back his horn. He began slicing the leather with his butcher knife. He made the moccasin with a double rawhide bottom. They'd last until fall. The sides and top he fashioned from buckskin. He had no gewgaws to add. She deserved some flash, so he fringed the tops. "Try these."

She sat on the ground and slipped one moccasin over her slim ankle. The top reached midcalf. He could see it fit, but decided to check for himself. Her leg was warm and her skin as soft as the tanned leather.

"It'll do," he said.

"They're wonderful. Thank you, Thomas."

Cordelia had washed her brown dress last night and hung it to dry by the fire. Sometime during the night the fire went out and the skirt froze. Her Sunday dress now dragged on the ground. The new moccasins had no heels and so she was two inches shorter. She squeezed the bottom of her brown dress. The fabric was so stiff it looked starched. It would have to do.

She glanced about the empty camp. Nash was nowhere in sight. But he had the annoying habit of appearing without a sound.

"Mr. Nash?" she called, then waited in the silence.

Quickly she worked the buttons on the front of her blue dress and slipped the fabric down, stepping out of the center.

"What?"

She spun around to find Nash standing before her.

She pulled the dress up and clutched the bodice before her bosom. Goose bumps rose on her arms and chest as his eyes scanned her.

"You called me, didn't you?"

"Yes."

"Well, what's wrong?" He scowled at her as she swallowed in a vain effort to push down her shock.

"I merely wondered if you were about. I wanted to change."

"Well, what do you need me for?" He sounded exasperated.

Her face felt hot at the same time her hands and feet grew cold.

"No, you misunderstand. I wanted to be sure you were not about."

"So you called me."

"Yes," she admitted.

"Women!" He spun in place and strode back into the forest.

She pressed her burning face into the fabric of her dress. *He's right. I am an idiot.*

What kind of game was this? She tells me not to touch her. Then she takes off her dress and calls me.

But she looked so shocked by his appearance. Well? She had called him, hadn't she?

Nash exhaled deeply, driving down the desire, then he went back to scraping the deerskin. The sooner he had her in buckskin the better. That damn blue dress was driving him crazy.

Last night, she had slept in her white cotton chemise. Her brown dress was bloody, and she didn't want to sleep in the blue. The night was cold enough

to ice the edge of the pond and her arms were bare.
She had inched against him during the night. He
hadn't sent her away. Instead, he had waited until her
soft breathing told him she slept and then he had
stroked her hair. Now he felt like some kind of thief,
sneaking around, trying to pet her secretly in the dark.

He scraped clean the larger skin and threw the wet
hide of the second deer over the log. The bristly hair
felt nothing like hers.

She was ruining his trapping. Now he thought
about her pale shoulders instead of where to try for
beaver. She was so skinny, he could see her collar-
bones sticking out. He'd dig some thistle root to go
with dinner. She'd asked for vegetables. Maybe
they'd help put some meat on her. Damn, but he hated
digging in the dirt like a squaw. He'd put farming
behind him when he'd lost Elizabeth. Never again, he
vowed. Now he lived single and traveled light. At
least he had.

He couldn't hold back the growl that broke from
deep inside him. She was his responsibility now.
Damn her husband for being too stupid to stay home.
Damn him for putting her at risk.

He scraped the last of the hair from the second hide
and rolled it with the other. When he entered the
camp she was scribbling in her journal again. She
wore her drab brown dress. He sighed with relief.

"Got to run my traps."

She stood and followed him.

"What are you doing?"

"I'd like to come along."

He closed his hands into fists in frustration.

"I can't take a piss without you tagging along."

"I'm sorry."

"Stop saying that! I already got a shadow. I don't need another one."

She stood before him, her eyes huge and pleading. If he said stay, she'd just sneak after him again. He was sure of it.

"Oh—all right. But keep quiet!"

Her shoulders slumped with relief. She walked silently behind him. He heard the rustle of her skirt against the river grasses.

He waded into the water to check his first trap. It was empty. He held his breath, opened the vial of beaver scent and used a stick to dab a bit onto the stake that held the trap. He replaced the wooden cork into the antler casing.

Farther upstream, he recovered three beaver. He drove the stakes tightly into the riverbed with the back of his ax. Then he set the trap and dropped the ring over the stake, carefully settling the trap to the bottom.

He glanced up at her. She smiled, causing his stomach to flutter. That made him scowl. He was sure that questions were burning a hole in her mouth, but she spoke not one word. Coming along was important to her, more important than answers. He wondered about that.

She carried her ax as they walked along. She didn't have a gun. What kind of a man leaves his woman alone with only an ax? He was glad her man was dead. It banished the possibility of having to kill him. Now he was stuck with her. Only until the fall, he thought. He'd teach her how to shoot his shotgun.

You don't need much aim. At close range, she'd hit whatever was in front of her.

They must have crossed some invisible barrier, because as they approached the camp the questions began. Why this and how that. He'd never talked so much in his life. His head hurt from all the answers she wrung out of him. You'd swear she planned on going into business as a trapper.

He started a fire as the sun disappeared behind the high peaks. They ate beaver tail and deer liver. He roasted the tubers in the coals. He had one and she ate three. He'd never seen a woman eat so much. Where did she put it all?

"Is something wrong?" she asked.

"Nope."

"Thank you for taking me along today. It was fascinating. What do you call that beaver scent again?"

"My medicine," he answered.

"Yes, that's right. Potent, is it not? And from the glands near the tail?"

He nodded.

"Why should that attract? I would think you would need a bit of meat to lure them."

"Beavers don't eat meat!" He shook his head. She looked confused. "They think another beaver is invading their territory. You got to place the medicine a few inches above the waterline. When he steps on the bottom to reach the scent, his foot's trapped."

"Why don't you place the trap closer to shore? Then you wouldn't have to wade into the stream and get your feet all wet?"

He slapped his head in frustration.

"Then the beaver would climb up on the bank, chew off his foot and get away."

She raised both hands to her mouth. "Oh, how awful."

"Damn right. I've lost one that way a time or two."

"I meant for the beaver. Poor little things."

"No worse than drowning, I 'spect."

"Oh, that's terrible, too."

"Whose side are you on?"

"I just don't like to see them suffer."

"That's why there's no women trappers." Ha! She had no answer for that!

He raked the coals into two piles and set a green wood tripod above each.

"What are you doing?"

"Smoking the leather."

"Whatever for?"

"You want your clothes to be weatherproof?"

"The smoke will do that?"

He nodded, then drove the wood into the ground. He drew the hides around the wood frames and staked them. Then, he tossed back the flap, where the pieces overlapped, and threw rotted dry wood over the coals. Smoke began billowing out of the opening at the top of the hides.

The breeze took the smoke straight for her. She coughed and rubbed her eyes but remained sitting.

"Move, you idiot!" Startled, she jumped to her feet and sat beside him. "Don't you even know enough to come out of the rain?" he asked.

"I won't need to. I will be waterproof."

Chapter Four

"I don't think this will do," Cordelia said, as he tried to drape the buckskin over her head.

"Hold still."

The hole was too small and the opening was ringing her scalp. He sliced a three-inch slit and the large skin fell to her shoulders.

The hide reached her knees front and back. He nodded in approval.

"Hold out your arms."

She did as he asked and he marked the place where the skin must be tied and trimmed, then pulled it off her again. She watched him cut the leather and puncture holes half an inch apart down the sides of the dress. He skillfully fringed the sleeves and cut the excess buckskin into thin strips. These he drew through the holes along the length of each side of the dress and tied.

"Try it on."

"Over my dress?"

"No—as your dress."

"Turn around," she said. He did and waited, listening to the rustle of fabric. "All right."

He admired his creation. It fit loosely from shoulder to knee. His eyes lingered on the slight swell of her bosom hidden beneath soft hide. His hand ached to touch her, so he checked the side seam for gaps.

"Now, I'll measure your legs."

She stepped back. "You will not!"

"How am I going to make you leggings without knowing the length?"

She thought for a moment. "Tell me what measurements you need and I shall take them."

He gave her a length of rawhide and instructions. She disappeared behind the wigwam. A few minutes later she returned with the knotted cord. "This one is my inseam." She pointed to the first knot. "This one the length from hip to ankle."

"I made you a belt while I was waiting." He handed her the band of leather. Each end had a hole bored through. A narrow bit of rawhide threaded between the holes. "I used your brown dress as a guide."

The belt fit perfectly about her tiny waist. He frowned considering the hollow beneath her ribs. A woman should be full and round in the hips. He gritted his teeth and vowed to see that she filled out.

"Where did you learn all this?" she asked.

"I spent my first winter with Flathead Indians."

"Did you learn a great deal?"

"Enough to stay alive the second winter on my own."

Cordelia followed his instructions exactly. This could not possibly be right. She was certain that Flat-

head women did not tramp about the countryside
wearing no undergarments.

She tied the soft leather about her waist and slipped
the loops that held the leggings at her hips onto the
belt beneath her dress. The leggings fit from hip to
ankle. But they did not cover her nether regions. If
she wore her bloomers under the leggings she doubted
she could get them off to relieve herself. She decided
to pull her bloomers over the leggings instead. She
glanced down. The bloomers showed beneath the
fringe of her dress.

The dress was too short. Nash said the Indians wore
shorter garments, so they didn't drag or catch. That
did make sense. Still, her ankles were exposed,
though sheathed in leather. She pulled her bloomers
up above her knee. That would have to do.

What would her Bible-study group think if they
saw her now? They'd never recognize her. She must
have lost forty pounds.

She stepped back around the wigwam.

"Ah, they fit?" asked Nash.

"I believe so. They will take some getting use to,
I'm afraid."

"Oh, they are a damn sight more practical than
your dress. More comfortable, too." He was right.
"Now the briars won't prick and them trappings
won't tear, neither."

She didn't like them, but he had spent a great deal
of time making this ridiculous outfit, so she thanked
him. He grinned. Her heart accelerated at the sight of
his straight white teeth. She smiled in return.

"Pack up."

"Are we hunting?"

"No, we're leaving. This area is trapped out. Time to go up the Musselshell into the Bitterroot."

"Musselshell?"

"That's the river we'll follow. This here's just a branch."

She watched him roll up the hides that covered their small dwelling and pack the skins with his furs, traps and other gear upon his horse.

"What about the sticks?" she asked.

"You don't pack wood, you idiot—you can find that anywhere."

"Mr. Nash," she said, not trying to disguise her irritation, "I would much appreciate it if you would cease calling me an idiot. I have a healthy mind. I am just unfamiliar with the nuances of trapping."

"Well, you talk smart, but you ask powerful dumb questions."

"I was once told there is no such thing as a dumb question."

"You was misinformed." He mounted the black and held out his hand for hers.

She had to hike up the skirt in order to straddle the horse.

"What's that?" he asked.

She hovered with her leg in the air. The lacy edge of her bloomers peeked from beneath the hide dress. She yanked down the buckskin.

"Tarnation! Is that bloomers? I told you not to wear bloomers. You don't need 'em."

She lifted her chin. "Well, Mr. Nash, I do need them."

He gave a suffering sigh but said nothing further. She waited. At last he offered his hand again.

"We're burning daylight."

By the afternoon they reached the Musselshell. She learned that this course eventually drained into the Missouri. The river was wide and fast with the runoff from the winter snowmelt. He kept the horses in the tree line rather than taking the easier game trail by the river.

"Why don't you—"

"That's it! I run out of patience. Get off the horse!"

"What?"

"Get off, I says."

He slid her to the ground. She clung to his leg. Panic, heavy and dark, swelled in her belly.

"Don't leave me!"

His eyebrows shot up.

"I'm not leaving you. I'm just giving my ears a rest. Go walk behind the horses and keep quiet."

The buzzing in her ears affected her hearing.

"You're not leaving me?"

"Delia, I stay with you until the Rendezvous, now scat!"

She walked behind the horses. Her stomach growled at midday. She wondered when they'd stop, but couldn't ask, of course. A gray fox appeared briefly in the forest then vanished. She saw several berry bushes, but the fruit was green and hard. How could she find out if they were edible without asking Nash?

By afternoon, she had stopped wondering. All her energy focused on keeping up with the horses. Each mile she dropped farther behind. Her feet throbbed with each step. Finally he stopped.

"You tuckered out?" he asked. She nodded. He reached down and tossed her up behind him again. He handed her some jerked meat and then kicked the horse. She gnawed at the thin strip of elk in silence.

The horse plodded along. She yawned, then let her eyes close as she nestled against his broad shoulders to rest.

She woke when he pulled her down from the horse. Her eyes opened to find he carried her.

"Put me down. I'm not a child," she said.

He never slowed his steady pace.

"Sometimes I wonder." She didn't struggle. There was something comforting about being held in the strong arms of a man. She relished his warmth and the comforting smell of his smoked buckskin. Beneath that was a now-familiar scent all his. She no longer felt comforted—his nearness did strange things to her heart rate. John's touch had always been pleasant, but never had he caused this jangled confusion of her senses. He walked to a fallen log and set her upon it, then strode away. She watched him. The man was all brawn and sinew and his touch was like no other's.

Cordelia rubbed her eyes and yawned again as she watched in silence. The place he chose was up against a large boulder with two smaller ones on each side. The rocks broke the wind and she assumed they offered some shield from observation. Though she hadn't seen any Indians, he told her they were about.

Nash unpacked both horses and hobbled them before setting them loose to graze. Then he laid out a sleeping pallet of buffalo robes. He made no shelter. When he began to gather wood she joined him, carrying smaller twigs and branches and laying them beside the pile he made. Finally he sat on a rock by the river. Cordelia watched him bait a white bone hook with a fat earthworm and throw the line into the river. Before the sunset he had four fish.

He made a small fire and gutted the fish. She silently retrieved her plate and flatware. When she returned, the fish hung by their gills above the coals. She watched the skin begin to sizzle. She loved trout.

Nash's voice broke the silence. "All right! Go on, talk. Damn it. Your quiet's worse than your chatter."

"Thank you, but I have nothing to say."

"That'll be the day!"

"Just one question."

"I thought so."

"How do you expect me to learn without asking questions?"

"I expect you to watch and listen and do. Them's the best way I know to learn." He poked angrily at the fish with his knife. A small white flake of meat fell into the fire. "They're done."

He slid two fish onto her plate. When they had finished eating, he lit a candle and doused the fire. He placed his guns and knife beside him and took off his hat.

"Come to bed," he ordered. She sat beneath the furs and opened her journal. She stared at him and then began to write in angry little strokes. "Oh," he growled, "you writing about me?" She nodded. "Well, don't take too long, candles is dear."

* * *

She still wasn't talking to him the next morning. Nash could get no more than a word from her. This was not the silence he craved and decided he preferred her idiot questions to her angry silence. He packed the horses while she wrote in that damn book. Finally he called to her.

"Come on!" He extended his hand and pulled her up onto the horse behind him, taking her journal from her and adding it to his pack.

The sky was changing fast. He began searching for cover. The best he could find was a large overhanging rock. He unpacked the robes and covered his gear with oilskins, then tied the horses to a nearby tree. He didn't want the lightning to spook them.

"Gonna be a real gully-washer," he said at last.

"What?" She sat beside him on a robe.

"A gully-washer, the storm."

"You mean it will rain?"

"Look at the sky and the wind picking up—it's blowing cold as well. See them leaves flipping over. That's all signs of rain coming."

"Is that why we stopped?"

"Of course, what'd you think?"

"I had no idea, thank you for clarifying." She turned her back on him.

He felt the urge to spin her about on her skinny bottom and shake her until her teeth rattled. Then he decided he didn't care what she did, it was nothing to him.

He chewed on some jerky and watched the storm roll in. The thunder followed the rain. She inched a bit closer.

"Do you like storms, Delia?"

"Like them? No, they terrify me, especially lightning."

As if summoned by her word a streak peeled to the ground. The valley flashed pink for an instant, and then came a mighty boom. Horses and the woman shrieked together. He was glad he had secured the mounts.

Delia was now sitting on his thigh, her arms wrapped about his middle.

"Easy, now. We're safe under these here rocks." He took the opportunity to stroke her hair. She didn't pull away. "You call this a storm? Why, I've seen hail the size of turkey eggs rain from the sky. This here's a bitsy storm, be gone in just a while."

"Are you certain?"

"Course I am. Hear that." Thunder rolled from beyond the river. "It's moving off already."

"How do you know?"

He stared down into her whiskey eyes. Her fear made them huge in her small face. His heart felt as if she squeezed it in her fist. She was worse than chiggers the way she wheedled under his skin. And the itch she caused was a hundred times more irritating.

"Why, you count the time from when you see the flash till when you hears the thunder. Try it." She counted to eight before the thunder reached them, still clinging tightly to his chest. He hoped the storm would never pass. He dipped his head to inhale her scent. "That's already two miles off and traveling west."

Her arms began to relax their hold upon him. She slid off his lap.

"Thank you."

He nodded. The place where she'd rested against him turned cold.

"Could I have a piece of buckskin?"

"What for?"

She shifted uncomfortable beneath his gaze.

"I'd like to make some alterations in the leggings."

"Some what?"

"Changes, that is," she said.

"What's wrong with them?"

"Nothing. But I would prefer britches."

"Britches? Squaws don't wear britches. Leggings is what the Flathead women wear."

"I am not an Indian squaw. I simply cannot go about without undergarments."

He rummaged in his pack and withdrew a piece of tanned leather. She ordered him to cover his eyes, which he refused to do, but looked straight ahead as she moved to the back of the overhang to remove her leggings.

His suggestion of adding a loincloth was rejected. Together they made, punctured and tied the leather to the leggings. She would not let him check the fit. A few moments later she sat beside him and sighed.

"This is so much better. I was getting a draft."

He laughed, a full, hearty belly-roller. She scowled for a moment and then joined him in laughter.

The rain tapered off to cold drizzle. Nash left the horses hobbled so they could feed.

"We'll camp here tonight."

He gave her the journal and sat down to sharpen his ax and knives.

* * *

She woke to find him gone again. Her heart began hammering when she noticed his horse was missing. She bolted to her feet and ran about looking for the horse's trail. Then she realized he'd left his gear. She sank down beside his pack. He was coming back. At least he meant to. Why didn't he take her along? She bridled the bay and was just mounting up, when she heard him call.

"Hello, the camp!"

"Hello," she called. Relief washed over her. He was safe. She dropped the reins and dashed to meet him. He held three grouse out to her. She accepted the fowl.

"Going somewhere?" he asked looking at his bridled horse. His crystal-blue eyes were on her again searching for answers. For a moment she wondered what his face looked like beneath his coarse beard.

"I was going after you."

"You can't keep doing this. You'll get lost or kilt or taken by Blackfoot."

"The same thing could happen to you," she said.

"You got to stay put."

"I can't."

"Why the hell not?"

"I just can't. Please let me come with you." She was pleading again, holding his leg. She hated her weakness, hated her fear.

"I'll come back, Delia. I'll always come back."

She lowered her head. "John said that, too."

He slid off his horse and held her in his arms. She rested her head upon his chest, taking the comfort he offered. His hands swept up and down her back. She noticed the change instantly. Her body trembled as she looked up at him. The compassion she'd seen reflected in his clear blue eyes melted into desire. Her breath caught in her throat. For a moment she thought he meant to kiss her. She gasped as she realized she'd let him. She looked to the ground, focusing on controlling her rapid breathing. His arms slipped away.

"I scouted the area. There's no Indians, hereabouts. Maybe if you knew how to shoot, you'd feel better 'bout being alone." His voice rasped, lower than normal.

"I do know how to shoot." She dared a quick glance at his face. He clenched his jaw, his gaze now inscrutable.

"Do you?" He didn't sound as if he believed her.

"But I have no gun."

"Can you shoot a rifle or shotgun?"

"I've fired both."

He set up a large chunk of wood against the hillside, then stood back about twenty paces.

"Hit that," he said. "Careful, my Bess has got a powerful kick. I used a half load. Still, it's a wallop."

He checked the placement of the gun upon her shoulder then stood back. The gun was longer and heavier than any rifle she'd ever held. The barrel wobbled and she was unable to hold it steady.

"Here," he said, "kneel down and rest your elbow on your knee, like this."

She copied his position and was able to hold the barrel still. Her gaze traveled down to the bead, which she sighted over the target. She took a gulp of air, exhaled half and held her breath, then squeezed the trigger.

The gun exploded against her shoulder, throwing her to her backside as the barrel kicked skyward, then fell from her hands. The jarring ride rattled her teeth. She groaned and rubbed her bruised shoulder, and the echo of the shot rolled back down the mountain.

"Damn close," he said. "Let's try the shotgun, then the pistol."

She preferred the pistol. The kick was small. Her aim was best with the shotgun. She hated the Hawkins rifle he called Bess.

"Not bad," he said as she fired the shotgun and sent the chunk of wood jumping.

"Can I come with you now?"

"Well, I can't hobble you like the horses, though I've a mind to."

"Then you'll take me hunting and trapping?"

"I reckon."

"Oh, thank you, you won't regret this."

"I regret it already."

The next day he woke her before dawn. She crawled out of the pallet without complaint. The air was cold. She ignored the rumbling in her belly as she mounted the packhorse, and followed quietly behind as he rode out. The sky turned from gray to violet as the sun crept closer to the horizon. They came to another river and followed it upstream. As the sun beamed over the mountains, she recognized the landscape. They were back in camp. There was no second river. It was the same one.

"Why, we've just ridden in a circle," she said in astonishment.

"Not much of a sense of direction, have you?"

"John used to say I could get lost between the barn

and the henhouse.'' She smiled. It was the first time she thought of him without feeling desperately sad and hollow inside. Now his memory warmed her. She turned her attention from within, back to the man dismounting before her. ''Why did you do that?''

''Just cutting for sign.''

Sometimes she wondered what language he spoke. ''I don't understand.''

''Looking for signs of Indians or game. I want to head upriver today.''

He cooked the remains of the grouse for breakfast. She tied her bundle on the horse and then began gathering up the bedding as she'd seen him do. He inspected her knots and the distribution of the gear and nodded. She smiled, knowing she had done it correctly.

Shortly after they set out it began to drizzle. He didn't stop this time. She looked at the sky and wondered how he could tell this storm held no threat. The man could see things invisible to her. Perhaps he couldn't read, but he was bright and resourceful and had knowledge that could keep them both alive.

She spent the day doing as he suggested, watching. She watched where he looked and followed his line of sight. By doing so she saw the little marmot darting along the top of a fallen log. An unfamiliar birdcall came to her ears. His body tensed, instantly alert. His head pivoted toward the river. She couldn't see beyond the reeds growing high along the bank.

He led them farther into the forest and up along a ridge. From the rocky outcropping, she saw the river below. Then she noticed peculiar objects floating on the water. They looked like large hollow bowls. Inside, Indians paddled along.

"Blackfoot," he whispered.

So that was what they looked like. She'd heard nothing good about them. These Indians were killers. They did not trade or take prisoners.

"What kind of boats are those?"

"Buffalo boats. They're made from the skin of one animal stretched over a green-wood frame. Much as a wigwam turned upside down."

She watched the men float downstream in their little leather boats. From up here they didn't look imposing.

"Come on," he said. "Time to pull foot."

They headed over the ridge. He stopped in a pine forest and cut the chunks of crusty yellow pitch off the trunks of several trees. These he carefully wrapped in leather and stored in his fire-starting pouch.

He chose to camp beside a huge white pine. The boughs hung down to brush the ground. But beneath the branches was a dry protected circle large enough to sleep. The pine needles made a soft bed for their pallet.

"No fire tonight," he said.

"Because the wood is too wet?" she asked.

"Naw. I can collect dry wood still on the trees. Blackfoot is why."

"Have you seen signs?"

"Not since the river."

They tied the horses beneath one tree and crawled beneath their own. She chewed on the jerky he offered and drank from the water skin.

"Do you think I could sew a pocket in this dress?"

"There's no pockets in buckskin, you idiot. Water will get in. You tie your possibles to your belt."

"My possibles?" she asked.

"Your personal gear, everything you might possibly need. Like this." He held up the little pouch that was always on his belt. "My possibles. You could carry your comb, sewing kit and such."

"What do you carry?"

"My bullet mold, awl, a small knife, tobacco and pipe. This one's got ball and patch, flint and my fireglass."

He kept everything close at hand.

"I should have a bag and case for my knife," she said.

He nodded.

She didn't miss the fire that night. His body kept her warm as always. His solid mass stood between her and all the dangers in the wilderness. She pressed her back against his side, feeling hopeful for the first time in many months.

Three days later he found his new trapping grounds. They followed a tributary of the Musselshell past the Three Forks and up the mountain to find several beaver dams climbing the hillside like steps.

She walked with him as he set his traps. This time she studied exactly where he placed his line. He was right. There was a different way of learning than by questions. Before, she did not really see what he did. Her eyes merely collected the images without thought.

She helped him cut green wood for the frame of

their shelter. That afternoon, she went hunting with him and shot a duck for supper.

That evening he roasted the duck over the coals. He handed her a leg. The meat was sweet and juicy.

"This tastes better than any duck I can remember," she said.

"Because you provided for yourself," he said.

The silence between them felt more natural to her now. She was comfortable with the quiet. She smiled in pleasure as she watched him bite another piece of her duck.

She took out her journal after dinner to record her triumph at taking the duck. The smell of his tobacco rose up about her. She inhaled the scent, which was now as familiar as the smell of leather.

He woke her the next morning so they could run his trap lines. Cordelia carried the shotgun and he held his Hawkins. His gun was never more than a foot from him. He even rode with Bess resting across the horn of his saddle.

The last trap, closest to camp, was not where he'd set it. She glanced about the water, searching for the wooden stake, which floated when torn from the pond bottom.

"There it is." She pointed to the stick. The trap ring was visible several feet from shore. He hadn't lost his trap.

Nash waded out toward it. The pond bottom must have dropped sharply, because the hand holding his gun went up suddenly to keep it dry as he slid into the water to his waist.

"Damn!" He waded out of the water. He glanced

about, took off his knife, powder horn and possibles bags and lay them beside Bess on the bank. Then he waded in again. She shivered thinking of the icy temperature of the water. He was chest deep when she heard the snorting of a large animal.

She turned to see a huge bear charging straight at her. Terror rooted her to the spot. She could not even scream. From beside her, she heard Nash hollering and splashing.

The bear turned toward the sound and raced past her, so close she could feel his fur brush her leg. The great brown monster leaped into the water at the same time Nash dove beneath the surface. The bear stood and bellowed. She thought it must be eleven feet tall. Nash surfaced some distance from the bear, which dove after him.

''Run,'' he shouted to her.

She couldn't move. Her heart fluttered uselessly in her throat as her legs refused her brain's command to move.

Twice more he dove. The last time he misjudged the bear's position. Nash breached the water right beneath the animal's jaw. The bear grabbed his head in his mouth. She heard the scream leave her body as she watched Nash shaken like a dead rat in the mouth of a terrier.

She raised the shotgun to her shoulder, sighted the beast's ear and pulled the trigger. The kick threw her off her feet into the reeds. The shot echoed for a moment and mingled with the scream of the angry bear. She rose to her knees and watched the monster drop Nash and charge out of the water toward her. She turned and ran toward the camp, knowing it would catch her and tear her apart.

Chapter Five

The sharp retort of the Hawkins rifle split the air. She ran on, turning toward the bear as she fled.

The beast lay facedown, unmoving on the ground.

"Nash!" She heard no answer.

She charged past the bear, expecting it to reach out and grab her. Nash lay on the bank with his legs still in the water. The gun was clutched in his hands. She turned him to his back. The sight before her nearly caused her to let go. Blood poured from a gaping wound across his scalp. His skin and hair dropped forward across his face. The white bone of his scalp glistened.

He began to sputter. Somehow, he was still alive.

"Nash?"

She half dragged, half pulled him up the bank. He kicked his feet, aiding their progress through the reeds and onto the river grass. With trembling hands she cradled his head in her lap.

"My rib is broken," he told her.

She saw the gashes across his side now, where the bear's claws had torn through his clothing. A quick glance revealed the bear was still lying motionless, facedown on the ground.

''Your head is bleeding. What should I do?''

''You'll have to stitch up the gashes, Delia,'' he whispered. He collapsed on the bank.

''I can't.''

''You can!'' He looked unconscious, but his voice was strong. ''I seen your stitches in that dress. This is much the same.''

She ran to the camp and grabbed her sewing kit. When she returned, the sight of his blood on the grass made her blanch.

''Thomas?'' He gave no answer. ''Thomas, please don't die.''

''I don't aim to,'' he whispered.

She flipped his scalp in place. The gash ran from the top of his head past his left ear. She used her shears to cut away much of his hair. There were two more gashes on the right side of his head.

Her fingers shook as she drew a needle from the ivory case. Finally the white thread cleared the eye. She quickly tied a knot and pierced his skin for the first time. She winced as the thread turned red as it ran through his scalp. She lost track of the number of stitches as she worked her way over his head. He lay so still she believed he'd passed out.

She lowered her head to his back and held her breath straining to hear his heartbeat.

''I ain't dead, Delia.''

''Thomas, your ear is nearly torn off. I don't think it's all here. I can't save it.'' She looked at the mangled bit of flesh.

''Well, you have to, is all. Sew it back, Delia.''

"Yes, Thomas."

She didn't know where to begin. Only a small patch connected the tissue to his scalp. *Just do it.* She sewed a blanket stitch to hold the torn ear together, then backstitched to hold the skin to his scalp. The bleeding stopped as she closed the last gash.

"Is it back on?" He opened one eye to look at her.

"Yes, Thomas."

She wet a piece of leather and gently washed the blood from his face and hair. Then she used her shears to cut the ties that held his buckskin shirt closed. As soon as she released the leather, the gashes began to bleed again. They weren't deep. Thank God, his lung wasn't punctured. She retrieved her petticoat and tore it into strips for bandages.

"You'll have to sit up, Thomas," she said.

He did, but wobbled slightly as she folded a pad over the claw marks and wound the cloth snugly around his chest.

"You done?" he asked.

"Yes."

"Good," he said, then fainted. She tried to drag him to camp, but he was too heavy to move. She collected his horse, but had trouble getting the beast to the water. The horse's eyes rolled white as it danced sideways. Cordelia knew the smell of blood and bear terrified the animal.

Finally she got the beast calm enough to tie a rope to the saddle horn and then beneath Nash's arms. She stopped before she finished the last knot. This would surely do more damage to him, dragging him over the uneven ground, getting dirt in his wounds.

She brought the buffalo robes to him and rolled his

body between the warm hides. His heart beat steadily. She sat back on her heels to think. The sweat covering her body turned cold.

She skinned the bear where it lay, running back to Nash periodically to check on him. He seemed to be sleeping now; soft little snores came from his nose. Returning to the beast, she finished removing the hide. Next she began butchering. She cut away the meat from the great hind legs and took the long back muscle. She placed the meat in the hide and she pulled the entire thing up into the trees fifteen feet from the ground and five feet from the branch as he'd shown her. Back at the pond, she splashed water on her dress. The blood rolled off the buckskin with the water.

She made a fire pit beside him, then gathered dead wood from the trees. She cooked some bear meat in its grease then added water to make a broth. As evening approached she hobbled the horses so they could graze without wandering. The sky was cloudy. Perhaps it would rain again.

She retrieved the green-wood frame he'd made for their shelter and restaked each pole. By the time she set the skin above him, the sky was dark.

She realized the bear carcass would draw scavengers. But it weighed hundreds of pounds. How would she move the thing? She let her eyes wander about their camp until they came to rest on the horses. It took some time to tie the bear to the horses. She led them forward. Their nervous steps were high and mincing. Her steady voice lured them on. They pulled and the bear remained inert. She clicked and coaxed. The animals strained and the bear carcass slid forward. Finally they reached the far edge of the pond and she freed the bloody remains.

Back at the camp, she worried that the firelight might attract Indians. She doused it.

"Nash," she called. He gave no answer. She gently patted his shoulder. "Nash!"

"What?" One eye popped open.

"Drink this broth." She held the horn cup to his lips. He finished three full rounds.

"We kill that bear, Delia?"

"Yes, Thomas."

"That's my girl," he said, and closed his eyes.

At night she heard the wolves devouring the carcass of the bear across the pond. The fearful fighting and growling brought her out in front of their shelter with the shotgun. Blackfoot be damned, she thought and struck steel to flint. The spark caught the dry tinder and lit. She added some of his dry pine sap. The flame leaped higher and she cautiously inserted twigs, branches, finally logs.

All night she sat tending the fire with the shotgun resting across her lap. Gradually she began to see the forest around her. The sky crept from blackness to deep gray. The wolves disappeared before dawn.

She took his "medicine" and set off at first light to check his traps. There were ten beavers in fifteen traps. She reset and staked each one adding a dab of the foul-smelling oil to each pole.

Back at camp she skinned all ten beavers. Her fingers cramped at the work. Nash stirred only when the smell of beaver tail filled the air.

"Who's cooking tail?" he asked.

Delia stuck her head beneath the hides. He smiled. "Thought I'd gone beaver," he said.

She gave him a puzzled look. What was he talking about?

"Gone beaver?" he repeated. "I thought I was a dead man—like my plew."

"Well, you are very much alive."

He looked about him.

"Lordy, Delia. How'd you get me back to camp?"

"I didn't." She threw the hide back to reveal the beaver pond. "I built the camp around you."

He gave out one guffaw then groaned. "Don't make me laugh, Delia. My rib's broke."

"Hungry?"

"That I am." He reached for the plate of meat she handed him. His knife sliced a piece of the bear steak and he chewed a while in silence. Then he said, "I thought for a time it would be the other way around."

"What?"

He grinned. "I thought the bear would eat me."

She couldn't return his smile. The fear was still too close. He'd nearly died. She pressed her eyes shut against the images that filled her mind. Had such a beast killed her John?

"Oh, Delia, I'm all right."

"Yes, this time," she whispered. Her eyes met his and his face lost its jovial expression.

"Got to see to my horses," he said, trying to rise from the pallet. A gentle hand was all it took to lay him back in place.

"I took care of them. They are staked on the riverbank."

"My head feels like a cracked egg. Ain't felt nothing like it since last year's Rendezvous." His fingers gingerly dabbed at his wound. "Damnation, woman! What'd you do to my hair?"

"I had to trim it to see your skin."

He touched the bristly spots and short pieces. "I must look like a dog with the mange. This scalp ain't fit for a lodge pole."

"I don't understand."

"When a warrior takes a scalp he tans it and hangs it on his lodge pole. But they'd leave me because my hair's shorn."

Delia tugged at a piece of her own long hair.

"Perhaps I should take those shears to my hair."

"Don't you dare touch one lock," he ordered.

"Why not?"

"I like your hair. It's pretty."

"Why, thank you, Thomas." Warmth, which had nothing to do with the food, filled her belly.

He looked outside.

"Where's the grizzly?"

"That was a grizzly bear?" She shuddered again.

"Of course. You expecting something bigger?"

"I dragged it to the far side of the pond. The wolves were after it last night."

"That bear must have weighed close to a ton. How'd you get it around the pond?"

"The horses helped me drag it."

He chuckled again, then clutched his side and winced.

"I would have loved to take that hide." She heard the remorse in his voice.

"I skinned it."

"What? Impossible." He stared at her as if he'd never seen her before in his life. "Truly?"

She nodded. Pride filled her at the admiration in his gaze.

"Did you take the claws?"

She wrinkled her nose in disgust. "Whatever for?"

"Why for proof. No one will ever believe us, lessen we have proof. I'll make you a necklace and decorate my shirt with the others."

She didn't relish the thought of seeing what the wolves had left. They might still be about. His eyes twinkled brightly, like sun off blue ice and she knew she'd go.

"I'll have a look," she promised.

"That's my girl." He slapped her leg. That was twice he'd called her his girl. For some reason the endearment pleased her. She smiled and ducked out of the tent.

She rode his horse around the pond, his shotgun resting across her lap. Flies buzzed around the carcass. The wolves had gutted the beast and taken most of the meat from his ribs and limbs, and in only one night, she thought and shuddered.

The claws held fast despite her carving at the paws. Finally she cut through the digit at the joint. She wrapped the vile things in leather and headed back to the horse. She was certain she would never want to wear one of these nasty trophies about her neck. That bear had nearly killed Nash. She didn't want any reminders of that.

He was pleased with the claws. She staked one of the beaver pelts to the ground and began the process of cleaning.

"Where'd you get that?" he asked from his bed.

"From your trap this morning. You caught ten beaver."

"Ten!" His voice was excited. He tried to sit up and groaned again. "What'd you do with the traps?" he asked at last.

"I reset them."

He looked at her in disbelief.

"You *have* learned a thing or two, ain't you?"

She nodded and returned to her work.

Finally the hides were all scraped clean. She stretched her aching back. Then she gathered green wood to make the stretching frames for the pelts. It took her the entire morning to dress the hides. When she finished, she found him sleeping again.

Ahead lay the dreadful task of scraping the bearskin.

She brought the huge hide to the ground. She cut most of the meat into thin strips to dry for jerky. These she laid across green wood above her smudge fire.

She found a log nearby large enough to use for scraping the hide and threw the pelt fur side down over the bark. She hummed hymns to herself as she scraped the fat and flesh from the skin. When she was done, little bits of tissue spattered her arms and dress.

A quick check on Thomas found him still sleeping. His body needed rest to heal. She walked to the pond and pulled off her britches and buckskin. Standing waist deep in the water, she scrubbed sand into the dress and rinsed away the grease. When she finished, she draped the dress on the reeds to dry. Her hair felt dirty as well. She lifted her braid to her nose and inhaled the smell of wood smoke. Her fingers worked loose the overlapping strands.

She dove beneath the cold water. The mud and sand at the bottom oozed between her toes as she stood. Thomas told her sand would clean most anything. She rubbed the gritty mud across her arm and then rinsed clean. She washed her entire body quickly, then rubbed the gooey mess into her hair. Three dunks and vigorous rubbing removed the last of the sand.

When she finished, Cordelia stood knee deep in the pond and wrung the water from her hair, then straightened and breathed deep the crisp air. For the first time in her life she stood naked before God.

Thomas held himself painfully up on one elbow. His ribs stabbed at him like a hot knifepoint. He didn't care. It was worth it just to see her the way God made her.

He'd done it. He'd saved her life. Somehow it made Elizabeth's death more bearable. Maybe that's why he was still here on earth, to keep this woman alive. The grizzly nearly got him though. He'd said his goodbyes as that bear clamped on to his skull. That's all he remembered until he'd heard Delia's voice.

He watched her now.

"Delia," he whispered. Her skin was as white as his clay pipe beneath that hide. Before his eyes, the cold waters turned her pink. Damned if she didn't have breasts after all. He studied the gentle swell of her bosom, then frowned at the sight of her shrunken belly. She'd had a hard winter, no doubt. Her curves would return if he kept her fed.

He groaned. How would he hunt with broken ribs? Each breath was agony. Just drawing air made him dizzy and he wondered if his lungs were bleeding.

A fly buzzed above him, but he had no energy to shoo the blasted thing. If he could just get on the horse, he'd probably make it. *Unless the rib snaps and punctures your lung. Then you'll bleed to death.* The bear meat would last a few days and the beaver was plentiful.

She was on the bank now, ringing out her hair. Water streamed down her body. Her skin glistened as if she were oiled. His groin stirred. *Oh, no,* he thought, dancing with a woman now would surely kill him. Might be worth it though.

He closed his eyes and settled back to the pallet. A few moments later she entered the hut. Her hair was wet and tightly braided. Her cheeks glowed a rosy pink. He hadn't noticed until now. Her skin looked healthy, no longer sallow. Her eyes were clear and bright as well.

"How was your nap?" she asked.

He considered telling her about his dream of a naked water sprite. But that would surely reduce the chances of seeing her again.

"Why is your hair wet?" He scowled at her.

"I washed it."

"You trying to get a chill and die? I didn't save your life just to have you catch pneumonia."

If he couldn't bed her, at least he could heat her blood with words. He shifted on the buffalo robe, suddenly aware of a more urgent matter.

"Help me up."

"You need to rest," she insisted.

"All right, if you want me to wet the bed."

Her hand rose before her mouth. He waited for the pink flush and smiled as it colored her cheeks.

"What should I do?" she asked.

He tried to use her body to pull himself to a sitting position. The stabbing in his chest took his breath away. He saw spots—big white sparks of light exploding before him like the flash from a rifle. He eased back down.

"Can't do it."

"I have an idea." She brought him his horn cup.

His head was swimming. He raised the empty cup in dismay.

"I ain't thirsty, Delia, I'm bursting."

"When my father was ill he used a bucket to, ah, relieve himself."

"I'll never be able to drink out of it again," he moaned.

"Certainly you can. I'll wash it thoroughly, I can assure you."

"Would you drink out of it?"

Her eyes fixed on the buffalo robe.

"Well, no," she said.

He nodded. "Go to my pack and get the buffalo bladder."

"You have an animal bladder in your pack?" She looked horrified.

"It's inside my rabbit hat, fetch it quick."

She rushed out beneath the hides. When she returned she held his hat.

"This?" she asked.

He reached inside and drew out the bladder. A Flathead squaw had made it for him to carry water. The top was adorned with braided leather and a carrying handle.

"An appropriate choice to use it again for its original purpose," she said.

He grunted and reached for the ties on his britches.

"Wait! Mr. Nash, give me a moment to withdraw."

He called after her, "Damn skidderish for a woman that's been married."

He sighed as relief came at last.

"Delia, come back," he called.

She accepted the leather handle from him and inhaled sharply. The bladder was half-full.

"Oh my Lord, you poor man."

When she returned she handed him the empty bladder. "You should keep this at hand."

He nodded and met her gaze. Something was on her mind.

She sat on the edge of his bedding.

"Why did you holler and splash? You drew that bear on purpose, didn't you?" He smiled. "That was an idiotic thing to do, Thomas."

"So now I'm the idiot, you ungrateful bit of baggage. Next time I'll let the bear gnaw on *your* head."

"I'd prefer that to watching you die."

"That's real noble."

"It is not noble. How long do you think I'd survive out here alone?" He thought about that for a moment and his smile dropped away. She couldn't read trail and couldn't tell north from south. Her chances were slim.

"Not long," he admitted.

"So what right do you have to go and get yourself killed?" She slapped at his shoulder. "I'd rather have that bear kill me than be left alone again. Do you understand me? Don't you dare leave me alone!"

The tears burst from her like water from a leaking beaver dam. He patted her arm as she covered her eyes with her hands.

"I'm sorry, Delia. But it all worked out. See, I'm alive. You're not alone. In a few months I'll take you out of here. You'll see. You'll be back East for Christmas dinner." Her warm eyes were on him again. His body responded to her gaze, like dry grass beneath the fire lens. He nodded. "Christmas dinner," he said. "I promise."

Chapter Six

She was too quiet.

"Delia, is there anything troubling you?" he asked.

She shook her head. Her lips pinched tight as she scratched away in her journal. Nash had grown to hate those pages. Whenever she seemed sad, she opened that damn book instead of turning to him. He sighed. Why wouldn't she turn to him?

He tried again. "Why not tell me what's on your mind?"

She stared at him with those inscrutable cat eyes and closed her book.

"I have to check the traps." She laid the journal beside her belongings and strode away toward the horses.

Nash stared in silence at the book. He listened to be sure Delia was gone, then opened her journal.

He began in the middle.

October 26, 1834—The wolves came again last night. They whine and scratch at the door. They smell the slaughtered ox. I don't know why they do not leap onto the roof. Surely they could rip through the canvas. I sat in the dark trembling with nothing but the ax to comfort me. At daybreak I found tracks of a great cat circling my little cabin. My blood runs cold that I shall have to face them again tonight.

He closed his hands, snapping the journal shut. Why had this happened to such a good woman? She should never have left home. He wondered where she began her journey. His fingers flicked back to page one.

Dayton, Ohio, March 10, 1834—John says we are ready to begin. All my hopes and dreams are packed into our new wagon. The glorious West and a grand adventure lie ahead of us. What marvels will I see a year hence? I tremble with anticipation. I know my life will be forever changed by this journey. I place myself in God's hands.

He slammed the journal shut again. This was going to be harder than he thought. He was angry already with the men who had taken her from the safety of Ohio. Then he thought of Elizabeth's death. She was safely back East when the carriage ran her down, crushing her leg. The doctor insisted the amputation was the only way to save her. But he was wrong. Blood poisoning set in and nothing could save her. Ohio wasn't safe, nowhere was. He chewed on that for a while, then opened the journal again. He studied her handwriting. She had a pen at first. The blue ink was evenly drawn in neat loops and lines across the page.

He traced his finger beneath her writing to keep his place. She wrote a damn sight better than him, but his eight-grade education served him well enough. Some of her words were unfamiliar. What was "debacle"?

September 10, 1834—John has fixed the wheel. I want to set out immediately to catch up with the others. He says we need a full larder before we cross the Rockies. Snows come early here. So he has gone to hunt for elk.

Her husband was a damned fool. There was a space between this entry and the next.

Night is falling and my John has not returned. I am worried. I've made a large signal fire to guide him home. Where is my husband? I pray to God that he is safe.

"Hello the camp."

At the sound of her voice, Nash tossed her journal beneath her brown dress.

"Hello," he called back.

"Seven beaver today!" She poked her head beneath the hide and smiled. He shifted, suddenly uncomfortable beneath her gaze. She grew prettier each day.

Cordelia tied the last of the tanned hides on the stretching frame. The bearskin needed stretching as well. She had watched him stretch elk and fox, but never something this size.

She chose a tree with a branch ten feet up and nearly parallel to the ground. She sat on the horse to reach the branch. It was not enough, so she carefully stood on his back, expecting at any moment to be thrown. But the horse merely looked at her as she shuffled cautiously to his rump.

She looped the rawhide over the branch and cut it in long lengths so she could reach them from the ground. After dismounting, she drove stakes into the ground at one-foot intervals.

Her arms ached by the time she had the bear's skin hanging from the tree branch. The tree trunk, along with an adjoining tree, gave her the sides of her large frame. She yanked tight the rawhide, which held the bottom of the hide to the stakes.

She stared in satisfaction at the taut hide. Her back throbbed abominably and she was more proud than when she won the spelling bee at Harper Normal School.

She was so thirsty. The water skin was with Thomas. She crept back to the wigwam so as not to disturb him should he be napping. Just as she stooped to enter, she saw both his arms fly out in either direction.

His hand gripped the Hawkins rifle.

"Damnation, woman! You nearly took a year off my life. What are you doing creeping around like an Indian?"

"I'm sorry, Thomas. I didn't want to wake you."

"Wake me. I almost shot you!"

"I'm sorry."

"Next time holler first."

"But that will wake you."

"I was awake. If you walk in without calling I will shoot you. You understand?"

"Yes." His words deflated her pride and she turned to go.

"What you want, anyways?"

"I was thirsty after stretching the bear."

"You stretched the bearskin?"

"I just said so."

He handed her the water pouch and she drank. The water washed the dust away.

"I'd love to see it. Can you raise the buffalo robes a bit?"

Her arms hurt just raising the water skin to her lips. She looked at him. His blue eyes shone hopefully. His hair was a ragged mess about his poor head. His ear looked dreadful, swollen and purple.

"Of course," she said.

She had nearly caught him that time. Nash didn't know if he should hide the journal or grab his gun. So he did both. When she knelt beside him, he realized the journal was only partially hidden beneath her small pile of belongings.

She was out there skinning critters and stretching that bear, while he sneaked around reading her private thoughts.

He snorted. Well, he'd surely done worse.

The stakes beside him began to disappear one by one, as she knocked them away with the blunt end of her ax. What a remarkable woman. He wondered if he could have endured that winter. He didn't understand until now how very difficult it was. She'd had no skills and had to learn from mistakes. But she had survived and had finally seen a white man again. And what did he do? He tried to get the Flatheads to keep her. Then he did everything he could to punish her for something that was none of her doing.

Somehow he'd make it up to her. But how?

Delia went up the stream to try to shoot duck. The bear meat was gone, except for the jerky and she didn't fancy beaver tail again. Nash doubted she'd get lucky, but he gave her his pistol and shotgun. The Hawkins stayed with him.

He looked out from beneath the frame of his hut at the beautiful golden fur of the bear. The skin was enormous. He was lucky to have survived, lucky and grateful.

He reached for the buffalo horn. The surface was smooth enough now to work. He sketched a rough outline with a bit of charcoal, then set to work carefully scratching into the horn with his awl.

He tried to ignore the persistent voice in his head. It urged him to pick up the journal again. He resisted at first then snatched up the leather notebook.

October 15, 1834—As soon as I chinked the logs, I began gathering dry wood. Then I thought I had better bank earth around the outside of the shelter. I have cut logs for fuel and stacked them with the kindling against two outside walls. The stove is now inside the cabin along with the barrels of salted oxen. The snow is falling heavily now. I hope I am ready.

Nash flipped back several pages.

September 15, 1834—I searched up the mountain for John. I called until my voice went. I slept in the woods and searched again today. His trail ends just past the meadow on rocky ground. Where can he be? It has been five days! My heart is breaking with grief. What has happened to him? Please God, let him return to me or take me as well.

The next entry was ten days later.

September 25, 1834—No sign. I am alone. I do not want to live now. I wait for death. I am sure John is gone before me. All my prayers are unanswered.

September 27, 1834—I found John yesterday. Scavengers had ravaged his poor body. I could not recognize him save for his clothing, and I cannot tell how he met his dreadful end. I pray he died quickly, but I fear it is not so. Will I ever forget the sight? Terrible, terrible. How I hate these evil mountains.

I cannot find his gun and I have no shovel so I used my ax to hack a shallow grave and buried him there in the woods. I covered his burial place with rock upon rock so those vile creatures can never touch him again.

Lord accept him into heaven and protect me

alone in this wilderness. Forgive me, for I do not wish to live without him.

Nash held the journal to his broken rib cage. Poor Delia, to find him all torn up by animals. He'd seen such, and the memories lingered still.

A vivid image of his wife lying in white sheets, the smell of putrid flesh strong in the air, flashed in his mind. He shook it away and remembered her as she had been before the accident, young and whole.

Lizzy had picked him out as a project. Her attempts to civilize him began with her teaching him to read and ended with their marriage. For two years he pushed a plow, planted tobacco and loved his wife with all his heart. She never took his sass and her gumption always made him laugh.

He'd ignored his sad-eyed hound that seemed to call him to wander the woods and focused instead on building Lizzy a home. When she'd died something snapped inside him. He wanted to die as well. But first he wanted revenge. She'd known that, she'd known what he was planning, so Lizzy made him promise on her soul that he would not kill the man who ran her down.

He promised.

After her death, he sold his land and bought a good horse. Then he turned his back on everyone he'd ever known and found the most dangerous trade there was—trapping. Many of the men he had met at his first Rendezvous never made the second.

But God liked to play tricks. The Flatheads took him in that first winter and he had lived. Come spring, he had nearly drowned in the Yellowstone when his raft came apart. Lost horse and beaver that day, but he'd made it to shore. Now, he'd outfoxed a grizzly. It seemed God didn't want him.

The date told him it was twenty days before she lifted her pen once more.

October 16, 1834—The snow is deep now. I have rehung my door to open into the hut, as I could not push back the snow against it. There is four feet already and still it snows. I shoveled a path to the woodpile and climbed up onto the roof to clear the stovepipe. Thus far, the roof has held. It is dark as a crypt inside the cabin. I saw buffalo using their great heads to clear the snow and graze. But I have no gun.

"Hello, Thomas, do not shoot me!"
He slid the journal beneath the buffalo robe.
"Hello," he called.
The skin flipped up and her hand thrust beneath. In her small fist were two ducks.
"You got one!"
She peeked under the hides. "I got two."

Nine days after the bear attack Thomas was noticeably better. His breathing no longer came in shallow little pants. The fear that gnawed at her middle all week had vanished. She parted his hair to look at the stitches. The skin was pink and healthy. The scab had fallen away in places.

She saw him wince and withdrew her prodding fingers.

"Does it hurt you, Thomas?"

"Smarts a bit when you pick at it."

"I'm afraid your poor ear will never be right."

"It works all right from the inside. Don't care much for the outside. I never see it anyways."

There was a small piece of his ear missing and an angry scar ran through the center.

"Stop gawking, it can't be all that bad. Bear mighta taken my whole head."

"True. I thought he'd killed you. I was so frightened."

"I'll be right soon enough. And you're doing fine. Appears you don't need me."

She looked at him with those warm brandy eyes. His gut tightened.

"I need you, Thomas."

He looked away. The feelings she stirred in him were too disturbing. Not again, he thought. I don't ever want to care that deeply about a woman again. It hurts too much. But he already did.

"I need to get out of bed."

She nodded. He managed to crawl from the hut once a day. He rolled to his stomach and pulled himself up on all fours.

"Bring my rifle," he said.

He used his gun and her body to pull himself up. His weight nearly buckled her knees. She walked with him to the large rocks at the edge of the woods and then left him there with his gun, as always.

She sat beside the bearskin. Her fingers stroked the soft fur. Somehow now the great bear gave her comfort, like stroking a dog. She laid the shotgun beside her and picked up the first duck. Her fingers grasped the feathers tight and yanked them loose. She decided to save the down to make a pillow for her head. She could use what was left of her petticoat and bloomers for ticking.

Her mind registered the movement. She wondered how Thomas had got this far without her. Her smile died on her lips as a scream tore from her throat.

Before her stood an Indian.

His face was painted entirely yellow with a vertical red stripe running from hairline to chin. He held his metal ax at his side. Behind him several comrades stood silently, watching her.

"Thomas," she called.

She looked at the shotgun beside her. She could kill only one or two. There were ten men, motionless as cigar-store Indians.

Where was Thomas? She turned and found him missing from his resting place. Two Indians dragged his inert body between them toward the others.

"Thomas!" she cried, and dashed to his side. He groaned and she drew her hand over his head, finding a fresh lump forming. Fear momentarily flicked through her belly only to be replaced by a scalding rage. She looked at the man with his face painted yellow and raised a finger at his nose. "If you hurt him, I will kill you."

He held her shotgun. Another Indian gripped the Hawkins. What were they waiting for?

Their leader pointed at the enormous hide behind her, then at Nash. Perhaps they wanted the one who killed the bear. Nash told her bears and buffalo were sacred animals to the Indians. Perhaps killing a sacred animal was a sin of some sort.

She shook her head and lifted an imaginary gun to

her shoulder and fired. Then thumped her own chest and pointed at the skin.

Several eyebrows when up. The leader pointed at her again and she nodded. She moved to guard Nash, kneeling between him and his enemies. The Indians spoke to one another.

Nash groaned again and lifted his head.

"Are they Flatheads?" she whispered.

"No—Crow," he said.

"I thought they killed people."

"They may get around to that."

Nash rolled to his back. She dragged his head and chest up onto her lap. Her breath came and went in frantic cadence.

"I'm sorry, Thomas. I shall miss you."

"Delia, you're the most remarkable female I ever met. Most women would be weeping hysterical right about now."

"That wouldn't do any good."

"Practical to the end."

The Indian's leader turned to her again. He moved his hands together and apart, touching his head and then chest.

"What's he doing?" she asked.

"He's asking your name."

Nash then spoke words she had never heard before.

"You speak this language?" She was astonished.

"Just Flathead and Crow," he said. His eyes never left the leader.

"He asks if you are the white woman who lived alone through the winter? Seems them Flatheads have been talking about you."

Nash spoke to them again.

"I told him you killed the bear and skinned it yourself. Says his people call you Winter Woman. Seems you're big magic. I don't think they're going to kill you, Delia."

"What about you?"

"Don't know yet. Fetch my pipe and tobacco."

They blocked her way. Nash spoke to them and they allowed her to go with an escort. She snatched his possibles bag and the bear jerky and returned to the group.

"Fill the pipe," he said. She marveled at the calmness of his voice. He sounded as if he was leading a Bible-study group instead of a band of wild savages.

"I brought the jerky," she said.

He spoke to the men and they sat. She offered them dried meat and they each accepted a piece. Hope tickled through her for the first time. The little clay pipe was passed from man to man. Smoke curled above dark heads. After a stretch of silence, the striped man spoke.

"This here is the Mountain Crow. They ain't the cold-blooded killers the Blackfoot are. They're real curious about you, Delia. Want to know everything. Your hair is causing quite a stir. They never seen a white woman and you got special magic because you done what no one else ever has."

"Killing the bear?"

"Naw. Surviving the winter alone. It can't be done. But you did it."

The man with the yellow face spoke directly to her. She looked to Nash for explanation.

"He says such a woman will not die by the hand

of his people. He offers you this gift as a sign of peace between you.''

The Indian withdrew his knife and tucked it into his belt. Then he untied the sheath and handed it to her.

''Oh, it's lovely. Thank you. Look, Nash, there's a little green turtle painted on it. Thank him for me.''

''Delia, you got to give him something.''

The next man gave her a necklace with a large tooth in the center. Nash said the tooth was from a buffalo and very lucky. She looped the cord about her neck.

''What should I give them?'' She had nothing a man would want.

''Something of yours, something of equal value.''

She nodded to the men and went to the hut, returning several minutes later. She handed the leader a white lace handkerchief. He opened the little bundle. Inside sat a copper halfpenny and a bear claw. He nodded to her and held the packet before him with two hands.

''He's pleased,'' said Nash.

She gave the man who had presented her with the necklace a second handkerchief. He folded back a lacy edge to reveal a halfpenny and a brass thimble. He smiled at her and nodded.

The Crow warriors held their little tokens together and talked in disturbed voices. Delia felt a knot twist her insides. Had she insulted them?

''Nash, what's wrong?''

He raised his hand and gave her arm a little pat.

''They think that's you on the coin.'' He laughed. ''That's Miss Liberty.''

"They says it's you."

"But it's not. You must tell them."

"This proves the magic. Metal is real precious and there's your face on each one."

"It doesn't look a thing like me," she insisted.

"Delia, it's magic. We won't have no trouble with them Mountain Crow again."

The men rose and she followed them to the edge of camp.

"Goodbye," she said. "It was very nice to meet you. Thank you for my gifts."

They spoke to her in their language and she nodded politely, then watched them walk single file into the forest.

Nash's laughter brought her back to camp.

"Damnedest thing I ever seen. You *are* magic, Delia."

Chapter Seven

"I been thinking," said Nash.

"That explains the headaches," she said.

"Lordy, woman, are you jibbing me?" He squinted at her and she burst out laughing. "Well, it's about time."

"I'm sorry, Thomas. What have you been thinking?" She rested the linen pillow casing in her lap and focused her attention on him. He lay reclining against a wide split log, resting against a tree. The position allowed him to work on leather and see about him. It also eased his breathing.

"You've done real good. You're trapping and hunting and keeping a clean camp. I reckon I'd be dead by that bear or them Crow if not for you."

"There's no need to thank me, Thomas. You've kept me alive as well. I'm grateful for your chivalry."

"Will you hush up?"

She pressed one finger to her lips and nodded.

"I want to make you my partner."

A curious wave of excitement snaked through her. "What do you mean?" she asked.

"I mean you're doing all the work around here. I reckon that's worth something. How about ten percent?"

"You mean I'll get ten percent of the furs?"

"Ten percent of the profits when I sells them at the Rendezvous. You deserve a stake. It'll be enough to make a start somewhere. What do you say?"

She fell to her knees beside him, wrapping her arms about his chest.

"Oh, thank you, Thomas!" She kissed his cheek in joy.

His fingers slid through her hair as he gripped her. Her gaze met his. Blue eyes stared down, intent and hungry. Her body reacted instantly like powder to a spark.

She knew he would kiss her now. She lifted her chin and her lips parted. His mouth slanted over hers, starting a wave of pleasure that rippled through her. Suddenly she forgot to breathe and her heart threatened to burst with its frantic rhythm.

She hadn't been kissed in nearly a year. And never had a kiss felt like this. She yearned for this man.

John's kiss, pleasant as it was, never ignited this wanting. A sudden image of her husband flickered in her mind, and she pulled back from the warmth of Thomas's embrace.

"What's wrong, Delia?" He looked confused. She felt so guilty. How could she? She'd misled this man and betrayed her husband's memory at the same instant. She jumped to her feet, hand gripped tight to her traitorous mouth and raced away. "Delia! Delia, come back here."

Somehow he got himself up and followed her to the edge of the pond.

"Delia, I'm sorry. I shouldn't of kissed you like that."

He reached out his hand to stroke her shoulder, but she stepped away.

"Oh, Delia, you don't have to worry. I won't touch you lest you want me to."

Her bottom lip trembled. She wrapped her arms tightly before herself.

"That's the trouble, don't you see. I did want you to. Oh, Thomas, what must you think of me? My John's not even gone a year and I allow a man to kiss me."

"A year—bah!" His voice sounded cross at first, then tender. "This here's the mountains. Those rules don't go here. You're just feeling guilty about living."

She looked at him in astonishment.

"That's right, Thomas, I do. How could you know?"

"'Cause when I lost my wife, Elizabeth, I felt much the same. She died and I couldn't do nothing to save her. Then I got angry with God for not taking me instead. But he didn't take me or you."

"Sometimes I can't believe he is dead."

"He's gone, Delia."

The tears filled her throat now. They changed her voice into a wavering, unrecognizable thing. "I still love him. I always will."

"Of course. This don't change none of what you shared with him."

She allowed him to enfold her in his great, strong arms and absorb her sorrow.

Delia finally accepted his offer of partnership. Nash wasn't sure if it was the kiss or the hard words about her husband that convinced her. He wished he'd never kissed her.

There was a new tension between them now. She rarely smiled. She jumped when he called her. Worst of all, she never touched him. He watched her like a dog waiting for some small sign of affection.

She kept all her thoughts more secret than before. He yearned to know what troubled her, but could gain nothing in conversation.

The beaver were trapped out. They stayed so he could heal. His ribs only hurt if he stretched too far. He thought he could sit a horse now. He rubbed his fingers over the scar on his head.

"Stop scratching," she said without looking up. She punched a hole in the leather of the possibles bag she had made herself.

"They itch worse every day," he said.

"Perhaps it's time for the stitches to come out."

Then she'd have to touch him.

"Take 'em out," he said. She kept working the leather. "Take 'em out or I'll claw 'em out."

"All right, Nash. Let me retrieve my scissors."

She called him Nash again, instead of Thomas. He hated the stiffness of her tone. The laughter was gone. He missed that most of all.

He held still as she carefully cut the thread. Her businesslike manner irritated him no end. The first tug pulled at his scalp. This was followed by the next, until his head pounded from the little stabs of pain. The ear took her quite a while to work loose.

"There," she said at last. "That's all."

He looked at the little pile of blackened thread beside him.

"My head must have looked worse than your stockings."

She smiled at that. It was a start.

"I'm going hunting. I saw some rabbit tracks up by the briar bushes," she said. "Will you be all right?"

He nodded.

"Take this along," he said. He held out the powder horn that he had made her. "About time you had your own."

"Oh, Nash! It's beautiful." She admired the scrimshaw. He had carved a picture depicting her shooting the bear. "This looks just like the bear. You have such a talent. Thank you. But I did not shoot him, you did. I lied to those men."

"You shot him all right. Not the kill shot, maybe—but you hit him, just the same. Stood your ground against a fifteen-foot critter. Few can say the same."

She lowered her gaze, but did not move to hug him this time. He thought she might be choked up.

"I filled it for you. It's ready to go."

When she lifted her head, he saw her eyes were misty, but she didn't cry and he strung the horn across her shoulder. It hung to her hip beside the knife sheathed in the Crow casing. About her neck were two necklaces. The first was a buffalo tooth tied on a leather lanyard strung through bits of colored bird bones, also a gift from her Crow admirers. The other was the huge grizzly claw he had made into a necklace with blue trade beads and leather. She looked like some ancient goddess of the hunt as she strode toward the horses, holding the shotgun loosely in her right hand.

He waited until her horse was out of sight to retrieve her journal.

Nash recognized Delia's struggle was much like his own. She felt sorrow, just as he had and wished to die from it. It changed her. Well, he was changed, too. He understood now, why she needed to come with him. She was frightened it would happen again.

He opened the brown leather cover to the place he'd left off. He needed her words. Here he could share her secret thoughts, the part of her she kept for herself.

December 28, 1834—The snow is over the cabin now. I had to clear the stovepipe by digging down several feet. The snow is so deep the wolves and panthers do not come at night to prowl. I almost miss them. I feel at times as if I am the last person in the world.

My John lies beneath deep snow. He and I are both buried here. My mind grips this thought and I find no respite.

What had he been doing that day? He thought back to his own cabin on the Yellowstone. The trapping was good. A beaver's coat is thickest in the winter. He remembered the bitter cold and heavy snow. The sunlight was brief then and nights long.

March 8, 1835—The snow has melted on the mountain. Last night the water began flooding beneath the cabin door. I took what I could and moved to the wagon. Today, I moved the stove. I have no grease and am afraid it will rust. The canvas is back upon the wagon as well. The whole world is a river running two feet deep and covering the meadow.

March 22, 1835—Still the spring thaw runs by my wagon. I have been unable to light a fire. Uncooked Indian meal and raw salt beef again today. My gums bleed every day now.

Scurvy, he knew the disease. How she'd suffered. He realized he clenched his teeth against the anger he felt. She'd endured so much.

The next entry was in pencil. The line was light and hard to read.

March 30, 1835—My ink is gone. I knocked the bottle over. I was adding a log to the stove when sparks leaped to the wagon floor. I doused the flame, but lost my ink in the process. I have no more meal. I am afraid to eat the plants that begin to grow about me for fear they are poisonous. The beef is nearly gone as well. I have rationed myself to one meal a day in hopes it will last until I am found. Reverend Harcort will surely send help when the snow melts from the mountains. I have begun to eat the crop we brought for planting. One by one the corn, barley and pumpkin seeds disappear with my dreams.

He'd taught her how to find dry wood even in a rainstorm. She'd have cooked beef now, by God, he thought. She came to him in May. Only two months ago she wrote those words. What did she think of him then? He hadn't been very welcoming. Well, how was he supposed to know what a wonder she was? All he'd seen was another woman he might grow attached to and lose. Why should he take her in, get close to her? He swore he'd never leave himself open to that kind of hurt again.

Yet, that was just what he'd done.

May 7, 1835—Two Indians on painted ponies arrived in the meadow today. I was so frightened I forgot how to run. My mind raced with all the terrible stories of what red savages do to white women. My knees actually banged together in my terror.

As soon as they determined I was alone they began raiding my wagon. Suddenly I was more frightened of being left alone with no supplies than being savaged or killed. One man restrained me as the other bundled my possessions. They even took my ax. I begged them to leave my things alone. They did not understand me. I called out to God to protect me. In a thrice I was swept up onto a horse and away we went. Where, I knew not.

I must confess my anguish and lack of any strength brought sleep to me, and I did not wake until the men roused me. To my surprise, neither laid a hand upon me, but fed me and treated me kindly. Wherever are they taking me?

She was almost to him now. He turned the page to hurry to their first meeting.

May 14, 1835—I am at the mercy of a wild man. He is nearly as fearsome as the savages who found me.

Wild man, was he? He'd fed her, hadn't he?

May 15, 1835—My Indian friends have left me with a trapper. He is coarse and unkempt. What sort of man is this? And what will befall me now?

I was so distraught yesterday, I forgot to mention his name. He insists I call him Nash, though his full name is Thomas Nash. He has the most atrocious table manners. Food and grease cover his hairy face. It was all I could do not to be ill at the sight of him.

He slammed the journal shut and tossed it aside. This was not what he'd hoped to see. He did not like the picture she drew of him in her journal. Did she really see him as some wild man? This would not do.

Cordelia tied the horse to the branch and released the girth about the animal's middle. She balanced the turkey and saddle in one hand and carried the shotgun in the other. Her strength was returning. She noticed the change. She was never out of breath now, and it didn't hurt to sit on the horse because she had a bit more padding. She took a deep breath of the sweet spring air. It felt good to be alive.

She turned to face the stranger holding Nash's Hawkins rifle.

She dropped the saddle and turkey to aim the loaded shotgun at his chest.

"What have you done with Nash?"

He raised one hand to stop her.

"I *am* Nash," said the man.

She instantly recognized his familiar clothing, crystal-blue eyes and low voice. But his face, dear Lord, *that* she did not recognize. He was easily the handsomest man she ever seen. His jaw was square with a cleft in his chin. His mouth drew her gaze. That was the mouth she kissed, the lips that stirred such hunger with the briefest touch. A tingling excitement began in her belly and fluttered up to her breasts to bring a sweet familiar ache.

"You act like you never seen me before." His voice sounded irritated.

"I haven't, not really. Why did you shave your face?" Her voice sounded breathless. She wanted the beard back. It acted like a mask, hiding his masculine beauty from her.

"It's warm now. Beards are for cold weather."

She forced her eyes away from him. Her hand grabbed the leg of the gobbler she'd taken.

"I can hardly believe it's you."

"I'm running the traps with you tonight," he said.

She looked up into those amazing blue eyes, then looked quickly away. "All right, if you feel up to it."

"What is the matter. Have I got something stuck on my face?"

"No, Nash," she said.

"Then why won't you look at me when I'm talking?"

She stared. The change was remarkable. Who would have believed the removal of a little growth of beard could transform him to such a—

"Are you listening to me?"

"Beg pardon?" She realized he was speaking, because she watched his lips moving. What he said was a complete blank. Her cheeks burned with embarrassment.

"You hit your head?"

"I'm fine, I do assure you. Now what is it you wanted?" Listen this time, she told herself.

"I want you to cut my hair. Like I was saying. Can you even up the mess you made, sort of trim it all one length?"

That would mean touching him. A shiver of excitement climbed her spine. Oh, no—she couldn't do that, not with her heart beating with the speed of a hummingbird's wings.

"It looks fine." She wondered if she sounded convincing. He frowned.

"No, it don't." He ran a hand over his uneven mane then extended his hand to her. She jumped backward. "What has gotten into you? You're twitchy as a cat with wet feet."

"It will be much shorter," she cautioned.

"Well then, leave the back long. Maybe it could cover my ear."

She nodded and retrieved her scissors from her possibles bag. He sat on a log staring off at the aspen across the pond. She hesitated a moment longer, taking deep breaths in a vain effort to get a hold of herself.

"Well?" he asked.

"Yes, just coming," she said, and stepped up behind him.

She drew her tortoise comb through his thick hair. He closed his eyes. His face held a serene expression. She allowed her fingers to pet his soft mane as she prepared to repair some of the damage she'd done. She leaned forward, nearly brushing his back, hovering there, just beyond his touch. Her fingers held the hair and she snipped the scissors. The brown coil fell to the ground beside his foot. She worked quickly now, trying to ignore his earthy scent that seemed to beckon her.

When she finished she sighed in relief. She'd endured somehow. She stepped back, thankfully, and assessed her work. She frowned.

"What's wrong?" he asked. "Is it lopsided?"

He looked more handsome than before.

"No. It's even."

"All them little hairs tickle my neck. I'm going to take a bath."

"Oh—well, I...I'll just dress the bird." She left the pond and sat with her back to him, but his shouts brought her scurrying back to the shore.

"Thomas!" she cried. The pond was quiet. The surface showed ripples. Could some animal have pulled him under? "Thomas!"

He surfaced a few feet from her, his naked shoulders and chest gleaming in the afternoon sun. Her jaw dropped and she gaped at him. He *was* feeling better.

"You scared the life out of me," she called. "Why were you shouting?"

"The water's damn cold. Shriveled up my—ah, puckered my skin."

He stood now and she could see the muscles of his chest and stomach. His wide shoulders tapered to a narrow waist. Below the surface she saw a thatch of dark hair. She spun about. Her face was so hot she half expected to burst into flames.

"Oh, now Delia. I know you seen a naked man before."

"Nash, come out of there before you catch pneumonia."

"All right."

He walked toward her. She heard the water splashing as he approached. His voice came from just behind her as a whisper.

"Care to warm me up?"

Squeezing her eyes closed did not banish the image his words created in her mind.

"Nash, put on your clothes this instant."

"I forgot to bring my drying skin."

Droplets of water spattered her.

"What are you doing?"

"Shaking off."

She pressed her hands to her burning cheeks and hurried off to get the buckskin. She couldn't resist taking one look at him from within the wigwam. He stood tall and perfect within a circle of sunlight. His legs were long and muscular. She wondered about the scar that marked one thigh. His body radiated power.

She wadded the skin and flung it at him. She watched the leather sail through the air and land at his feet. Her skin was moist, as if she'd been the one swimming.

A few minutes later he stood before her dressed in only his britches. He somehow looked bigger to her now. She gripped the feathers and pulled them from the turkey.

"One of them feathers would look pretty in your hair."

"A feather?"

"The Flathead women tie feathers at the end of their braids. Like this." He gathered a few smaller feathers like a bouquet of flowers and held them to the end of her braid. His skin smelled clean. Droplets of water sparkled on the dark curling hairs covering his chest. His presence disturbed her more than his kiss. Her breathing came in short little pants.

"Yes. Perhaps, I'll try that."

She took the feathers from him. Her fingers brushed over his cool flesh. At last he moved away.

This was ridiculous. She'd lived with this man for over a month and had never been so affected by his physical presence.

But he'd shared his heart with her. He'd told her about his wife's death and how it hurt him. Now she understood perfectly why he had come to the mountains. It explained why he was so reluctant to accept her into his life. She was a reminder of a woman he'd loved and lost. She was another chance to suffer pain. The realization made him dearer to her. He touched her spirit. Now his physical presence drew her body.

She could not believe her battered heart stirred again, not after so much pain. But here she was feeling that strong desire to touch and hold. Somehow her heart was ready. Her mind held back. The pain was too fresh. She couldn't go through that kind of suffering again. Not again.

Chapter Eight

Nash could sit his horse. He announced they would move camp again. They followed the stream to the Musselshell. The main channel forked into three branches.

"This here is the Three Forks. We'll head East from here toward the Yellowstone."

They traveled for several days, hunting only for food as they climbed into the high mountains where the river narrowed as it fell down rocky slopes and danced through alpine meadows. The splendor of the Rockies took her breath away. Beautiful and deadly, she reminded herself. Nash kept heading upstream. The water ran calm now.

There were signs of beaver, she thought, noticing the stripped bark and felled trees all about them. There was good shelter in the high ridge of rock to the left and plenty of tracks indicating game.

"We'll stop here," said Nash.

She smiled in silent satisfaction. He'd taught her so much.

The gear was unpacked and the camp struck. By

midafternoon they set a line of traps and caught a fat buck for dinner. Nash did the skinning. She took the hide for tanning after he finished gutting and butchering the beast. Before dusk she collected cattail root to roast with dinner.

That evening, she turned a flank of venison over the low fire. From their new camp she could see the snow on the high peaks to the west. She gazed at the blue giants nestled in green foothills. The light receded and the mountains rose up, dark against the sky.

"Purdy, ain't it?" he asked.

She nodded dreamily.

"Delia, you haven't said nary a word all day."

She smiled. "I remember when you told me that I talked too much."

"I never said that exactly."

"No, you just made me walk behind the horse for ten miles."

"I was trying to make a point."

"Perhaps you made it too well." She slid the meat to a flat stone and cut a piece for him. The venison was placed beside the cattail tuber upon a tin plate. Some days she succeeded in getting him to eat from a plate. She had yet to see him use any utensil other than his knife. He refused to say grace. She offered him the plate and smiled as he accepted the tin.

"Just was wondering if there was something on your mind, is all. I known some women in my time that used silence as a weapon. Don't keep it all bottled up."

"No, Thomas, I do not hold you a grudge." That much was true. But there was much on her mind.

After dinner she would write down her thoughts. It helped her make sense of her feelings.

Nash looked to where she lay beside him, curled on her side with her head resting on her new down pillow. Her hair was wispy about her face. The early-morning light filtered through the hide. In sleep, she looked younger, like a girl. He wanted to brush the fine hair back and kiss her awake.

He flopped back onto the hides. This was driving him mad. He'd make her his woman, if she'd let him. He could read trail and weather. But somehow he could not read Delia. She gave him no information and, damn it, he tried three times to start a conversation. He wanted to hold her again. But he did not want to make a fool of himself, chasing after a woman who wanted no part of him.

He glanced at Delia in slumber, then lifted himself up on one elbow and reached over her body to the bag beyond her. Quiet as a thief, he slid the journal from its place and eased out of the hut. He crept off to the rocks above the camp and sat down facing their resting place.

June 1, 1835—I shot a grizzly bear. I can hardly believe my luck. The great monster had Nash's head in his terrible jaws. I don't know what came over me. I grabbed his gun and shot the beast's head. By God's miracle, I hit it. The bear dropped Nash and charged after me. I'm ashamed to say I ran for my life. Somehow Nash made it to shore and shot the beast in the head. It died on the spot. Nash is terribly injured. I prayed to God to spare him. I cannot lose another man to these wretched mountains.

What did that mean? Did she have some feelings for him? But her words were not clear. Perhaps, she just feared losing another protector.

June 14, 1834—Thomas kissed me today. I do not know what to think. I did not stop him, though I'm sure I should have. It was wonderful for a moment. I felt a bursting joy within myself. It was as if that kiss brought me back to life and gave me hope. Then I thought of John and felt so ashamed. He is gone from this earth and here I am kissing a man. And not just kissing him. I wanted him to do more than kiss me. I don't know what's wrong with me. Surely, these are not proper thoughts for a widow. I do not want my Johnny to be gone. But neither do I want to leave this man. I'll all torn up inside.

Thomas told me he was married. His poor wife was killed in an accident. This explains so much to me. Now I see why he was so cruel at first. He knows what it's like to survive and wonder why. Why me, Lord, and why him?

Oh, I nearly forgot—Thomas offered me a 10% share and I took it.

Nash slapped his forehead so hard it stung. Women were crazy. How could she shove his partnership offer there at the end, like an afterthought? He looked over the passage again. He had his answer. She wanted him. But she was still raw from her husband's death. He needed to be patient.

He turned the page of the journal and read on.

June 16, 1834—Thomas shaved his face today. I barely recognize him; he is so handsome. I cannot believe the change. I clipped his hair as well. My fingers yearn to touch him once more. He looks dashing. After all this grooming he decided to bathe. I think he is intentionally trying to stir my blood. I recognize my body answering his call. He plays games with me. I have been in love and—

"Thomas!" Delia snatched the journal from his hands and glared at him with accusing eyes.

"Damn, woman! When did you learn to sneak about like that?"

"You told me you cannot read."

"Now, Delia—"

"You lied to me! It's just like stealing." She clutched the journal to her breast. He noticed suddenly that she had filled out there as well. She no longer was shaped like a stick of dry wood. Now her hips and bosom pressed against soft buckskin.

"Now simmer down, woman. I was just—"

"Don't you tell me to simmer down. Of all the unspeakable acts. How could you?"

"I only wanted to know something about you."

"Some things are private, Thomas. You have no right to read this."

He felt a door closing, slamming shut in his curious face.

"Damn." It was all he could think to say.

"You should be. You surely should be. How long have you been reading my journal?"

"Since the bear," he admitted.

Her little fist was clenched tight, shaking before him. He wished she'd take a swing at him and get it over with. "How far?"

He stood silent, wondering how long this storm would blow.

"How far did you read?" she shouted.

"June sixteen," he said.

"You beast! I'll never forgive you if I live to be a hundred. Don't ever speak to me again."

"That's gonna make for a real interesting summer."

She whirled away. Moccasins were better for sneaking than stomping, he decided, seeing her storm away. He was going to miss reading that book. He waited up on the hill for a long while. His experience with Elizabeth taught him that he'd just get second helpings if he moved in too early. Generally his wife would shout at him and then he'd apologize and then they'd make love. His eyebrows went up. It was possible, he decided, and headed back down the trail.

Nash found her talking to her horse in the field beyond the rocks. The puffiness about her eyes told him she'd been crying.

He never meant to hurt her. If he hadn't been so crazy about her, he wouldn't have taken the journal today. He ground his teeth rhythmically together. Then she never would have known. But she did and was now embarrassed he knew these things. He was a skunk.

"Delia, I'm sorry I hurt your feelings," he said. That sounded heartfelt and he meant it. With any luck she'd be in his arms before breakfast.

She stroked the horse's face and said not a word.

"You don't need to be embarrassed. You didn't write nothing to be ashamed about. Now why don't you forgive me?"

"Let me get this straight, Mr. Nash," she said. Her voice was clipped and icy. "You are sorry for hurting me, but not for stealing my journal and reading my private thoughts. You feel I am embarrassed when by all rights you should be. And you have the audacity to consider yourself deserving of forgiveness?" She slapped him across his bare cheek.

Elizabeth had never hit him. She'd always accepted his apology. His face stung. He squinted at her.

"Now do you forgive me?"

"No, Mr. Nash. I will never forgive you."

This was unfamiliar ground. Sometimes flattery could get him out of a tight spot.

"You look pretty when you're mad."

"Pretty? Do you suppose I care what you think? I could kill you. I have never, ever been so mortally offended in my life. I can think of no way you will ever make restitution."

"Good, I guess, because I don't know how to make a restitution anyways."

She stared at him for a moment, appearing to size him up. Then she laughed at him. Not a friendly laugh, but a scornful, hurtful kind of laugh. The kind to make a man feel small.

"Of course you don't," she said.

The blood rose up within him. How dare she laugh at him? Maybe he didn't use those fancy words. He'd taken her in, hadn't he? He'd kept her fed until she looked like a racehorse instead of a mule.

He lashed out and grabbed her by the arms.

"Now you listen here, Delia." He spoke through clenched teeth and gave her a little shake to get her attention. "What I done was wrong. But you have to forgive me. It says so in your Bible. I ain't done you no bad hurt. I just read your words so I could understand you a little. I think you're a fine woman. Maybe I ain't got the best education. But I know spite when I see it. You're out to hurt me."

"You hurt me," she said.

"Forgive me, Delia."

"Why?"

"'Cause I need you to. You're the most important thing in the world to me."

Her eyes changed. They looked all velvety brown now. That's the way he wanted her, with her eyes looking at him just like that. His breath came rapidly now.

"Tell me why you did it." She was listening to him now. Looking into her rich amber eyes, he almost told her the truth. He nearly said he loved her. Instead, he settled on a half-truth.

"I have feelings for you, Delia. I was wondering if—I mean, I know you worry about me. But that's because you need me to get back East. I just want you to care about me a little as a man."

"You must think I am the most ridiculous woman alive."

"You're the bravest woman alive."

She smiled at him.

His fingers stroked her cheek. She didn't pull away. The flesh was warm and soft.

"Tell me what you think of me, other than that I'm a thief and a liar."

Her arms loop around his waist. She stepped toward him. He felt warmth swelling within his chest. What was that? Then he knew. It had been so long he'd nearly forgotten. It was hope. She made him feel hopeful.

"At first I was so frightened of being left alone again. Now it's worse, because I care about you."

He met her serious gaze. "That's all I wanted to know."

"You should have asked."

"I asked, Delia. You shut me out. Why'd you do that?"

His thumb brushed the shell of her ear.

"I was afraid."

His hands slid over her shoulders and down her back to the spot where her body was most narrow. His hands splayed about her waist and drew her in. Her stomach pressed against his hips. The pressure of her warm body raised an ache within him. She leaned forward now, pressing her soft breasts to his chest. The ache began to pound with the coursing of his blood.

He lowered his mouth to hers and watched her eyes flutter shut. She gave her lips to him. There was richness in her touch, a lush fullness pressing to him. Her mouth opened at his unspoken urging and his tongue slipped within. She tasted of fresh mint.

The hot stoking of the tip of her tongue brought a groan from somewhere deep within him. One hand delved into her hair and the other pressed her body close. She must feel him now, hard and wanting pressed against her own breathless body.

A cry reached him, but he did not stop to consider the meaning. His kiss was now a promise of what he would do to the rest of her sweet flesh, if she would let him. He heard the cry again.

A horse's whinny and a hoof pawing at the ground. He pulled her away and looked about the meadow. Something had frightened his horses.

"What is it?" she asked.

He cast a quick look at her. Her lips were swollen and pink from his kisses. The flush on her cheeks nearly made him lose his reason again. Instead, he lifted his Hawkins from its resting place against the tree.

"Stay here."

"I will not."

He scowled at her.

"Then follow close."

He crept slowly in the direction of the horses. He frowned at their snorting and dancing. It could be a wildcat, he thought. Not in the daylight, he decided. Then he silently prayed that they did not smell another grizzly. He cocked his rifle. Behind him he heard the double click of his shotgun cocking.

He peered over the rocks to the area of their camp. Several Flathead Indians stood near the fire pit. He released the hammer on his gun and eased it gently into place.

"Them's Flatheads," he whispered.

"Is it safe?"

He nodded then called to the men.

"Hello, brothers." He spoke in the language he had learned his first long winter in these mountain.

"Hello, Long Knife." The speaker looked familiar. This was the man who had brought Delia to him. "I see that Winter Woman is much changed. Now she looks strong on the outside as well."

Soon the men sat around the fire. Delia stoked the coals as Nash brought venison. The men ate and drank their fill. Nash did not bother them with questions. They would come to the reason for their visit in their own time. There was no use in rushing a Flathead. He'd learned patience in his time with them, and manners. Finally one of their group spoke.

"We have finished our fighting with the Blackfoot for now."

"Did you count many coup?" he asked.

"Yes, my warriors were brave and fought with honor. But not all of them are coming home with me. My younger brother has gone before. My mother has no one left in her lodge, now. That is why I have come. I remembered you did not want this woman."

Nash scowled. He remembered with shame his efforts to get the man to take Delia with him.

"I am wiser now," said Nash.

"You see the strength in her? This is good. I saw it before when she was skinny and weak. There is a light inside her. I could not stop thinking about this woman."

"I thank you for seeing what I could not. She is a rare woman to be sure." He looked at Delia. She shifted uncomfortably. It was obvious that they spoke about her, yet she did not ask a single question of him. He smiled at her control.

"I wish Winter Woman to become my wife," said Hunts Buffalo. "Strong children from her will begin to heal my mother's heart." Nash looked from the warrior to Delia. Her eyes were wide with questions. "Please tell her that she will live with my mother until she is accustomed to me. I will give her seven horses if she agrees and she may pick them."

He had no choice but to relay the proposal. He turned to her.

"Delia, I have to tell you something. But before I do you got to promise me not to raise your voice. Think before you speak and be sure what you say cannot be taken as an insult. This here's one of them men that rescued you."

"Yes," she said, smiling at the warrior. "I remember him. He was very kind to me."

"He's done making war on the Blackfoot and has come here to propose to you."

"Propose what?" He could tell by her expression of confusion and dread that she knew damn well.

"He wants to marry you. Now don't say nothing, just nod. That's a girl. He wants you to live with his mother for a while. He thinks you'll give him strong children. Oh, and he'll give you seven horses as dowry. That's more than customary."

"What should I say?"

"Well, unless you want to be a Flathead squaw, I'd say no."

She frowned at him. "Of course I'll say no. I want to know how to say no so I do not insult him."

"That's the part I ain't figured out yet."

"Marvelous," she whispered.

"Delia, this is a real touchy situation. Flatheads are peaceful, but they's still Indians. If you insult him, make him lose face, he'll skin me and you both."

Her eyes were wide with fear now.

"Tell him—wait, that's not good." She seemed to focus on the lush green leaves above them, then her gaze met his once more. "Tell him I will be forever grateful for his rescue, that I owe him my life. I hope to repay him one day for his kindness."

"That all?"

"Tell him that first."

She waited while he spoke to Hunts Buffalo.

"He says you could repay him by becoming his wife."

Chapter Nine

"He says he'll give me a hundred beaver for you," said Nash.

Cordelia wondered if he actually considered it. Not so long ago he would have jumped at the chance. She pressed her damp hands firmly against her thighs. She would show these men no fear.

"Are you going to take him up on it?" she asked.

He scowled at her. She'd never been so happy to see his irritation. Sweet relief flooded her body, lifting her spirits like a rising tide.

"What do you take me for? Sell my own partner? That'll be the day. Besides, I promised to get you to the Rendezvous and so I will, God willing and if the creek don't rise."

So he was concerned about his partner. Now she was frowning. Perhaps she had become a little too useful. He considered her an asset. She wanted to be more to him than his trapping partner, didn't she? She really wasn't sure what she wanted.

"Maybe I'll just go along with him and see what it's like to be a Flathead."

Nash's head snapped around and his gaze focused on her. Now she knew what a deer saw when sighted down the barrel of his long rifle. She shifted, suddenly uncomfortable at her challenge. He spoke to the chief in a calm voice. When he faced her, his eyes flashed blue ice. He dragged her up and away from the men. She found herself dancing along beside him as he strode to their wigwam.

"You crazy? He'll have you cooking and carrying. He'll work you from morning to night."

"And that would be different from my current arrangement in what way?" she asked.

He scowled. "You know Flatheads take more than one wife?"

This seemed to be the fact he was sure would convince her, when all she wanted was for him to tell her not to go. She stared up at him, holding her breath. Then she sighed.

"A second wife, wonderful, I'll have half the work to do."

"Are you actually considering this or just trying to lather me?"

"What difference does it make to you? You'll be able to keep your ten percent and you'll have a hundred skins to boot. What's stopping you?"

"Good Lord."

"I was just remembering how you felt about my coming here."

"I explained all that to you. I didn't want to get involved with a woman again."

"You still haven't."

"You're talking crazy. What do you want me to say?" She knew then what she wanted and it frightened her to death. She wanted him to say he loved her. She opened her mouth to tell him, but he spoke first. "He'll take you, if I let him. Damned if I know how to stop him if he decides to take you anyway."

Suddenly her impulsiveness frightened her.

"You mean they might take me?"

"What do you think, this is some kind of game? We need a reason you can't go, a damn good one. There's eight of them. I might kill one or two but not eight."

He was looking back at them now. She followed his gaze. Hunts Buffalo sat relaxed and patient beside his warriors. The men each carried a long knife and two had flintlock rifles.

Her skin felt as if she'd been dipped in ice water. Gooseflesh rose up along her arms.

"I'm frightened," she whispered. Then she turned to Nash. "What are Flathead afraid of?"

"Not much, Blackfoot, maybe, and spirits."

"What kind of spirits?" she wondered.

"Evil one, crazy ones, the ghosts of their enemies."

A seed of an idea drifted into her mind. She considered and the seed took root.

"I know what to say." She took one step and felt his broad hand restrain her.

"If you says no outright, they'll be insulted. You has to—"

She interrupted. "I'm not going to say no."

"Delia—"

"Trust me, Nash," she said.

He studied her for a moment longer and nodded. "Let's go."

The sat together, across from Hunts Buffalo.

"Tell him I am forever grateful for his rescue." Nash nodded and spoke to Hunts Buffalo, who smiled at her. "Tell him I agree to be his wife," she said. Nash raised one eyebrow and shook his head.

"I ain't telling him that, Delia. Damned if I will," he growled low at her.

"Tell him I do not think my husband's ghost will bother him, because he is an Indian."

"What?" Nash said. "You sure?" She nodded and waited until Nash and Hunts Buffalo finished speaking.

"You hooked him, Delia," said Nash. "He wants to know about your husband."

"Ask him which one," she said, smiling and nodding at Hunts Buffalo.

"What do you mean which one? You been married more than once?"

"No, now repeat what I say. 'Which one?'"

He did. Delia watched the warrior lean forward, his eyebrows high on his brow.

Nash said, "He wants to know how many husbands you had. You sure got him interested, I'll grant you that."

"Tell him I have been married three times, all white men. My first husband was a jealous man. He died in a war. Before he left me, he told me he'd kill any man who touched me."

Nash nodded. His direct gaze seemed to radiate approval. The icy fear within her melted and she warmed inside. Then he spoke to the group again. The men about Hunts Buffalo muttered to one another.

One looked behind him at the forest. Their relaxed posture contorted into nervous tension.

"Hunts Buffalo wonders what happened to your other husbands?" Nash said, seemingly eager for the next installment of her story.

"It was very tragic. Roger drowned. I can't understand it because he a very strong swimmer. And John, the finest hunter in Ohio, went hunting and never came back. Just bad luck, I suppose."

"Delia, you're brilliant," said Nash. He turned to tell the men the bad news. Then he nodded and listened for a time.

"Delia, Hunts Buffalo has changed his mind. He does not want to disturb the spirit of your first husband. He thinks you survived the winter because of his protection."

Delia nodded. That, at least, might be true. If such things were possible, John would have protected her.

"Tell him, I completely understand. I am sure he will always be my friend. Assure him, I remain in his debt and am grateful to him."

"Delia, not only can you trap and shoot, you're the smartest woman I ever met." She basked in the glow of his words for a moment.

The warriors seemed in a sudden hurry to depart. Her invitation to stay the night met with hasty refusals. She waved to the group. They forded the cold stream and vanished into the wood.

Nash grabbed her about the waist and spun her in a glorious circle.

"Damn, Delia, you ran them off!"

"Yes, I did, didn't I?"

He extended his arms and lifted her high in the air.

Then he lowered her gently to the ground. Heat radiated from him through the soft hide covering her body.

His lopsided grin warmed her.

"You really foxed 'em. Ha! What made you think of it?"

"You did! You told me they were afraid of spirits. I just followed your lead."

"The part about the drowning purely terrified them. And saying the man was the best shot in Ohio, that's like being the best bookkeeper in the Rocky Mountains." He doubled over, clutching his side in laughter.

The smile fell from her lips. She suddenly felt cold. John had won a shooting contest. It was one of the things that had convinced him to come west. He brought his Kentucky rifle along, sure he could provide for them. But it wasn't big enough to stop grizzly or buffalo. She didn't know that then and neither did John. So he walked over that hill one sunny morning, never came back.

Nash wasn't laughing now. He watched her with cautious eyes.

"Delia? What's wrong?" His hand rested on her shoulder.

She shook her head and pressed both hands to her lips. A swelling hot lump of pain rose up in her throat. Tears escaped the corners of her eyes, carrying her sorrow out to him. Then she was wrapped in the hard comfort of his arms.

"I feel so guilty," she gasped.

"For lying to them fellas, hooey!"

"John won a shooting contest in Cincinnati," she wailed.

"Oh, Delia, hush. I'm sorry. I didn't mean no disrespect to him. I surely did not." He rocked her. Her breath came in ragged gasps. His hand patted the center of her back. "I thought you made that up with the rest. I didn't know. Hush now, you'll make yourself sick."

She quieted gradually, pulling back the pain, letting part of it wash away with her tears.

"I miss him still. I feel so guilty being here."

"No reason to feel guilty for not dying."

"Not for that." She pulled away to look into the sympathetic blue waters of his eyes. "For starting to feel again, for laughing with you while my John—"

"Don't say it. Nothing good comes from these thoughts. That's mean thinking that tears you down, makes you feel bad for living. You couldn't do nothing to save him, Delia. The mountains took him. That's all."

She turned her back on him. Just looking into his dear face brought a fresh surge of emotion and pain.

He took her by the shoulders. She tried halfheartedly to shake him off, but he tightened his hold, drawing her backward into the comfort of his firm embrace. This is what she wanted—to be held by him. His body was as warm as a fire on a cold afternoon.

His breath brushed her ear as he whispered, "You can't stop living, 'cause he's gone. You ain't buried with him. You're here, with me. Would he want you to be miserable for not dying as well?" She made no reply. He squeezed the breath from her. "Would he?"

"No. He'd want me happy."

"Course he would. Living's hard, sometimes harder than dying. You have to keep trying and if you find some comfort, someone that brings you joy, don't push him away. Maybe it's only for a day or a year. That's why you need to grab it, grab it with both hands."

She turned to face him and gazed into the conviction shining clearly in his eyes.

"But it hurts so much to lose."

"I know that. Do we dry up and never try again? That's a coward's way and we ain't cowards."

"I just what to run away and find somewhere safe."

"I ran. Nowhere's safe. The pain tracks you like a wolf after a sick calf. I half hoped I'd die. But no more, because of you."

She turned to look into his eyes. His lips turned up into a sad smile.

"I don't think I can do this, Thomas. I can't be left behind."

"I come with no guarantee, Delia."

Cordelia needed some assurances that he would never leave her. A solemn promise that if death came, it would take her first and never, never leave her behind.

He held both her hands. "I know you think you need me. But is that all that's between us?"

"I think you are an honorable man." Her feelings were so muddled. The insistent tug of attraction still pulled. Her body tingled for his touch. The intensity of his stare made her tremble.

"Is that all?"

"You already know I need you to get out of here, that I depend on your wisdom and strength."

His brows dipped low over his winter-blue eyes. The pressure of his grip changed.

"What do you want me to say?"

"I want," he said, stepping so close that his shirt touched her dress, "for you to want me as a man. I want you to feel what I feel."

She could sense his desire now, like a beating heart. His hand reached up to clasp her single braid. Callused fingers removed the leather cord and combed her hair into blond waves about her shoulders.

"Your hair is so pretty, just like the mane of a palomino."

"Your hair has always reminded me of mink."

He cocked his head.

"Really?" She nodded. He slid his hands slowly down her back. She pressed her stomach and breasts against him and heard him sigh. "Put your arms around me, Delia. I need your touch."

She lifted her arms and looped them about his neck, letting her fingers delve into his long dark hair. His eyes drifted closed and his square chin rose, relishing her attention. She drew one finger around the shell of his damaged ear. His eyes snapped open. Somehow his gaze made her breathing come fast. Her blood coursed through her body.

"How do you do it?" she asked. Her throat went dry, her words the merest whisper.

"What?"

"Make me want you with just a glance?"

He swept her roughly from her feet and strode to

their sleeping pallet. She thought to stop him for a moment. This would change everything between them. She would stop him, she told herself, as soon as those piercing eyes left her.

The soft bearskin caressed her legs as she sat upon the hide. He knelt above her and drew off his shirt. She stared at the thick hair covering his wide chest. How many times had she wondered what it would be like to feel the muscle beneath his velvety skin? Her hands rose up to touch, reaching no farther than his stomach. At the contact of her fingertips, his muscles twitched and the sound of the intake of his breath reached her. She looked down to his leather breeches and saw the evidence of her effect upon him.

His hands were at the hem of her dress now. She stopped him.

"Delia, please let me see you. Until now, I only dreamed it."

"You dream of me?"

"Nearly every night. You're driving me crazy. I've never felt like this before."

"Never?" Surely a married man would know this pulsing desire, this quickening.

"Not like this. Never like this."

She wanted to please him. Anticipation surged through her as she considered his desire.

"You once said I looked like a boy." She reminded him.

"Not anymore. Now you're pure woman and driving me mad. Just let me look at you."

His hand fell to her hip. She'd discarded her bloomers and leggings weeks ago in the warm weather. He was right. She didn't need them. Her hand covered his and she rose on her knees and drew the dress away in one smooth stroke.

She watched him now. His mouth parted slightly. His gaze covered her breasts and then traveled down to the thatch of dark brown hair at the juncture of her legs.

Her skin seemed to hum; she could almost hear the vibration of her body trembling beneath his gaze.

"You're beautiful," he said. His hand reached out. She ached for him. Still some piece of her cried out in anguish. Images of her husband rose in her mind, comparisons and memories. John preferred the dark. He never looked at her in the daylight. He was not as beautiful as this man before her.

She grasped his hand before he could touch her.

"Delia, let me bring us back to life. Let me touch you."

She nodded but held his hand firmly. "I want—I need this to be different from ever before."

He nodded and she pressed him backward to the bearskin. Her fingers played along the sharp contours of his chest and stomach. She pressed herself against him and licked the shell of his ear. As she kissed him, her fingers slid beneath the edge of his breeches. Her fingers wrapped him tightly. He was warm and stiff beneath her touch. Never had she held a man this way, feeling the long length of him.

Thomas pressed himself against her palm. She let her hand glide up and down the length of him. He held himself still, as if movement on his part would break this spell cast about them. His desire must have grown too strong, for he rolled her to her back, struggling for the lacing of his trousers.

His large body settled between her legs, and he loomed above her. His hands covered her breasts. His mouth trailed close behind. He pressed hot kisses down her body, licking the curve of her navel. His touch sent a trail of fire over her heated skin. Her desire pulsed with each strong beat of her heart. His fingers moved toward her thatch of hair.

"No!" she cried.

He rose up above her.

"I just want to taste you." He stared at her a moment. Her hands pressed ineffectively at his chest. "Delia, have you never—you've done this with your husband, surely."

He said the words and the spell was broken. He was not her husband. Yet, she had let him touch her in ways even John never had.

She shook her head frantically now.

"Let me up, Thomas," she begged.

"Delia, please, let me love you. I just want—"

"No, Thomas, you are not my husband."

"He's gone, Delia." Thomas held her wrists above her head and stilled her squirming body with the weight of his own. "He's gone for good. I'm here, alive and burning for you."

"Thomas, I know you miss your wife. But I am not Elizabeth. Let me up."

He rolled to his back. The air cooled her flushed skin. She reached for her dress and pulled it over her head, letting the soft leather cover her shame. He lay motionless with one arm thrown over his eyes. He clenched his teeth, showing the muscles at his jaw. She resisted the urge to touch his shoulder.

"I'm so sorry," she said. "I didn't mean—I can't do this."

His arm slid away and his fingers coiled about one wrist. She met the intense gaze, feeling a flush bloom on her cheeks.

"You're wrong. I don't want a replacement for my wife, Delia. I want you."

She shook her head in disbelief and tugged at her captured wrist. He rolled to his side and stroked her cheek.

"I pushed too hard. You're still grieving him. I see that. I'll give you time, Delia. You tell me when."

He released her hand and she bolted from the little shelter, pursued by all the demons of her mind.

Chapter Ten

Nash lay on the hide for a few moments, thinking of her soft skin and the pink flush on her cheeks. Then he closed his eyes, rolled to her side of the pallet and inhaled the scent of her. A growl escaped him. He thumped the hides with his clenched fist and sat up. The pressure of his erection squeezed between the leather breeches and his body forced him back down again.

Why wasn't she ready? She'd been months without the touch of a man. He'd told her he loved her, hadn't he? He thought back to what he was feeling and doing nine months after Elizabeth's death. He'd been living with the Flathead, alone. He'd had opportunities, but he still felt attached to his wife. Now he couldn't quite see her face. How could you forget the face of the woman you loved?

He sat up again. Was Delia gun-shy or grieving? Maybe she just didn't fancy him. Her journal said she did—so much it caused her guilt. The look of her, flushed and panting, confirmed his conviction. Her body, at least, wanted his.

He stepped out into the afternoon sunshine and looked about. She was gone. He drew on his shirt and grasped his Hawkins. She couldn't avoid him for long. He debated whether he should search for her, then he decided to check his traps.

He saddled his horse and bridled the other. Then he rode to the stream and hollered, "Delia! I'm checking traps. You coming?"

He waited a moment, thinking she might appear. After looking for some sign of her, he sighed and turned his ponies upstream. The thudding of running feet stopped him.

He swung about in his saddle and saw her dash down the trail. Her blond hair flew behind her. She ran with a grace usually reserved for four-legged animals. He could see her red eyes and damp cheeks. She jumped onto the packhorse without a boost or stepping stump. Damn, what a woman! She straddled the horse and her dress rode up her bare thighs. He stared at her long tanned legs. She would not look at him, choosing instead to stare at the horse's mane. He clucked to his mount and off they went to the beaver pond.

He checked the traps and she held the horses. They rode a slow circle about the pond, collecting his catch. He tied the beaver behind his saddle. Then he walked to her and placed a hand on her leather-clad ankle. At last, she looked down at him. His smile yielded no reflection in her face.

"Delia, I'm sorry if I hurt you," he said.

She gazed at him. He kept his hand still upon her leg, resisting the urge to pull her down, into his arms.

"I don't want to give my heart to a man who plans to leave me at the Rendezvous."

He nodded. That was the original plan. So much had changed since he had spoken those words.

"Would you want to stay with me, Delia?"

She blinked as if she couldn't understand him.

"What do you mean?" she asked.

"I don't want to leave you at the Rendezvous. It just seemed like what you wanted and maybe what's best for you."

"What do *you* want, Thomas?"

"I want you to stay with me."

She smiled at last. Slowly the smile melted away like last year's snow. A chill seeped through him as he studied her tranquil expression.

"And trap the mountains, run from Indians, grizzly bears and who knows what else?" she asked.

She was right. Of course she was right. What was he thinking that, just because she had learned to shoot and trap, she wanted to make a living at it? What else could he do? He had always hunted for a living, even back in Kentucky when he owned a little farm. But she was educated, a preacher's wife. Likely, she was used to cities and congregations, books and quilting bees. Even if he did leave the mountains, could he give her the kind of life she was used to? He had no answer. Suddenly he felt full of insecurity.

"You're a fair hand at trapping," he said at last.

"Oh, Thomas, this is no life for me. I can't live here in the wilderness."

"Yet, you were ready to do just that with John." He was unable to keep the venom from his voice.

She straightened her back and peered down her pert nose at him as if judging him and finding him lacking.

"I did. Now I have seen this great wilderness, this terrible, unforgiving land. I want to go home."

"Where's home?"

"Ohio."

"And who is waiting for you, Delia?"

She pressed her lips together. He knew the answer; he had read it in her journal.

"You know I have no family."

"Home is where you make it. Make it here."

She looked away and he knew. He'd lost.

"I can't," she said.

He released her and mounted his horse.

How had it happened? How had she fallen in love with the absolute wrong man for her? Cordelia couldn't stay here with Thomas. She'd never survive another winter in the mountains. The land had rugged beauty, the sweeping vistas and tiny miracles. But it was a wilderness. They were alone and at the mercy of unforgiving nature.

She lay beneath the hides, only a foot from him. Her traitorous body whispered for his touch. She clenched her fists at her sides. Now that she knew the feel of his arms about her, how long until she lost this war within herself?

The gripping tension in her body finally exhausted her enough to allow sleep to take her. The night sounds that had once terrified her lulled her to sleep.

She woke to the smell of coffee and crawled out to meet the day. He handed her a rabbit leg and a cup.

"I'm going to check the traps," he said.

She nodded and stumbled down to the river to wash. She chewed a birch twig to fray the green wood, then used it to polish her teeth. The cold water did more than the coffee to rouse her.

When she returned, he was already mounted. In a moment she was rocking to the walking rhythm of her little bay.

She wondered about her future as they rounded the circuit of his traps. If he'd leave the mountains, she'd go with him. She watched him move through his tasks with silent efficiency. Would he ever leave them?

They rode back to camp. She saw his posture change. Her hand moved to the shotgun and held it ready. She halted at his signal and waited for him in the trees as he rode in first. After a long silent stretch, she kicked her horse forward, breaking the tree line and sighting the camp.

The wigwam was destroyed and their hides scattered. The bearskin was gone. She looked to the empty place where the tanned beaver hides had been stacked and wrapped in the waterproof deer and elk hides. Thomas studied the ground, running back and forth across the camp.

"What happened?" she asked.

"River Crow."

"How do you know?"

He held up the banded shaft of an arrow. "This here's their mark. Damn! River Crow are born thieves and dangerous as rattlers."

"When?"

"Not long, we just missed them."

"How many?"

"I'm just figuring that—ten, maybe."

He reached for her and pulled her to the ground.

"Stay here," he ordered.

She grabbed his shirt, clenching her fists in soft leather.

"What are you going to do?"

"I'm going after them. They got our catch."

"Don't! Stay here. We can catch more beaver."

"Delia—it's July. We ain't got time to catch enough furs to live through the winter, let alone make a profit. Let go."

She wouldn't. He had to pry her fingers away one by one.

"There's ten, you said. They'll kill you, Thomas. What good are the furs if you're dead? Stay with me, please."

"Let go." He freed himself and pushed her away. She fell in the dirt. Before she could rise, he was on his horse. He grabbed the reins of the bay and kicked his mount to a canter.

"Thomas!" she screamed his name. He rode away. Her feet pounded along the uneven ground. The distance between them grew. "Thomas, don't leave me!"

"I'll be back," he called.

She fell to the ground beside the babbling stream. She lay there for some time. He'd left her. He'd left her with the shotgun, a water skin and no horse. How long could she live without him? Could she find the Rendezvous alone? No, she could not. She rose and walked back to the camp. The bag of jerky still hung safe on the white pine. She lowered it to the ground and filled the water skin. Into her shoulder bag went all the jerky she could carry without removing the shot, powder and rags. The water skin went over her opposite shoulder. She rested her hand upon the butcher knife he'd given her. Then she followed the path of ten Crow and one stubborn trapper.

Nash should have left her a horse. But then she would have followed him, sure as hell. Then again, a horse meant she'd have a chance of getting out of these mountains. That was if she could make it past the wolves, bears and Indians. But he needed the horse to pack the furs once he recovered them.

He checked the trail, staring at the ponies' footprints in the mud. They were just ahead now.

Without those furs he'd have no chance of ever having Delia. He needed money to make a fresh start, buy land in St. Louis or Ohio or wherever the hell she liked. If he lost them, he'd lose her. He couldn't ask her to stay in the mountains during the winter and trap. That was no place for her. She should be home, in a house, with a real wood floor and a hearth. She should have friends and neighbors and perhaps a child or two.

Watch the trail, you idiot, or you'll run right into them.

He'd wait until they slept, than steal back his goods. He and Delia would need to hightail it out of the area, before they came swarming down on them like wasps.

They'd forded the stream here. The ground was still

wet from the horses' passing. He stopped, deciding to scout ahead on foot. He hoped they wouldn't travel all night.

Cordelia's legs were so tired. Don't think about it. He's just ahead, just ahead. She hadn't lost their trail. John's trail had vanished after only a mile, as if he had stepped off the earth. She would not lose this trail.

She gritted her teeth and continued walking. The first stars appeared in the dark blue sky. She'd find him.

The moon rose, adding light and sending long shadows across her path. The sound of a screech owl rattled her nerves. She gripped tight the warm wooden stock of the shotgun.

Terror walked with her through the night. She feared the past and what lay beyond the small circle of her sight. Above all, she feared failing. She struggled to cast off the images of Thomas lying on the ground with his scalp removed. She saw arrows protruding from his back. A shiver shook her body.

The moon was falling now, slowly dipping into a bright orange ball. She looked to the East hoping to see the sky brightening. When the moon disappeared she halted, crawling beneath the roots of a fallen pine.

The sound of birdsong roused her from an uneasy slumber. Her muscles groaned in protest as she rose stiffly from the ground. Now the light was growing in the East. The day approached.

How much farther?

She heard the shot and recognized the sound. The echo rattled past her. It was his Hawkins. Another

shot rang out and she was on her feet, running toward
his discharging gun.

When she came upon the horses, she stopped. First
she found the bay and black. Farther along was a
string of ten unfamiliar mounts. The painted markings
on the legs and unusual halters told her they belonged
to Indians. She stood panting before the questioning
stare of ten horses. Now what?

She crept forward, slowly slipping from tree to tree.
This camp seemed empty. She glanced at the beaver
skins tied in neat bundles. A hundred yards beyond,
the Indians squatted behind rocks and leaned against
trees. Above them came an occasional shot from
Thomas's rifle. They had him cornered on a rocky
bluff.

She had to do something. But what? Her heart hammered so loudly she wondered that the Indians didn't
hear it.

She crept back to the pelts and carried them bundle
by bundle to the horses. Then she untied the Indians'
beasts and walked them back to Thomas' pair. She
mounted the bay and led the entire string away from
the camp, back to her fallen tree and the small grove
of briar bushes beyond. She tied them there and hid
the hides. She chose a pretty pinto of black and white
for the return trip. The beast had intelligent pale blue
eyes. Red stripes were painted upon the mare's front
legs.

The horse allowed her to mount and ride bareback
toward the camp. Where the horses left the animal
trail, she stopped to sweep the ground with a bough
from a white pine. Covering her tracks, Thomas
called it.

She didn't know if her plan would work. Perhaps they would kill her. She clenched her jaw. Her gaze lifted to the treetops swaying against the blue sky. Better to die and go to heaven than to stay here alone. *God help me save Thomas,* she prayed. Some Indians respected her, feared her. Please let this band have heard of Winter Woman.

She rode boldly up behind the Crow warriors.

"Thomas," she called.

All eyes focused upon her. Drawn bows pointed at her. She did not flinch. Several men pointed at her horse. The sound of their muttering reached her. None of the men fired. She held her shotgun aimed at the closest man.

"Delia? Good God, woman, is that you?" She'd know his voice anywhere.

"It's me," she said.

"Where are you?"

"Down below with the Indians."

There was silence for a moment, as the entire world seemed to stop.

Thomas yelled to the Indians. They shouted back.

"They knows you, Delia. They don't want to shoot you. They say to drop your weapon and they'll not harm you."

"What about you?"

"Me they plan to kill," he shouted.

"Tell them to drop their weapons or I'll shoot the man wearing the blue necklace. Tell them I have their horses and the furs."

Thomas spoke to them. The man behind the tree lowered his weapon.

"He says that's his horse, and nobody but him can ride her," said Thomas.

She smiled at the Indians and tightly gripped the rein, hoping to disguise her racing heart and trembling hands.

"Apparently he is mistaken. Tell them I'll trade with them."

There was another exchange between Thomas and the Crow.

"He says he can kill you and take his horse back."

"Not before I kill this man." She motioned with the barrel of her gun, her eyes never leaving the sight. She kept her weapon raised, holding the stock firmly to her shoulder. Nash's translation drifted down the mountain. "I'll give them half the horses in exchange for you."

"They can find the horses, Delia."

"Just tell them."

He did. The men spoke between themselves.

"They want all the horses and furs," he called.

"No furs and all the horses but ours and I don't kill this man."

Thomas's words rolled down off the mountain.

"They agree."

She lowered her gun and smiled. The bows dropped to each man's side.

"I'm going to fetch them," she said.

She wheeled the horse about and cantered off toward her cache. After retrieving the horses and switching to the bay, she rode back to the group. Thomas had crawled down off the rocks and was speaking to the Indians.

She handed the reins to the man wearing the most

feathers. He nodded and pushed Thomas forward and spoke. She looked at Nash, who stood mutely wearing a stubborn expression.

"What did he say?"

Nash scowled. "He said I ain't worth ten horses."

"You are to me."

Nash cocked his head and appeared to be considering a moment.

The leader called to his men. The group quickly mounted up and rode off.

Thomas stood motionless until the forest swallowed up the sound of the horses' hooves. Then he spun about and pulled her off her horse.

"That was a damn stupid thing to do," he said. His finger pointed, like a pistol, toward her chest. "If those were Blackfoot instead of Crow, you'd be dead right now."

"So would you." She managed to get the words out before her trembling body took over. Her knees turned to water and she sank toward the earth. He caught her before she slipped away and held her quivering against his solid body.

"They could have killed you," he whispered. His breath ruffled her hair.

She closed her eyes, inhaled his earthy scent and then sighed. "They didn't."

"You can't keep relying on them thinking you're magic. You should have stayed put." He pulled away far enough for her to see the scowl on his face.

"I stayed put once and look where it got me." She shook her head in disbelief. "You still don't understand, do you? I'd rather be dead than left alone in these mountains."

He looked momentarily chagrined but quickly recovered his composure to continue his tirade. He paced back and forth before her and spoke.

"You have to do as you're told. You're my responsibility."

"You are not my husband. I'll do what I think best." Her control evaporated and her voice rose sharply. "They would have killed you. Are those furs more important than your life?"

"Yes," he shouted. Her jaw dropped open at the vehemence of his response. "You think I give a damn what happens to me? All I care about is getting back those furs."

She knew he wanted his pelts. But it hurt to know they were all he cared about. Especially when her own feeling for him nearly overwhelmed her. She was a fool to love a man who cared nothing for her.

"Well, you've recovered them." She turned her back on him, walking through the lush grass growing beside the stream. She couldn't look at him, couldn't stand there and stare into his cold eyes without crying. Then she changed her mind, determining to go back and face him. She turned about, startled to find him just behind her.

"Why are those furs so important?" she asked.

His intense gaze stopped her in her tracks. He stepped closer and placed a hand heavily on each shoulder, rooting her to the spot.

"Because without them I can't have you."

"What?"

His voice was calm now, and sure. "Without them pelts, I got nothing to offer you but my sorry carcass. The money from them furs will give us a stake."

"What are you talking about?" A tingling excitement swept through her like a brush fire.

"I'm talking about a stake, Delia, our stake."

"Thomas, I don't want to stay in these mountains." She wanted him, but he had to understand, the winters here would kill her. The loneliness and isolation were harder on her soul than the lack of food was on her starving body.

"I know that."

He drew her into his arms. She let her body mold to the hard planes of his chest and belly. He'd said nothing of marriage. Would she marry him if he asked?

"I won't see another snowfall here. Never, never again. I'm afraid of the snow now."

"Afraid, you, who faced Flatheads, Crow and an eleven-foot grizzly? Not my Delia, she ain't scared a nothing. Bravest woman I ever met, you are."

"I'm not brave. I'm full of fears."

"Marching into a nest of Indians is a funny way of acting scared."

"I just wanted you safe."

"And so I am." He petted the hair upon her head in even strokes. "Delia, I should have left you a horse."

"Yes, you should have. I would have been here yesterday."

"You need me to get down to the Rendezvous," he said. Something about the stubborn tilt of his chin made her wonder if he dared her to deny it.

"I need you for more than that."

His eyes grew intense. The black pupils seemed large, crowding out the circle of vibrant blue.

"We'll get there. I promise."

She knew then, he would kiss her. Her eyes fluttered closed and his mouth found hers. The warm pressure sent desire rippling through her, tightening her nipples into hard buds.

His hands slid down her back, drawing her in and deepening the kiss to a sensuous blending of tongues. He delved into the hidden recesses of her mouth. She could feel the hot thrusting rhythm of his kiss stoking her until she glowed from within. It was difficult to stand. Her body seemed weak with the longing he drew from her.

He guided her gently to the ground. The smell of soft grass surrounded her. She cried out in a throaty moan when his lips left hers. The sound changed to a sigh as his kisses moved to her neck, climbing with exquisite leisure to the hollow behind her ear.

His lips milked her lobe, sucking like a babe. She reached for him, near frantic. He allowed her to draw him close. Her fingernails scored the hide-covered shoulder. Her hips rose up to press against his hovering body. From deep within her came the velvety moisture of wanting.

She needed to feel his skin pressed tight to hers. As if in answer to her desire, he rolled her to his stomach and dragged her buckskin dress slowly up her legs. He gave her time to refuse. Instead, she tugged at his shirt lacing. The afternoon sun touched her back for just a moment. Then she was lying in the grass. He swiftly removed his clothing.

She stared at him, kneeling by the brook. John was too modest to reveal himself so boldly. Looking at Thomas, she suddenly felt cheated that John had denied her this pleasure. Thomas was beautiful, just as hard and rugged as these mountains.

His shoulders were so broad. The labor of trapping and hunting had sculpted his brawn into well-defined planes. Even the muscles of his stomach bulged and knotted. Her hand ran over the sensitive skin of her soft belly and her eyes moved to the most obvious difference between them. So that was what it looked like. She'd touch it in the dark, knowing the feel of a man moving within her body and wondered.

Her gaze returned to his eyes. She found him studying her body as well. Knowing his gaze was upon her caused the throbbing anticipation to grow more urgent. She reached for his hand and pulled him down beside her.

"Delia, you're so beautiful, lying there. I can't believe my eyes."

He held her face in his two large hands, keeping her from lowering her head. She blushed.

"Not skinny anymore?" she asked.

"Only in the right places. You filled out real nice."

His rough hands caressed her breasts. His head lowered to take her hardened nipple into his mouth. The heat and moisture of his kiss fired her blood. She arched back in his arms, giving him full access to her aching breast. One hand reached down between her thighs. He groaned as he found her wet and ready.

She opened her legs to him, rocking her hips up to meet his. He never paused, as if hesitation might allow her to think, consider, deny. Swift as a diving eagle, he plunged himself into her warm body.

He held her tightly, kissing her mouth, and thrust into her again and again. She matched the driving rhythm he set. Then her graceful movement changed into a wild, desperate thrusting. Need made her frantic. An avalanche of sensation spun out from her core, sending exquisite shock waves through her. A long moan escaped her lips.

He held her shuddering body in a rigid embrace. A throaty cry reached her ears and he fell slack upon her. He crushed the breath from her for an instant, then rolled to his side, drawing her along until she lay beside him.

She stared at the blue sky. Impossible to believe she gazed at the same sky that had snowed and snowed until she had been buried alive.

"Is there anything you ain't good at?" Thomas whispered into her ear. Then nipped at her with sharp teeth.

She smiled, basking in the sunshine and the gentle hand that stroked her hair.

Gradually the world drifted back into perspective. Her limbs were no longer heavy and relaxed. Her breathing settled into a slow steady draw. The grass beneath her began to scratch. The weight of Thomas's leg across her middle became oppressive and she wondered how she could possibly be lying naked on the ground? Next came guilt. This was not her husband. Thomas had never mentioned marriage, only a stake. He had not told her he loved her. No, she was his partner. Regret rose up like a filling well. Her face flushed with embarrassment. How could she be so stupid? What if she became pregnant? Fear washed down her spine.

His voice broke into her thoughts.

"I didn't understand at first why I lived through the pain and through the dangers. Now I do."

Her hands pushed frantically at his leg. He shifted and propped himself up on one elbow to look at her.

"What is it, Delia?"

"Let me up."

He frowned. His lips pressed into a grim line and his eyes darkened with anger.

"How could I do such a thing?" she cried.

He sat up and dragged both hands through his thick hair in frustration.

"We didn't do nothing wrong."

She quickly drew the dress on and shook out her hair, dislodging the bits of clinging straw.

"Not wrong? My husband is gone only eleven months."

"He's dead, Delia." She raised her hand to strike him. "You ain't," he said.

He waited. Her hand hit his cheek with a loud clap. He barely moved. Regret filled her. This was not his fault. His eyes never left her.

"I still ain't sorry. You are the most magnificent female I ever met, and that is what man and woman was made for."

Chapter Eleven

He'd kept his eyes forward even when the sounds from behind him told him she was crying. Her hand left his waist to wipe her nose. He heard the little sniffs and her ragged intake of breath above the sound of the horse's steady hooves. She was obviously trying not to draw his notice, so he gave her privacy.

The stifled sobs tore at him like the claws of a bobcat. All he wanted to do was put his arms around her. Look what had happened the last time he had. She mentioned her husband and he couldn't control the anger. Her face had gone pale when he harshly reminded her the man was dead. He was gone and Nash was tired of her throwing him between them every time he got too close.

Hadn't he just told her that he needed the furs to get them a stake? Once he had the money, he could buy her a farm or a business. He'd take her wherever she wanted. He planned to start again, with her.

She still lived in the past, clinging to the memory of a dead man rather than accept the one who was aching for her.

Maybe he wasn't good enough. She was polished, educated and had religion. She probably thought of him as some kind of brute or hermit. Was she ashamed to love him? He ground his teeth together until they squeaked.

How he dreaded making camp. The meal, the evening and after that—pure torture. Their lovemaking was precious to him, but not to her. She was crying and everything was spoiled between them. Somehow he had to patch this up. Three weeks remained before the Rendezvous. Three weeks to make amends and win her heart before he brought her out of the mountains.

Delia managed to stop the flow of tears before they reached camp. If her face was swollen and her eyes red, he said nothing. How she wished she could ride with the pelts. Instead, her arms were looped about his narrow waist. His warm body urged her to lean against his broad back. She denied herself the pleasure, sitting stiffly behind him. She was a fallen woman. Somehow she had let her desires override every shred of moral decency. She'd never forgive herself.

A God-fearing woman waited until she was joined to a man in holy matrimony. Her eyes looked up at the billowing clouds. *Please God, forgive me.*

She couldn't blame Thomas. He was a man. Men were expected to find their pleasure if a woman allowed them. He never even said he loved her. All he mentioned was sharing his stake with her and making her a ten-percent partner. And when she explained that she must leave the mountains, he didn't try to dissuade her. He didn't ask her to stay or vow to never leave her. He merely said he understood. Well, what did she expect? Did she think he'd leave his trade to follow her East? He had made it quite clear that he hated the States. He'd never fit into her world in any case. She tried to imagine what the women of her congregation would think of Nash. She pictured him sitting in a pew clad in his buckskins, with his powder horn slung over his shoulders and his Hawkins rifle gripped in his right hand. A groan escaped her. She had never seen him without that blasted gun.

Another thought slashed through her mind. What if she bore his child—a bastard? How would she explain a child born so many months after her husband's death? Cold dread sank into her stomach.

The night crept up the mountains, bringing with it a change in sounds and sights. Above her, bats darted and dove for insects, silhouettes against a dark blue background. She heard the tiny frogs singing in symphony. They almost seemed to be crying in one long wail.

She raised her head to see the stars while the horses crossed a meadow. How much had changed since the last time she had looked at them. Thomas was rescued and she was lost.

A coyote's howl caused her to tighten her grip on Thomas's shirt. Their echoing chorus sent a shudder down her spine. The little brothers of the wolves, she thought. She remembered the wolves, scratching and whining at her shabby hut until she thought she'd go mad.

"We're back," said Nash. "Stay put. We ain't staying."

She sat numbly on the horse and he slid to the ground and quickly gathered their belongings, adding them to the packhorse.

He mounted up. "Where are we going?" she asked.

"Downstream. We'll be heading East now. Toward the Rendezvous."

Her heartbeat quickened. Conflicting emotions jumped within her like a bucket full of crickets. She'd be leaving him soon. And he'd be leaving her. Why had she allowed herself to surrender to him so close to the time they'd be parted? Perhaps that was exactly why. She forced herself to consider the possibility. Did she want to leave him? No, she did not. But she needed to leave this place. She wondered if he would ever consider going East and starting again? She shook her head. He belonged here.

She leaned her cheek against the flat plane of his back and fell asleep listening to the comfort of his beating heart.

She woke to the rushing of water. The sound overwhelmed even the birdsong. A new day was well underway before she opened her eyes to greet it.

She nestled into the warm fur. This was not her pillow beneath her head. Her eyes blinked open. Thomas's arm lay under her neck and was wrapped intimately across her ribs. His large hand splayed across her stomach. She turned her head to look at his sleeping face in outrage. That was when she saw the cheeks rough with a two-day growth of whiskers. Beneath his dark lashes were black circles. Her indignation ebbed. Had he ridden all night?

She eased away from him, trying to slip from beneath the hides. He rolled toward her and dragged her back against his body.

Her breath came in a quick gasp when her bottom pressed flush into the fold at his waist. His grip tightened and he groaned. A surge of desire so strong it frightened her shot through her chest and seemed to squeeze her heart. The feel of his hot breath upon her neck sent her into action. Not again, she vowed. She slapped and tugged at his arms until he roused enough to release her.

"What the—Delia, what?" He blinked tiredly at her.

"Let me up."

The hands were instantly withdrawn. He groaned again and rolled to his other side, dragging the bearskin with him.

She pulled herself stiffly to her feet and surveyed her surroundings. They were camped behind a large boulder and several hardy trees. Through them she could see a river.

"Careful of the waterfall," he muttered.

She looked back at him. Obviously he was not ready to rise. She took the shotgun and went to find a little privacy before exploring. The horses were tethered to a tree on a long lead. They stood head to tail, brushing away the flies from each other's faces. She led them to the river and wrapped their ropes around the thick cane that grew along the bank. The pair began nibbling at the cane leaves.

She followed the roaring sound of the river. The ground was damp and mossy here. She inched along until she saw the water drop from sight. The height was dizzying, so she sank to her belly and peered over the edge. The river tumbled and crashed into a frothing pool some hundred feet below her. Along the lower banks, she saw tree trunks cast up like scattered matchsticks. The water calmed only a few feet from the falls, seeming very deep and very blue. She crept back from the edge, wondering what the falls looked like from the bottom.

Returning to the camp, she found Thomas still asleep, snoring now in long sawing strokes. She smiled. In sleep, he seemed younger. She could nearly imagine the boy he had been, before the loss of his wife, before the scars and the cynicism, before she knew him or loved him. Her body ached with the urge to strip off her dress and crawl back beneath the hides with him. She turned her back on the compelling sight.

He seduces me even from his dreams.

She knew this lusting was wrong. This desperate desire to have him again was so urgent. Now that their time was limited to days, the struggle to do what was right grew more difficult. Why was this wicked temptation so strong?

She moved beyond the rocks to reflect and pray. After a few minutes of contemplation she remembered her surroundings again. The sound of running water drew her notice. She felt better, confident of her own admission of sin and God's forgiveness.

Before heading back to camp, she wandered toward some shrubs in the woods. Delight bubbled up in her as she realized they were blueberry bushes covered with ripe berries. She picked and ate until she had her fill. Then she picked a heaping handful for Thomas. She cradled the little round berries against her stomach with one hand and retraced her footsteps. She stared at the plump morsels, the first fruit of the season.

A sharp pain in her foot brought her suddenly to the ground. She looked down and discovered a pointed stick protruding from the earth like the blade of a knife. The end was covered with her blood. She grasped her foot and saw the wood had missed the tough rawhide bottom of her moccasin and sliced through the buckskin on the side. One tug released her foot from the leather. There was a small slit in the fleshy pad of her heel. The skin had closed up again. There was only a trickle of blood.

The initial shock waned and her foot throbbed steadily. It almost felt as if the wood was still in her heel. She stared at the stick again, wondering why it stuck from the ground like a spear. Her fingers grasped and pulled, but she was unable to withdraw the thing from the ground.

She looked at the scattered blueberries, muddy shotgun and began to cry. Her foot hurt and she wanted Nash to have his blueberries. She gathered up the ones in her reach. Slowly she rose from the ground and looked at the bits of dried leaves on her skirt. She sniffed loudly, still cradling the berries, and took her first step. The pain of weight bearing brought a cry from her lips. She sat again on the damp ground. The musty smell of fallen leaves was all around her.

She allowed herself to cry a few more moments then decided she needed to call Nash. No doubt her cries would scare the wits out of him, but she could think of no other way to get back to camp.

* * *

Nash rolled to his back and stared up at the green canopy of leaves above him. Something was wrong. He grabbed his Hawkins and rose to his feet, throwing off the cloak of hides.

"Delia?" he called. He waited and heard no answer. The damned waterfall likely drowned out his call. The falls were why he had stopped just before dawn. He didn't fancy facing the steep trail riding double in the dark with a horse heavily burdened behind him.

He found traces of her on the mossy rocks.

"Delia!" Indians be damned, he thought. Where the devil was she?

The worry changed over to pure terror. He stood at the edge of the falls and peered over. Had she fallen? He scoured the traces of her footprints to a sign of a slip or fall. He found no trace of such a thing. He sighed, then pressed his hand across his mouth. A more horrifying possibility occurred to him. Had she jumped?

She was upset that they had made love. She had cried most of the trip, except when she slept. Why hadn't he comforted her instead of plodding along? *Fool*, he thought. Was she so distraught she would take her own life?

No! Never that. Delia fought for life. She was here and he had to find her.

He hovered at the cliff edge in fear. Below his feet, the water plunged and frothed with awesome power. He'd never forgive himself if something happened. How could he bring such sorrow to a woman who meant the world to him? He realized it now. This gut-twisting fear proved it. He loved Delia. He loved her with all his heart.

Dear God, don't take her. I'll send her back to you. I'll never touch her again, I swear. Just let her be alive.

He dashed back from the brink and ran toward the woods. He had to get to the bottom and search. She was here. He had to find her.

How could this happen twice? How could he lose Elizabeth and now Delia? You haven't lost her. She's here. She's alive. Think.

He raised his rifle skyward and fired. The blast echoed loud above the sound of the rushing water. He waited, listening to the hammering of his own heart and the pull of air into his lungs. Then came the sound of a shotgun. He had never heard a sound so sweet.

He bounded over the carpet of fern. There she was—a little flash of tan amid the brown leaves.

He scanned the area for bear, wolf or man.

She waved one hand over her head.

"Thomas," she called.

He ran the few steps that separated them, knelt beside her and pulled her roughly into her arms. Relief, sweet as spring water, welled within him. His hug was greeted with a groan.

"Thomas, let go. You'll squeeze the life from me."

He pulled away to look at her. He saw no blood. Her color was normal. The ground was littered with blueberries.

"What happened?"

"I cut myself on that stake." She pointed to a sharpened sapling. He frowned at the dried blood on white wood.

"Where?"

She indicated her foot. Carefully he held her foot. A puncture wound about an inch wide slit her skin. He looked again at the stake and judged that the tip had traveled into her flesh at least an inch.

"I tried to pull it out of the ground. It almost appears rooted."

"That's a sapling chewed down by a beaver, likely for the green bark."

She stared at him a moment, then laughed.

"The little fellows are having their revenge on me, I think."

He did not return her smile. He didn't like a wound without blood. He couldn't see how much damage was done. Memories of another wounded woman filled his mind. With them came a rising fear swelling within him like a stream in April.

"Can you walk?"

"No."

"I'll carry you then."

"Eat your blueberries first."

"My what?"

She gathered the berries from her lap and held them out.

"I picked them for you."

He accepted them and tossed the entire handful into his mouth. They were warm from the heat of her body. The sweetness coated his tongue.

He poked at her foot and she jumped.

"Don't do that," she scolded.

"I want to see if it's clean."

"It is, so don't go poking me with dirty fingers."

Calmly, he handed her the shotgun and rifle. His

stomach twisted like an injured snake. He didn't show her the fear blasting through him as he scooped her into his arms and held her round firm body close.

He wouldn't give her up, not to the Indians or the mountains or to God himself. A realization dawned— he had promised God he'd send Delia back East if he found her alive. Nash clutched her tight as he strode back to camp. He'd be damned first. And besides, God owed him one.

Chapter Twelve

"I think I'll have a look-see at that foot," said Nash.

He eased her gently to her seat on a large rock.

"Does it involve cutting or poking into the wound?" she wondered aloud.

"Delia, I got to see if it's clean." His expression told her he was worried. Until now she had considered herself lucky the damage was so slight.

"Thomas, it's not even bleeding. How serious can it be?" His frown deepened. A stab of fear pierced her gut. Serious, she thought. "All right, do what you must."

"I wish I had some whiskey to give you."

Her tone was indignant. "I do not indulge in spirits." Then she added, "Why would I need to?"

"I have to see if there any splinters stuck in there."

Queasiness rolled through her belly as she watched him draw the awl from his possibles bag.

"Thomas, I don't think I can do this."

"Look at something else." He handed her a scrap of rawhide.

"What's this for?"

"To bite on so you won't scream."

She stared at the vile bit of hide.

"If I feel the need to scream, Thomas, I most assuredly wish you to hear it."

She flinched when he gently touched her foot as if his fingers were branding irons.

"You got to hold still, Delia. Hold your foot so," he said, positioning her.

She nodded mutely. Her voice had gone with her courage. Staring at the awl, she was certain her voice would return within moments.

Thomas rubbed the awl on a bit of stone until the metal shone like silver. The end was now blunt and the metal clean. He held her ankle with a force that terrified her. There would be no escape.

The awl slipped between the flaps of torn skin. The metal burned like hot iron. She jumped but managed to keep from crying out. He wiggled the thing within her wound. Tears sprang to her eyes and she gritted her teeth. Then he poked again and she cried out. He looked up for an instant. She raised her other foot and was preparing to kick him when the awl slid out.

"It seems clean," he said.

Now her heel was bleeding. Throbbing pain traveled up her ankle and into the back of her leg.

She swabbed the tears, which continued to roll down her cheeks. "Oh, Thomas, it hurts terribly now."

He lifted her into his arms once more and carried her. The nearness of his body did nothing to distract her from her bleeding, aching foot. At the edge of the river he lowered her to the mossy ground and dipped her ankle in the rushing water.

The icy river caressed her trembling ankle. The pain dissolved and a blessed numbness crept over her skin. She sighed and closed her eyes for a few moments.

She could feel his presence beside her, watchful, worried. Her face relaxed. Gradually she noticed the feel of the sunshine upon her face and the warm rock beneath her hands. The world no longer centered on her pain. When she opened her eyes, she found his gaze upon her.

"You look so pretty in the sunshine," he said.

She smiled. "You're trying to distract me."

"Maybe."

She knew he wanted to move on, to leave the danger of the Crow behind. Would her foot begin to throb again if she pulled it from the numbing water?

A sharp bite on her little toe brought a scream to her lips. She yanked her foot out of the water and held her ankle with both hands.

"Something bit me!"

"Trout, maybe. Your foot is bleeding and it's the same color as the underbelly of a fish. Honest mistake."

She scowled. One minute she's pretty and the next she reminded him of a dead fish. She turned her attention to her heel. Blood seeped out of the puncture and ran with the water down her foot. She inspected her little toe and found no damage.

"I think I can ride," she said.

He nodded. "Let me bandage it first."

Her foot was wrapped and settled carefully into her

high-topped moccasin. He loaded the horses, lifting her up last. She felt like baggage when he plopped her on the black gelding.

Her foot began to throb shortly after they set out. The pain was no worse than a headache, so she did not mention it. Of course it hurts, she thought. *I was stabbed twice, bitten by a fish and now it is hanging there. Think of something else.*

"Thomas, are you a Christian?" she asked.

He looked over his shoulder at her. She was accustomed to waiting for answers. Sometimes she forgot the question by the time he responded. She watched a meadowlark flit across the trail.

"My Momma did her best to raise me up right," he said at last.

"Are you a member of a congregation?"

"Nope."

"Do you pray?"

"Not so you'd recognize it. God and I have come to an agreement."

"What agreement?"

"I don't blame Him no more for taking Elizabeth, and He don't bother me with details."

"You have to pray, Thomas and go to church or you're not a Christian."

Another snort.

She didn't want him to jeopardize his immortal soul.

"Thomas, you don't want to go to hell, do you?"

"I been in hell. Hell is here on earth. God don't put you in hell, men do."

"That may be true, but you can't go to heaven unless you follow God's word."

"You mean to tell me God won't accept all them Flathead men and women or their little babies, because they ain't been to church?" He shook his head. "Don't think so. They got their religion. Who says yours is right and theirs is wrong?"

"It just is." What nonsense he talked.

"Do you know about their religion?"

"Well, no."

"Or the Crow or even them Lakota?"

"No, but I am sure—"

He interrupted her. "But you can dismiss something you never heard of and knows nothing about because that's the way you was raised."

"Thomas, you were raised that way, too."

"But I kept an open mind. Don't you think you should hear a man's point of view before you try and change it? It's all right to have beliefs, just don't go pushing them on others because theirs is different."

"But this is the one path to righteousness."

"I never been nowhere that's got but one path leading to it."

"Thomas, how could you reject everything you have learned?"

"I ain't rejected it. I changed it to fit what is. Take church for instance." He released the reins and held both arms out wide. "Where would you be if you was God, in a cold little clapboard church full of hypocrites or here in these mountains?"

She thought about her church and then looked at the trees above her, green and full of life.

"But God is everywhere," she said.

"Exactly, so why do I have to haul my ass to a church just to say hello?"

"Thomas, your language!"

He sighed. "Delia, why are we talking about this?"

"I was trying to take my mind off my foot."

"Did it work?"

"Yes."

"I'm glad, because it gave me a headache."

She took his none-too-subtle hint and remained silent while she considered his words.

At midday, he handed her a few strips of jerky from his bag. She sighed, knowing they would not stop. By late afternoon, she was certain that she could feel each step of the horse's hooves echoing through her foot.

She gave up. "Thomas, my foot feels worse."

"Chew on this," he said, handing her several twigs. "We'll make camp at the first likely spot."

She gnawed on the bitter bark. "It tastes awful. What is it?"

"Seven Barks root. Flatheads gave it to me for gravel. Helped with the pain, until I passed the stone."

She continued to pulverize the fibrous root between her teeth, extracting the bitter medicine. She couldn't say exactly when it worked. Gradually her mind turned back to her surroundings. The breeze stroked her hair and brought Thomas's reassuring scent. The pain was still there, but held down somehow, so it did not intrude.

"Stay with the horses," he said.

"Where are you going?"

He pointed up the hill to several outcroppings of yellow rock. "Finding camp."

She waited while he scrambled up the ledge. He jumped from one boulder to the next, briefly disappearing and then reappearing in a different spot. She would never be able to climb that cliff. When he returned, she could tell by his expression that he had found what he was looking for.

"I'll bring you up, then see about the horses."

She leaned forward, resting her hands on his wide shoulders as he eased her from the horse. She enjoyed the feel of his hands about her waist. He swung her across his body and climbed the slope steadily, seemingly unencumbered by her weight. She squeezed his neck when he jumped from one rock to another.

"I'll never be able to get down," she said.

"Nope, you're my captive."

She smiled. "Why not camp by the stream?"

"Defensible position," he said. "Still in Blackfoot country."

He climbed around a gigantic flat rock shaped like the head of an ax. Behind the boulder was another flat rock jutting out from the hill to form an overhang of several feet. She could see to the back. No animal was about.

"Snakes?" she asked.

"I checked."

He laid her in the sand beneath the rocky ceiling. From her seat she could see the tops of the trees and the valley below. The horses were hidden from view by the ax-head rock.

"I'll be back," he said.

She sat quietly watching. A chipmunk appeared and, seeing her, raised the alarm with a loud chirp. She heard the sound of a large bird in flight, its feathers pushing back the air. A crow darted through the treetops. Thomas's question rose in her mind. *Where would God rather be?*

She decided to look at her heel. Gently she released the leather wrapping Thomas had so carefully coiled about her ankle.

She raised her eyebrows and opened her eyes wide at the sight of her foot. The wound was sealed with a black line of dried blood. The skin about the puncture looked red and swollen. Her anklebone was no longer visible. She could see an outline of where each piece of leather pressed into her skin.

Your foot was hanging down all day. Of course it's a little swollen. The ankle was worse than a little swollen. She pressed one finger into the spongy skin over her bone and watched it sink a quarter inch. Then she removed her finger, leaving a yellowish imprint.

Trepidation filled her. She craned her neck for Thomas and listened for a sign that he was about. The fright rose up and she battled the urge to shout, knowing her call might reveal them to enemies.

The first thing Nash saw upon returning to camp was the amber fire of her eyes burning with fear and pain. Then he saw the ankle, red and swollen. Alarm rang in his entire body. He dropped the bundle of hides and rested his gun atop the pile. He knelt beside her and pressed his hand to her foot. Internal heat blazed like rock beside a fire, radiating through his fingers. The wound was infected.

Not again! Sweet Lord, don't let her die of fever, too.

''What do we do?'' she asked. Her voice was tiny,

helpless. Gone was the woman who had fought a grizzly and outfoxed the Flathead. In her place was a frightened child.

"I'll make a poultice to bring down the swelling. You stay put and rest awhile."

Her hand gripped his wrist, preventing him from rising. Her touch was cool. She had no fever.

"Thomas?"

"We'll fix it up, Delia. Don't you worry." He wondered if he kept his own terror from seeping into his voice. She smiled and nodded, seeming to put her faith in him.

Don't let me fail the trust in those eyes.

Her foot was nearly double in size. He had to get the swelling down. The bindings seemed to have done damn little. Why had he moved her before he knew she was all right? Regret burned in his belly like banked coals.

He was lucky to find Horse Tail growing in the gravel beside a rock. He yanked the plant, roots and all and stuffed it into his bag. He hunted for Squaw Weed by the stream, then turned into the woods to search for dark mossy places. There beneath the poplar he found a Yellow Moccasin flower. He knelt beside the delicate blossom, using his fingers to carefully uproot the plant. On his way back he found a beaver meadow. Growing there was Blood Grass topped with small yellow blossoms. He tore the tops off several plants and watched the juice turn red.

He returned to the camp and hobbled the horses by the stream. Then he climbed up the steep hill and found her rocking nervously back and forth. Relief flooded her face as she saw him. The movement stopped.

"You were gone a long while," she said.

"I had to find these." He held up the Moccasin Flower and Blood Grass.

"You brought me flowers?"

"They're medicine," he said. She nodded and reached for the Moccasin Flower.

"This one is lovely. Do I eat the flower?"

"You might, though I don't know what would happen. The root is where the medicine's at."

She looked at the Blood Grass. "This has no root," she said.

"We use the flower on that one. But don't eat it, you crush it and put it on the wound."

"Where did you learn this?"

"Flatheads."

He set about starting a fire and gathering his pots.

"Does it hurt you now?" he asked.

"No, but it looks like it should, doesn't it?"

He was certain it would hurt soon enough if he couldn't get the swelling down.

He suspended the pot of water over the fire with a green branch through the wire handle. He crushed the Blood Grass and Horse Tail together on a rock with the blunt end of his knife. After removing the pot from the coals, he poured some water into a tin plate. Then he added the pulverized weeds and set it on a rock to seep. The Yellow Moccasin root was also mashed and then added to the pot to cook awhile.

The medicine man had told him the remedy was very strong. The Flathead used it to treat cholera, and Nash had seen it taken in ceremony to induce visions with frightening results. His own experience still sent an icy shudder down his back. He hoped Delia wouldn't need this particular medicine.

"It looks ghastly, doesn't it?" she asked.

He heard the challenge in her voice. She dared him to deny her words. Right now she needed reassurance, not the truth.

"I seen worse."

But never on someone who kept his foot.

He placed the green mush of Blood Grass and Horse Tail in a clean cotton cloth, the remains of the dress she had once worn. The ends were folded together and tied closed. He applied the poultice to her ankle. The leather bindings held the medicine in place.

He patted her calf in what he hoped was a reassuring gesture. "That'll take down the swelling. Mind, we have to keep it wet."

"It looks like everything will be wet soon."

He followed her gaze to the sky. The gray clouds rolled past, turning over the leaves of the trees, their billowing bellies an ominous black.

"I got to tether the horses and gather more wood."

He shook out the skins and helped her climb between them. He rolled the wigwam skins in a bundle and propped up her foot.

"Is this another Indian trick?"

"Nope, I learned that from Doc Gilbert in Kentucky."

She smiled at him. Her eyes remained worried. If anything happened to her—he didn't finish the thought. It was too terrible to consider.

He descended the steep slope at a trot and quickly

saw to the horses, securing them under a rock out-cropping similar to the one he had found above. Then he dashed back to the stream and cut a great armful of river grass, dumping it before them.

He threw a leather strap on the ground and began tossing dried branches and logs hurriedly upon it. Then he wound the strip about the load and hefted it to his shoulders, resenting even these few minutes away from her.

The heavens opened up and the rain poured from the sky. He swore as he dashed up the incline carrying the load of wood and trying to shelter his rifle from the worst of the rain.

"Oh, Thomas, look at you," she said.

It was good to hear her laughter again. How long had it been? Too long, he decided, unable to remember.

"You look like a drowned beaver."

He tossed the wood back beneath the overhang and crouched to crawl into the rock shelter. It was a good camp, he thought, as he watched water run in rivulets away from them.

"Damn, my Bess is wet."

"Give it to me. I'll dry and oil it for you."

He handed over his Bess. Water ran off his buck-skin, pooling at his feet. Raindrops dripped from his hair and rolled beneath his shirt. He shook himself like a Saint Bernard, violently throwing his shoulders from side to side. Water droplets sprayed in all directions.

"Oh, stop that! You're getting me wet!" she howled. She held his gun before her with both hands like a shield. He shook his head again and was rewarded by another squeal.

"Quiet now," he said.

She grew still. Her neck seemed to grow longer as she craned to look about.

"Why?" she whispered. "Did you see signs of Blackfoot?"

He knelt beside her and whispered back.

"No, but I'm afraid a mountain lion will mistake you for a wild pig."

She pushed his shoulder and he allowed himself to roll backward in the soft sand. He lay there a minute enjoying the sound of her laughter. When he rolled back up he heard her quick intake of breath.

"Thomas! You've got sand stuck all over your shirt. Pull it off so I can beat it."

He looked at the wet shirt coated with mud.

"You'll not beat this shirt over my bed," he said.

"Then you do it."

He peeled off the shirt and shook it near the rain line, then thumped it several times.

"Lay it on a rock until it dries," she said.

He turned to find her gaze fastened on his bare chest. His skin felt as if she had doused him in whale oil and set him ablaze. When she lifted her eyes to meet his, he saw desire burning bright within her golden eyes.

Chapter Thirteen

Delia stared at his bronze chest, wet with rain. A flash pan of fire ignited within her belly. Her fingers curled as she imagined running her hands over the warm slippery skin.

Nash pinned her with his eyes, as if sensing her desire. His glance revealed smoldering heat beneath clear blue eyes.

He waited, still and powerful, for some sign. She knew she could withdraw by merely looking away. Her voice could rescue her. But the throbbing of her own heart seemed to close her throat.

He was moving now, slowly, stalking her like the mountain cat he had just mentioned. His step was silent, his movements graceful as he glided ever closer.

He sank to his knees upon the soft furs. She raised her hand to touch his moist skin. Her fingers scored his flesh. The shudder of his body seemed to travel up her arm and shake her to the core.

"I've never felt this way before," he said. "I can't

control this wanting.'' His hands gripped her shoulders, blaming her for his passion.

"I feel it, too," she said.

"It's like wildfire down a mountain."

He pulled her tight against his chest. The rain dripped from his hair to her neck. He lowered her to the soft furs. His teeth scored her neck, taking tiny bites of her flesh as she arched to give herself to him. His hands caressed her breasts rousing a shudder of delight. His descending mouth captured her moan of pleasure. The force of his kiss dashed all thoughts from her mind. She writhed and moaned in pleasure as the rain beat down upon the rocks above them. Her hands tugged at his shoulders, insisting, demanding. His fingers slid the leather dress over her hips.

His warm body nestled between her thighs. She lifted for his thrust, rising to meet him. He grasped her hips, holding her captured against his embedded flesh, as if her movement caused him pain. She thrust again and wrenched a cry from him. Some internal dam burst within him. Now, he was all frantic motion. He drove into her body again and again. She absorbed the wild thrusting, throwing her hips against him. The wave rose within her, cresting and breaking in a violent surge of pleasure. She gripped his shoulders with all her strength.

Her cry seemed to be a signal. She heard him groan as he gripped her. Then her body was falling, weak and replete, into the soft furs. He followed, resting half upon her. *Too sweet,* she thought, as their bodies lay motionless but for their rapid breathing. All about them the rain seemed to envelope them in a curtain of seclusion. The steady fall of water soothed and her eyelids drooped shut. *How I wish I could stop here and hold this moment forever.*

After a time, her strength returned and she stretched like a cat. His head jerked as if her movement stirred him from sleep.

The bandage on her foot had loosed and the poultice slipped to the fur. The steady ache returned, rising slowly to the center of her awareness. She reached for her foot with one hand.

"I'll do it," he said. "How does it feel?"

"I didn't notice it until now." She smiled. His method of distracting her was wonderful. He did not return her smile. He furrowed his brow as he studied her ankle. She saw the worry reflected in his gaze. Apprehension coiled within her belly, like an angry rattlesnake. He pressed his lips tightly together, squeezing away the color.

"There must be something wrong with me," he muttered. "To fall on you like a rabid dog and you injured to boot."

"I'm not that injured," she said. Her smile again yielded no harvest.

"You deserve better."

She glanced away. This passion he stirred frightened her. Desire changed her. Somehow her thoughts dissolved, leaving nothing but the feral urgings. This made her no better than a beast. Embarrassment heated her face and neck.

It was this place, this wild, dangerous country. She had no anchor—her husband, her church, her entire world seemed far, far away. How could she ignore this virile man? He was as rough as these mountains, and as beautiful.

No, she shook her head. It wasn't the mountains and it wasn't the man. The wildness was inside her. Even in Ohio, she had sensed the stirring, baying at the moon. She kept the animal caged. All these years, she'd locked her hunger away, denying her passions and hoping the animal would die. Now this man and this place had unleashed the monster within. Suddenly she knew she couldn't go back. She would never again be satisfied with rigid rules of her old life, with the tame, tepid emotions.

She'd changed into someone she hardly knew. This new woman ran about with no corset or underclothes, indulging her basest desires.

Who was she now? How could she look into the eyes of a proper God-fearing woman? She was wicked, fallen, wild. *I can't stay here.* The fear rose up, overtaking the guilt. Her throat was suddenly dry as chalk. *But I can't go back.*

He shook her shoulder and she focused on him once more.

"Delia!" She looked into his crystal eyes. "It ain't that bad. The heat just dried the poultice a bit. I'll moisten it up. I think the swelling's gone down."

She looked at her foot, but she did not recognize it. Her toes stuck out of the end of a puffy red mass. Her skin was stretched tight and shiny. The distended flesh looked as if with one pinprick her foot would explode like a bursting balloon.

Then she saw the red streaks. She pointed, speechless.

He lifted one of his eyebrows and considered her silently before pressing one broad hand to her forehead. "Lay down, Delia." He pressed her firmly to the hides. His hand remained on her, holding her down. She wiggled beneath his restraint. "You got a fever, girl. Lay still."

"I've fallen."

"No, you ain't."

"I'm going to die for my sins, Thomas."

Something needed to be done. She had blood poisoning. Nash had seen that before. Once it traveled to her heart, she'd die. He'd have to take her foot. She'd never forgive him. Elizabeth hadn't. She'd blamed him for allowing the doctor to take her leg. Before she had died, she had made him swear not to seek revenge against that devil of a driver. He would have promised her anything. After she'd died, he knew he'd break his vow if he ever saw the man again. So he had left and had come to the mountains.

He studied Delia's damp, flushed face. The orange firelight sent strange shadows dancing across her fevered body.

Why did she have to mention dying? Because death was a real possibility, that's why. There was no guarantee that she would not die of infection after he took her foot.

The fear gnawed at him like a dog at a bone. He was strong, but not strong enough to lose another love. This one would kill him. She had brought him back to life after Elizabeth and all she had asked in the world was to go home. But he had kept her here, where she didn't belong and look what had happened. This was his fault.

"Don't die, Delia," he whispered to her in the night.

He waited through the darkness. Using a wet scrap of buckskin, he wiped away the sweat from her fevered brow. When he could see the treetops silhouetted against the sky, he boiled the water. When the liquid bubbled, he drew it from the fire. He reached into a small leather pouch and dropped the dried fragments of a crushed plant into the steaming water. A familiar sweet odor of the seeping plant instantly emerged. Damn, he hated this little flower. Images of the medicine man holding the ladle to his lips spun in his mind. Then the pain was gone, and the visions began. He shook his shoulders, driving away the memory. It was necessary to bring down the fever and stop the pain so he could take the foot. Her visions might not be so terrible.

He threw his hunting knife and awl into the pot. The medicine man said the Squaw Weed would give the cutting blade power.

As the sky grew brilliant crimson, he began offering the yellow liquid to Delia. Her color changed first. The flush disappeared and her cheeks grew pale. He saw her breathing slow. He called to her. She opened her eyes but seemed unable to focus upon his face. Her pupils were huge black moons rimmed with gold.

He looked at his knife and felt his body break out in a cold sweat. He thought of all the animals he had butchered. He could cleanly slice through any joint without nicking the bone. But not on a living being, not on the woman he loved.

You have to. She'll die otherwise. Firmly he clasped the knife and gathered his resolve. He raised a trembling hand and laid the sharp blade against her swollen skin. His stomach clenched and coiled. For a moment he thought he'd vomit.

It was the only way! He fell back to his heels. His wrist swept across his damp brow. His breathing came in rapid gasps.

Elizabeth had died anyway.

He grasped her ankle and pressed the knife into her soft flesh.

She screamed when he cut. Her fingers, curled like eagle's talons, clawed toward his face. He dodged and managed to capture her wrists.

He grasped her ankle tight and cut along her heel until he hit bone. He had to try. He could still take the foot if this didn't work.

"Easy, Delia. Rest now."

She trembled like a spent mare. He'd never forget the sight of her eyes rolling white and wild. Her body stilled and she looked about. Her gaze seemed to focus on some point beyond him. Now her hand jabbed at the air, pawing at the creatures only she could see.

"Where is he?" she asked.

He looked at the clear blue sky.

"I'll find him for you. You lie back."

She nodded and he eased her back to the fur. Her eyelids drooped.

He turned back to her foot, pulling her skin aside, and peered past the gore. The smell of putrid flesh rose up. He used the awl to search. The metal struck a hard mass, resting in a pocket of yellow pus. He flicked it from the wound. The little pellet landed in the dirt. He scooped it up and examined the thing. It was a fragment of the wood, no bigger than his thumbnail.

"You little bugger." He had missed it! All the while it had festered within her. *My, God,* he thought. *I almost took her foot.* He looked at the draining wound. The danger was still great. Infection could travel or she might spike a fever.

"Please, not that," he muttered.

He poured the seeped Squaw Weed water over the wound. At last only clear fluid and blood ran from the incision.

He made a new poultice of the Blood Grass and Horse Tail. He threaded his needle with rabbit gut and stitched the wound. Then he bound the compress about her foot.

When he was finished, he knelt. For the first time since before Elizabeth died, he prayed.

"God, it's me. I know I haven't been speaking to You. Truth is I was angry 'bout Lizzy. But I don't hold no grudge now. I'm asking You to help Delia through this. She's a good woman, too good for me. But she could sure be of use to You down here. Besides, you got enough angels. Ah—amen."

He sat watching her. She lay still but for the gentle rise of her breast. There was nothing for him to do now but wait.

Chapter Fourteen

Surely this was hell. Little red devils poked at Cordelia with spears. She ran along the black path, the coals burning her flesh. A lance ripped at her foot and she fell. The devils jumped upon her, grabbing her arms.

Thomas was there, holding her, shielding her from the demons. But he could not see the bats. Hundreds of little bats, swooping and shrieking. Sharp white teeth snapped at her.

He was gone. Somehow she was alone again. She screamed for Thomas and hands pinned her to the ground.

With each bite, they took a tiny bit of her flesh. Sins of the flesh, she thought.

"I'll get them for you," Thomas said. "You lay back. They won't get you on the ground."

He was right. But here the coals slowly burned her skin away. It was better than the bats.

She burned away and floated up in the smoke.

"Cordelia." She knew his voice. Her husband called.

"John, where are you?" She could see him now and she saw through him. The air about him was silver, like moonlight through the clouds. "John, what happened to you?"

"My body melted with the snow, but my soul rose."

Her grasping fingers could not touch him.

He gave her the crooked little smile she'd nearly forgotten.

"Be good, Cordelia."

His image melted into light and fell cold upon her. Then, like a passing lantern, she was alone in darkness.

Hands to God, hands to God. She looked and her hands were gone. Now what would she do? Without her hands she could be of no service to God.

Nash watched her twitch and tremble. Her muttering ground his nerves like acorns beneath the pestle. The Flatheads said not to touch. This disturbed the vision. But he couldn't stand to watch her lost inside her mind. He thought of his visions, nightmares really, running after carriages, running to save Elizabeth as the wheels cut into her soft flesh. His hand reached out and clasped her arm.

"Delia!"

He gave her a little shake. She screamed. The sound raised the hairs on his neck. He released her and she settled back to her panting and tremors.

By nightfall she stilled. He thought the worst was over. Never would he use that damned moccasin again. He'd tie her down or hold her. Pain was better than this. Quick and soon forgotten.

He crawled beneath the bearskin, careful not to touch her. He watched. In the heart of the night she rolled to her side and groaned. He heard her say something that sounded like his name. He clasped her extended hand and felt their fingers entwine. She sighed. He gathered her close, tucking her head beneath his chin and breathed in the smell of her hair. She was back.

Cordelia woke cradled in his arms. What strange dreams, she thought. He released her gently and she rolled to her back. His arm draped, familiar, across her chest.

The pain in her foot drew her attention. The poultice must be dry again. An uneasy feeling crept through the fog that separated dreams from day.

Her hands! She held them up to see. There they were, slim and callused. She sighed in relief.

John.

She had seen him! He was an angel. Then he must know she had sinned.

Her hands flew to her cheeks. Nash groaned and dragged his hand across her breasts before rolling away. *Be good,* John said.

The little demons rose in her mind and she cried out.

Thomas was there now, leaning over her. He studied her closely with red-rimmed eyes.

"Delia? Do you know me?"

Know him? What was he talking about?

He stared at her. "You awake?"

She nodded. "Don't you see me looking at you?"

He gently held her head between both of his broad

hands. She did not understand the relief that flooded his face. He smiled wearily.

"Yes, I see, at long last."

"I had, I don't know what to call them. Worse than nightmares," she said.

"I gave you some medicine. It brings on dreams, waking dreams."

Dreams? It was only medicine. Somehow the unease would not be so readily shaken.

"It didn't feel like a dream."

"Flathead call them visions and set store by them."

"They believe they are real?"

"In a manner."

He unwrapped the bandage. She sat up to see and gasped at the change. The swelling was nearly gone. How long had she slept? He pulled away the compress and she saw the three-inch scab on her heel. A row of even rawhide stitches knit the skin together.

"What happened?"

He held up a dark brown pebble for her examination.

"I took this out of your foot yesterday."

She reached for the grisly trophy.

"Why, it's wood!"

"The sapling," he corrected. "Must of broke off in there. You'll mend now." Quickly he applied a clean bandage. "How do you feel?"

"Fine. I have a headache."

He nodded, then offered her a cup of water and elk jerky.

"I have to see to the horses. Do you need anything before I go?"

She shook her head and watched him disappear.

When she was certain he was gone, she rose, trembling slightly. Her foot felt so much better. She stepped gingerly forward keeping her heel from touching the rock. Slowly she left the overhang and made her way behind a boulder to relieve herself. Cautiously she tried to put weight on her heel. The hot poker instantly sprang to life. Too soon for that, she decided, and walked back to the skins using only the toes of her injured foot. Once there, she lay panting, her body trembling like a leaf before a thunderstorm. Why was she so weak?

She returned to the hide and sank gratefully onto the soft fur. She dozed on and off throughout the morning. He brought her two grouse and roasted the birds with wild onions. The sweet bulbs gave the meal a rich flavor. After eating, her strength returned, seeping through her like coffee into hot water.

"Your color is better," he said.

She smiled, then noticed his tired lines and red-rimmed eyes. He looked exhausted.

"I'm sorry to be such a bother."

"You patched me up. My turn to do the same."

He moved close. She shifted, suddenly uncomfortable. Her body longed to accept the arm that was wrapped protectively about her shoulders. The image of her husband haunted her. This was wrong.

She lifted his arm and slipped away. He let her go, only his gaze following.

"Tell me about the dreams, Delia," he said.

The silence stretched on between them, stark and lonely.

"I don't want to talk about them."

"That was from the Yellow Moccasin. 'Tweren't

real. They are visions, the Indians say. I say they are nightmares.''

''They were horrible.'' She shuddered and held her hands to her eyes as the tiny devils danced through her memory. Evil, twisted faces delighted in her pain.

''I'm sorry I gave it to you. I didn't want you to feel the pain of the knife.''

She looked up into his sad eyes. He tried to help her. Were they just dreams? No, they were more.

''I saw John,'' she said. Nash's brows descended low over his eyes. ''He said, 'Be good.'''

''That was your own mind talking to you.''

''No, it was more. I could feel him. He's with me even now.''

Nash moved uncomfortably and cleared his throat.

''Delia, I think you should forget about them. Try to put them aside.''

''I never will. It was he. He spoke to me. Oh, Thomas, I am so ashamed of what we've done. So ashamed.''

''You got no cause.''

She looked into his eyes. Men were so different than women. He really thought this was all fine.

''Thomas, I want you to keep your distance. I'll work and cook, but I refuse to be your, your—''

''My what? My whore?'' He was on his feet now. His fists spoke of the anger surging through him. ''I treated you with respect, always. If that's what you think we had, I feel sorry for you and all your shriveled-up, self-righteous Bible-thumpers!'' He shouted at her.

''At least I've read the Bible. You don't even say grace.'' She heard her voice rise to a shriek.

"I treated you like my woman. And you—you turn it into something dirty."

"You never made an honorable proposal."

"They was all honorable." His voice was low now, like a growling bear. He turned his back and stalked down the trail.

She held her bottom lip tight between her teeth until he was out of sight. Then the sob came rapidly, making her shoulders jump up and down like a dancing man.

Now she had lost Thomas, too.

Nash was angry enough to spit blood. She had made him lose his temper. He shouted, as if the woods weren't a nest of hostile Indians and she wasn't sick with fever. He had taken care to hide their tracks and avoid the river, and had secreted her in the cave. Then, he stood before her and howled like a rabid coyote. This was the cost of bringing a woman along.

She didn't care about him. Oh, she wanted his body. But afterward their lovemaking made her feel dirty. He wasn't good enough, oh no. She was God's chosen one, for Pete's sake. And what did that make him, the devil's instrument? He snorted and kicked a stone into the river.

Why was he so upset? If she didn't want him, better still. He wouldn't have to feel guilty leaving her at the Rendezvous in a few weeks.

He didn't feel any better. Somehow her opinion of him was the most important thing. He wanted her body, of course he did. But he wanted more. He wanted her respect and her love. If she wasn't always looking down her nose at the way he ate and talked, and the fact that he didn't attend church, he might have asked her to marry him. Not now, that was certain. Now he knew just what she thought of him.

And where was he supposed to find a church and a minister out here? Men he knew just took a squaw and that was that. They'd have a wife until they made their fortunes and moved East. Some men stayed—a few did. Delia would never settle for that. No, she'd want a church built right here in the damn woods. Probably make him ride back to St. Louis to get her a veil. Well, he'd be damned first, if he weren't already.

He picked up a stone and skipped it. The rock bounced off the surface four times before disappearing into the water.

He heard the arrow strike the tree beside him. He was on the ground and aiming before he even looked around. No more arrows followed. He looked up at the red bands near the flashing. Crow.

Delia heard Nash approach. She didn't call out. He had told her the area was loaded with Blackfoot. When she saw the Indian behind him, she held back a scream. Where was her shotgun? Her gaze fixed on the weapon beside the cold fire pit. She grabbed a gun and crept silently back into the shadow of the overhanging rock.

Then she noticed Nash still carried his gun.

''Delia,'' he called, ''Come out.''

She did so, rising cautiously to her feet.

''Who are they?'' She studied the three men before her.

"Mountain Crow. Show them your foot."

"What?"

"I'm afraid it will fester again and they knows things I don't."

She sat on the fur and untied the leather binding. The three men squatted about her, staring at the injury. She listened to their strange garbled speech and watched their faces for some reaction.

"Do you understand them?" she asked.

"Not a word."

Then they stood and faced Nash. They signed to him and he nodded.

"We're going with them," he said.

"What? I don't want to go with them."

"We're going."

A few minutes later she sat on the horse behind Nash. This was too close. His scent raised memories of his body lying on hers. How could she be so weak? Think of something else.

After several hours she didn't have to search for a distraction. It was there with each beat of her heart magnified in her foot. She could feel her toes grow stiff with the swelling. Could there be pieces of that infernal stick still in her foot?

She heard the barking of dogs. A moment later they appeared, yapping and jumping around the horses. Next she saw several sentry on the rocks above the river. They waved to the men before her.

"How do you know they don't mean to kill us?" she asked.

"Could have done that anytime. Mountain Crow are thieves, not killers. They never done no harm to nobody I know, except Blackfoot."

She considered this as she saw the tops of their
dwellings appear before her above the high grass.
There were perhaps forty large conical tents covered
with the hides of buffalo neatly stitched and stretched.
She studied the paintings that decorated the outside
of several of the dwellings. Drawings of horses and
buffalo were most common. All about her was the
smell of wood smoke and roasting meat.

In a few moments the entire village seemed to be
gathered to see the strangers. The warriors descended
and spoke with several old men. Chiefs? she wondered. They were not dressed any differently from the
rest. Nash slid off the horse and strode gracefully to
the group. He raised his open hand and they did the
same.

He spoke to them. The chief did not seem to understand. He held up a hand for Nash to stop. A few
moments of silence passed. Nash helped her to the
ground. Then they were ushered into one of the large
tents.

Inside, the grass was covered with animal hides. In
the center of the tent a fire burned low. The men sat
around the pit. A young girl with twin black braids
motioned to her to sit behind the men. She eased herself down and stretched her sore foot out before her.
The girl offered her a horn cup filled with what tasted
like berry juice. Delia smiled and nodded her thanks.

The man already seated in the tent spoke to Nash.

"He speaks Flathead," Thomas said. "He was captured eight years ago." He turned his attention to the
conversation, and Delia was ignored for several
minutes. One of the younger men rose and left

through the little tent flap. He returned with an old man.

"Delia, this here's their medicine man, Smoke Rising. Let him look at your foot."

"My foot is fine," she insisted. His eyes narrowed at the lie. She could barely stand the burning itch, which grew by the minute.

Nash unwrapped her foot. Delia's eyes opened wide at the sight. The swelling had returned and yellow pus oozed from the punctures of his stitches. She raised her gaze to Thomas.

"You'll be all right now. Smoke Rising will take care of it."

She allowed the old man to pinch and poke at her with thick fingers. She winced but did not cry out.

"He says you're a brave woman," said Nash. "You're going to his tent, now."

"Don't leave me." She had no right to ask it, not after what she had said to him. She told him to leave her alone. Now she was afraid he would.

"I'll be with you."

He lifted her into his arms. If only she had his strength. Nothing frightened him. His gaze held hers and she drew peace from the blue depths of his eyes. He was with her.

Nash strode behind the silver-haired man. His long braid was the color of smoke rising. The Indian opened the flap to his tent and motioned them inside. Within was an old woman with thinning white hair and few teeth. The captured Flathead Indian followed Nash into the dwelling.

She listened to the medicine man speak for a time. Her gaze moved about the interior, considering the bundles of plants tied to the wooden supports. The dwelling was full of the sweet, musty smell of drying plants. Before her, coals in a central fire pit glowed around an earthen jar, blackened from smoke.

Smoke Rising lit a bundle of dried grass the size of a cigar. The smoke smelled fragrant, like a spice.

"What is that?" she asked.

"Sweetgrass. It purifies the spirit."

The old man fanned his hand, bringing the smoke to him as he inhaled.

The old woman washed Delia's foot in some kind of green oil, then gently dabbed her skin clean. The pounding ache grew worse.

"Drink this," said Thomas as the woman handed her a cup.

"What is it?"

"Running Fox tells me it will just deaden the pain. Drink."

She looked at the brownish water and remembered the last time she'd deadened the pain. The little devils with sharp spears rose up in her mind. Thomas said it was the medicine.

"Go on," he urged.

"No."

She wondered if he could see the determination in her eyes.

"It's gonna hurt like hell," he warned. She was silent, but her gaze never left his. "All right then."

He returned the brew to the woman. The medicine man showed Thomas how to hold her foot. Her skin grew damp as fear and anticipation washed together.

Smoke Rising grasped a short blade. He sliced through the leather stitches that held her skin closed.

The blade seemed to cut her flesh. Her muscles tensed but managed to keep still. The air rushed in and out of her lungs.

She peered past Nash to see the pus draining around the black scab. Smoke Rising grasped the gut thread in his thick fingers and gave a sharp tug. She gasped as the leather passed through her skin. Before she could exhale, he pulled the next one and the next. One drawing pain followed the next. Her hair was wet with sweat when the pain stopped.

"Is he finished?" Her hopes were dashed by the slow shake of Nash's head. The medicine man spoke to the woman. She handed him a gourd filled with water and a brush with stiff bristles. "What's that?" she asked.

"Boar's hair brush," said Thomas.

A shiver of fear stole up her spine. Then Nash's hands clamped tight about her ankle and a burning agony captured her leg. This is how the beaver feels, she thought, when the trap closes. She understood now how they could chew off their own foot. If only she could reach her foot. Anything to stop the pain. A scream tore from her lips as the torture continued. Her senses dimmed suddenly. She welcomed the blackness that enveloped her.

She woke to a rhythmic prodding. Each touch sent a bolt of searing pain. They were burning her. She sat up and was immediately restrained by Thomas. He held her, keeping her arms pinned to her sides.

"Nearly done," he said.

The old medicine man hunched over her foot. She could see the raw tissue. Her skin was rubbed away, leaving a sticky, oozing wound.

"It looks dreadful," she said.

"Not for long. Lie back." He didn't wait for her to obey, but pushed her into a reclining position. He was right, better not to see. She gritted her teeth at the jabbing. When his hand finally left her, a dull throbbing ache remained.

She lay with her hand draped across her damp brow. The sound of conversation drifted past her. She focused on the wooden poles above, watching the gray smoke curling to the sky.

"It's done," said Thomas. She looked into his blue eyes. They were brighter than the piece of sky she saw through the smoke. "Rising Smoke says you are strong."

"Are they going to leave it uncovered?"

"Yes. Walks About, his wife, will look after you."

They placed a little frame made of sticks over her foot and draped the wood with a deer hide. "That will keep the flies off until it scabs up."

"Where are you going?" She started to reach for his hand and stopped. He stared at her, as her withdrawing fingers fell back to the pallet.

"I have to speak with the elders," he said and waited for her reaction.

The anticipated panic at separating never came. She glanced at the stranger beside the fire who blinked at her and then back to the man she trusted. He needed to go and she could not follow. She would not be more of a burden than necessary.

"I'll be back," he said.

She lifted her chin and smiled. "I know you will."

Chapter Fifteen

Nash followed Smoke Rising to the largest tepee on the plain. He stooped to enter. On the inside of the tent, he found men sitting in a circle around a small fire of hot coals.

Nash nodded at Kicking Elk, the Flathead translator.

The man turned to a serious-looking fellow with black hair and a wrinkled face and spoke to him. Nash waited patiently. "This is the chief, Grazing Bull. He wonders if you have seen our enemy recently?"

Nash gazed at the chief while speaking to Kicking Elk. "I saw a group of five Blackfoot warriors yesterday near where your men found us."

The chief asked several more questions about the direction they traveled, how they were armed and if they were mounted. Nash answered them honestly, for he had no love for the Blackfoot.

Nash waited as the men discussed his information. He noticed how each man gave his full attention to the speaker. No one interrupted and each spoke methodically in turn. The air was still and warm. Nash wished his chest was bare as well. His shirt stuck to his damp flesh.

"Is there anything else you wish to say?" asked Kicking Elk.

"Tell him I am grateful for his kindness to my woman. The Crow are a great people to help those in need. I wish to make him a gift to show my respect for your tribe." Nash pulled his trade goods from his possibles bag. He laid red ribbon on the hide before the chief. Beside that he added pearl buttons and a handful of metal awls. Finally he rested a metal knife blade, still without a handle, beside the other offerings.

Grazing Bull distributed the ribbon, buttons and awls to his men, keeping only the knife for himself. Kicking Elk's deep voice rumbled again. "He accepts your gifts. You and your woman are welcome to stay as long as you like. He also extends a great honor. He invites you to join them on a raid. Our braves will find these Blackfoot warriors. He says you may be lucky and take a scalp."

Now he was stuck. He had no desire to run off and fight this man's battles. To refuse would be an insult and he would have to leave. Delia was too ill.

"I am honored."

At sundown they came upon his old camp. The fifteen braves slept with him on the little ledge above the river.

Nash lay on the warm sand, his head resting on his bag. This was the first time he'd been apart from her since her arrival in the spring. He hoped the pain did not keep her awake and wondered if the wound had begun to mend.

He rolled to his back again trying to find a comfortable position. He needed her little body to coil about. *My God, I can't even sleep without her.* The night passed in restless longing. He was happy to see the stars grow dim and the sky turn steel-gray.

He checked his rifle again and readied his shot and powder. Without his horse, he carried only the essentials of war: his rifle, pistol, shot, powder and knife.

He let the Indians do the tracking, choosing to chew on some jerky as they trotted along the animal path. The fringes of their leggings dragged in the wet grass as they crept along. An hour after sunup they spotted the enemy.

The five men all stooped about a deer carcass. Two skinned and the others butchered. The warrior before him gave a bloodcurdling scream and all eyes focused upon them. Arrows flew from the bows of the Crow. He sighted a Blackfoot warrior, but did not fire. One man fell with four arrows protruding from his chest. Two others dropped behind the fallen deer using the carcass as a shield and returned fire.

From behind a tree he watched the Crow take down another man with their arrows. Five of the Crow circled behind and now ran from the woods screaming as they fell upon the three remaining men. This was not war—it was a massacre. Another Blackfoot warrior fell and was slit from throat to crotch like a fish, his punctured intestines spilling out on the ground. Nash exhaled sharply against the smell. The remaining two warriors writhed on the ground beside their butchered comrade, and the Crow beat them with their fists.

Thomas lowered his rifle. Bile rose in his throat, but he forced it back. The dead men lay beside the deer. He smelled enough blood for ten lifetimes. The savagery of the warriors' attack sickened him. The Crow set to mutilating the bodies, slashing away pieces of the corpses and throwing them at the captured men. Nash turned away. He knew the Blackfoot would do the same if they had won the day.

The victors tied the hands of the battered warriors and cinched a rope about their necks. Then, the band turned back toward the village, herding their bleeding enemy along before them.

Thomas knew the fallen warriors were the lucky ones.

He wondered if these two men were strong enough to bravely endure the tortures ahead. Nash had heard stories at the Rendezvous of what was to come. The words of fellow trappers filled his mind as they approached the village.

The cries of victory brought an echoing trill from the women of the tribe. People streamed out of the encampment to greet the triumphant warriors and their miserable captives. Sticks and rocks were hurled with insults as the men were dragged forth.

Thomas turned away and washed in the river. Their blood was on him somehow. The sooner they were away from here, the better for them both.

Sick at heart, he headed toward the only one capable of quieting him.

* * *

Delia slept in the middle of the hot afternoon. Her face was covered with a sheen of sweat. He frowned.

Walks About smiled and motioned for him to enter. As she spoke, Delia's eyes opened. Her amber gaze fell on him and instantly lit a familiar fire within. He smiled.

"You're back," she said.

"How do you feel?"

"Better." Her voice sounded weak. He forced a smile for her benefit.

Walks About flipped back the hide covering her wound, showing the black scab that covered her ankle. He leaned close. The wound was closed and he could not smell any putrid flesh. The skin was only slightly swollen.

"Do you have a fever?" He pressed his hand to her moist forehead.

"I did, but I'm better now."

He stared at her hot pink cheeks. She was too ill to travel.

He wanted to leave this place before darkness, before the torture began. He wondered why he felt such urgency. His skin prickled. This uneasy feeling had warned him of danger in the past when he was wise enough to listen. Why now? They were safe enough inside this village.

"Your foot looks much better," he said. She smiled. He noticed her eyes glowed too bright. Surely the danger he sensed came from moving her in her present condition. She needed rest.

He glanced up and noticed Walks About was gone. Someone had named her well. She was no doubt drawn by the excitement of the prisoners. He settled on the fur beside Delia.

He rested with her while the day melted into night. The pulsing of the village drum woke him. The beat echoed in his chest. He squeezed his eyes shut as he thought of what was to come. Soon the ritual slaying of their enemies would begin.

"Did you find the Blackfoot?" she asked.

He nodded.

"Are all the Crow warriors all right?"

"No injuries." Images of the massacre he'd witnessed rose before him once again. His forehead grew damp as memories exploded in his brain. He would spare her this.

"Are the Blackfoot dead?"

"They soon will be." His gaze traveled to the opening of the tepee. The fire's orange light shone through the gap in the thick buffalo hide.

"Oh, no—Thomas, what will they do to them?"

He wouldn't fill her head with the gruesome stories he'd heard of Indian torture. Even in death the captive would find no peace. They'd slash the corpses, mutilating their spirit, so the men could never again fight against the Crow.

"They'll kill them, Delia. That's all."

Her eyes were wide and round as the drumbeat ceased, heralding the beginning.

"What shall we do?"

"Nothing. This is their way."

"But Thomas, it's a sin to kill an unarmed man. It's a crime against God."

"Delia, this is their country, their tribe and their way of doing things. They never heard of your God.

You can't stop this. All you can do is get well so we can leave.''

"You're right, Thomas. Of course you are."

He stroked her hair as the chanting began. Her body trembled against his. Her skin was still too warm. He lowered his head and prayed her fever would break.

She fell asleep after a time. He studied her lovely face illuminated by firelight. He would see her through this and to safety. She was right about not belonging here. And he thought she'd be happy here with him. His gaze traveled over her body. But oh, how he'd miss her. She was his partner. Somehow, the notion of taking a new trail without her filled him with melancholy. What could he do? *You better think of something—or you'll lose her.*

"Thomas? I was wrong, you know," she said, waking up.

"About what?"

"About everything. I've been blaming you for all my faults. I'm so sorry."

That's the fever talking. He checked her forehead. Her skin still felt warm. Not too warm.

"Don't talk now—rest," he said.

"I missed you. If anything happened to you, I don't know what I'd do."

What would happen if he did not return? She'd be adopted and marry a Crow warrior, if she'd have him. They wouldn't bring her home. No, that was his job.

"We got to get you back East," he said.

"I don't want to leave you."

"What are you saying?" He tried to see her face,

now merely an outline in the dying firelight. He could see no detail, no expression to guide him.

"I realized something. I've been fighting so hard, I couldn't see it until now."

"Hush—now, rest."

"I don't want to rest. I have to tell you. First, I was fighting to find John, and then I was fighting to stay alive. Then I came to you and I've been fighting ever since."

"You're not making sense."

"I didn't want those feeling for you. It was too frightening. So I fought them and you. I blamed your heathen ways and rough language. They were all excuses. I couldn't admit it. Now I can. I'm not afraid anymore."

"Admit what, Delia?" This rambling frightened him. Fever was the same as whiskey. Both loosened the tongue.

"I'm in love with you, Thomas."

He sat up. "What?"

"I love you. I don't want to leave you, ever."

He held her shoulders tight, wishing, praying this was real. His eyes stared into the darkness at the face he could not see. What was the matter? He knew her face better than his own. Please, let this not be the fever.

"You won't," he said. "We'll sell the furs and then take our money and go anywhere you say. We could buy some livestock or land, maybe we could open a trading post."

"Thomas, you feel the same?"

"I do."

"I think you are the most wonderful man in the world."

She threw her arms about him. He held her close, inhaling her heady scent. *Give me the chance, Lord. I'll do right by her.*

The eerie sounds of singing filled the air. Here in this little circle of leather, he'd keep her safe and she'd keep him warm.

He dozed for a time, then startled awake. The night sounds changed. The chant grew in volume until the screams rang in the air. She gripped his shirt.

"What is it?"

"They're nearly done."

"It's horrible. I'll never forget the sound."

How much better that she did not have the images to go with it. Her body trembled like a captured bird.

"It's all right. I'm here. We're safe. Close your eyes." He murmured, replacing the sounds of terror with words of comfort.

His fingers brushed her cheek. She was cool. He sighed in relief. Her fever was gone.

"Delia, do you remember what you said before?"

"About loving you?"

"Yes." He sighed. "That was it."

In the morning she took her first steps. Thomas held her about the waist and helped her along. The scab cracked, blood trickled down her foot and onto the yellow grass.

He led her away from the center of the scattered group of tepees. Whatever horrors had taken place during the night, Delia saw no traces now.

They passed several men and women. Each nodded, some smiled. They acted as if this was an ordinary day, not the day after a barbaric execution. Thomas had tried to protect her from the torture by whispering in her ear and changing the subject when the screams forced her to ask what the Crow did to their enemies. The questions and possibilities were worse than seeing. She would never understand these people.

"Let's sit awhile," he said. Thomas guided her to the grass beside the Bighorn River. The water rolled gently along.

"It's nothing like the mountain rivers, is it?"

"Nope. There it dances along like it's in a hurry. Here the water just sidles."

He broke off a blade of grass and chewed on the end, twirling it around and around in his fingers. She followed his gaze to the southeast. Jagged mountains tore at the sky. This delay must frustrate him.

"Is that where we are going?" she asked.

"Down the Bighorn. We'll follow that a ways. We still have nearly a hundred and fifty miles of rough country ahead."

No wonder he was anxious. His packhorse was staggering under the furs he had collected and the fur companies would soon gather to lighten his load.

"When will we leave?"

He tossed the grass away and lowered his gaze, from the mountain peaks, to her face.

"Soon, Delia, very soon."

The next day she managed to walk about without assistance. Her scab held, thanks to the ointment Rising Smoke gave her.

Thomas found her that afternoon with Walks About. They were slicing elk into small pieces for stew.

"We'll leave tomorrow."

"All right." She gave him a broad smile, but he did not return it. Instead he rubbed his neck. She knew that gesture. "What's wrong?"

"I don't know. Something don't feel right."

She stared into his eyes. His gaze darted up to the mountains then down to the river. She'd never seen him so restless.

He stood before her. "I got to check the horses. Come along."

She pointed in the direction she would go and Walks About nodded, shooing her with a hand.

The moccasin did not pain her foot as she walked along with him. His step was slow, making it easy for her to keep stride. His horse caught his scent and nickered before she could even see the animal. The packhorse was staked on a lead to a grove of white poplar. Within the cover of trees and brush, his horse escaped the heat and ever-present flies.

She stroked the velvety nose of his mount as Thomas checked the hooves.

"I got our gear all packed, over there." He motioned with his head.

She saw it then, a pile of furs and sundries peeking out from beneath a buffalo robe. She clenched her jaw. Her injury had delayed him and all because of a misstep.

"I'm sorry," she said.

"For what?" He dropped the last hoof and looked over the horse's withers at her.

''For keeping you. Will we still make the Rendezvous?''

''We'll make her all right.'' He gave the horse's chest two quick slaps and watched the dust rise in the air. Then he turned from the cover of trees. She watched him look about the village. ''I don't know why, but I'm jumpy as a bug on a griddle.''

She ambled toward the packhorse. It blew heavily from his nose in greeting.

A wild cry tore the still air. Her body startled and the horses' ears lay flat.

She turned to Thomas to find his gaze pinned on the clearing.

''What in the world?'' she asked.

''Blackfoot,'' he said, already pulling her to the ground.

Answering cries rose from the village as the Crow warriors grabbed their weapons and braced for the attack.

She watched Thomas draw a rope from his bag and throw it over the horse's neck. Then he grabbed her hand and pulled her back to the cluster of trees. From the glade she peered onto the plain below. Indians poured from the woods behind them onto the open field.

''Blood tribe, a whole angry mess of them. Damn, my harnesses are down there.''

''What should we do?''

He handed her his pistol and checked his rifle. The shotgun remained tied to his back.

''We'll stick here and hope they don't see us.''

Below them the Crow warriors ran up the hill toward their attackers. She could see Grazing Bull lift

a bow and fire. Her gaze shot to Rising Smoke's tee-
pee. There on the edge of the village, Walks About
ran toward the river. Behind her the Blackfoot forces
closed in. Delia saw a club lifted high and swing
down. Her gaze crashed to the ground with her
friend's limp body.

A cry tore from her lips as she began to rise. "We
have to help them."

His strong hand gripped tight and she spun about
to face him. "You can't help them by getting killed."

"But they're dying!"

"You can't save them, Delia. This fight is as old
as these plains."

His image swam before her as the tears welled up
and over her lids, running fast and hot down her
cheeks. She threw herself against his wide chest using
the soft leather of his shirt to muffle her sobs.

The cries and screams went on and on. Now came
the smell of burning. She looked up to see black
smoke billow above the village.

He set her away from him. "Stay there."

He went to his furs and began to tie the beaver
plew onto the horse. He fashioned two rough halters
from his rope and tied the packhorse to his own.

"We got to go, Delia. They'll comb the woods for
stragglers."

He boosted her up and led the horse from their
protective island in the sea of grass. The tree line was
fifty feet away. They'd never make it unnoticed. Her
head pivoted about at the mayhem below.

"Thomas, how do you know they aren't watching
from the woods?"

His voice was grim. "I don't."

She gripped the horse's mane more tightly as they entered the forest. Here the cries died away and the birdsong came to her. The smell of smoke was replaced by the smell of warm cedar. He paused only long enough to mount behind her. She leaned against the reassuring mass of his hard chest muscles.

He avoided the animal trail to their left, heading instead through the brush and rough ground. Her ears strained for some sign of pursuit. The rattle of dry leaves brought both their heads swinging about to find a jay searching for bugs on the forest floor.

For several miles they picked along, silent except for the fall of the horses' hooves.

"Have we lost them?" she asked.

"Maybe, if they don't find our trail. Damn, I should have known better."

"Where are we going?"

"South, we'll follow the Bighorn."

Thomas stopped the horses. She sighed and stretched her tired back. He sat erect, listening. At first there were only the usual sounds, the wind in the trees. She wondered why there were no birdcalls. Then she heard the pounding of many hooves.

"Damnation," he cried, and kicked the horse to a gallop.

She clung to the horse's mane, craning her neck to see past him. The trail was empty behind them. She glanced ahead and saw a rocky hill. He spurred the horse, wheeling for the high ground.

"I see them," she yelled.

Chapter Sixteen

Several Blackfoot warriors rode hard on their trail.

Thomas drew his knife and cut the line holding the packhorse. The animal veered to the right down the hill. Four men followed the loose horse.

The rest rode on, like the hounds of hell, screaming as they closed the distance.

The ground rose sharply. She gripped the horse's mane as she slid back against Thomas. Fear swelled in her throat. What if an arrow hit his back?

Below the Indians slowed, picking their way more carefully. The boulders about them blocked her view of the enemy for a moment.

They'll kill Thomas, if they catch him. She knew they would. What would they do to her? A vision of the war club coming down on Walks About's head filled her mind.

Thomas slid to the ground and pulled her after him.

"Too steep," he said, and slapped the horse back down the trail.

He grabbed his rifle in one hand and her hand in the other as they dashed up the rocky cliff face. He dodged behind boulders and over rock, pulling her along. Her foot burned white-hot with each step. She knew if she stumbled, he would stop. *God, please don't let me fall.* He stopped before a crack in the rock at his feet. The fissure was three feet wide and filled with dead leaves.

Thomas looked back and she followed his gaze. They were not there. He probed the gap with the butt of his rifle. The barrel disappeared to the stock.

"Down you go, Delia," he said.

"Don't you leave me!"

"I won't."

She sat on the rocky edge and slipped into the gap. Her body fell down through the dry leaves coming to rest in the soft lining. She heard his body rustling along as he descended and burrowed toward the sound.

Her fingers touched him, gripping tight to his arm.

"How far?" she whispered.

"Ten, twelve feet. Quiet now, they're coming."

The warriors' screams pierced the air as they charged up and over the rocks above them. If they found them here, there would be no escape. They were trapped in this narrow grave.

The men were right above her now. She pressed her face to his shoulder and held her breath.

Soon the cries came from a greater distance. She strained to hear as they faded away. A hiccup escaped her lips. He pressed his hand across her lips, muttering a curse.

She listened as his heartbeat began to slow, taking comfort from the steady rhythm. Her legs trembled from the run up the rock and her foot pulsed like a sore tooth. Finally her spasms ceased and his hand slid away from her mouth.

She tried to wait for him to speak first, but the minutes dragged by with no sound from above.

"Now what?" she whispered.

With her ear pressed to his chest, she felt his whispered words vibrate beneath her cheek. "Sit tight until nightfall."

Nightfall? That was hours away. She let her legs fold beneath her, crumpling to the ground. She brushed away the leaves before her face, trying to clear a space to breathe. The musty odor of rotting leaves choked her.

He sank beside her. "Keep still. They're close."

She heard them again, their voices clear as they crossed above her once more.

His lips brushed her ear. "They'll keep searching until dark. Hold still."

She pulled the neck of her dress over her face to keep the leaves from tickling her nose. She could smell her own fear. She as sat unmoving as the stone behind her.

Back and forth the Blackfoot traveled through the hot afternoon, searching for their prey. Each time they leaped the gap she was sure an arrow or spear would descend upon them. Sweat trickled down her back. Tiny branches pricked at her skin. She stifled the urge to scratch. Why don't they quit and go home?

Beneath the pile of leaves, the world was dark. How would he know when evening came?

Then she heard it. The sound of a coyote cry pierced their cavern, heralding in the night.

The voices of their pursuers came no more.

"I'm going up," he said.

"Me, too!"

"No, Delia, stay here where it's safe."

"What if you don't come back?"

"I'll come back—I always come back." There was a pause. "And if I don't, you wait till tomorrow night and then follow the river back up to the Crow."

She'd never make it with her foot. If she insisted on going, she'd put him in danger.

"All right. I'll stay."

His fingers brushed her cheek and he was gone.

Nash knew he'd abandoned her again, knew that she was most afraid of being left behind. But she was safer there, hidden in the crack in the earth. And she'd not insisted—she had let him go.

He crept along the ridge of rock, keeping low. His moccasins whispered over the stone as he swept along.

They had taken everything, a year's work, all his furs, his horses, everything.

His fingers coiled tight about the smooth wood stock of his Hawkins. Without those furs he had nothing. Worse than nothing, he'd be in debt for the traps.

He'd get them back, every pelt, by God, he would.

The moon was a tiny sliver in the starry sky. He was invisible.

He climbed down the rock. This was where he'd cut loose his packhorse. Damn them!

He smelled the air but caught no sign of their camp. The night was so dark he had to feel his way along through the blue spruce.

He heard a soft sound, like a sigh. He sank to one

knee and raised his knife against the night. His ears strained to hear. Then he saw them, warrior after warrior lying on the ground before him. He could touch the nearest man with the barrel of his rifle.

He had nearly stepped on them.

His heart jumped to a pounding rhythm, so loud he feared he'd wake them with the mad beat. He edged backward up the rock.

No fire, no lookout, just fifteen warriors lying on the ground. There might be a scout. He can't see any better than I can.

Fifteen! That many he had seen, there might be more. Good God, he could never kill that many. Where was his horse? He had to find it.

It would be guarded. Blackfoot never left the horses unattended. Still he might slit the man's throat before he could sound the alarm.

He thought of Delia, trembling in that hole in the rock. Even if he recovered his plew, what then? They'd never outrun them riding double with a loaded packhorse trailing behind.

Damn.

If I was alone, I'd chance it. I'd steal it all back. I'd make a run for it. But I'm not alone.

He crept back up the mountain. The warriors hadn't given up, or they'd be gone. They'll be back in the morning. Should they run?

Blackfoot were the best trackers he'd ever seen. *They'd find the trail and, with us on foot, we'd have no chance.*

The crack foxed them. He'd have to hope they wouldn't find it tomorrow, that they'd widen the search.

He climbed up the rocks to the spot where he had left her. He almost missed it himself. This was damn good cover.

"Delia."

"Nash? Oh, thank God. I prayed so hard." Her voice was muffled. His jaw clenched in anger. He dragged her over half the Rocky Mountains and put her in danger. Despite his best efforts, he could not keep her safe. She deserved better than he could provide. She deserved to go home.

"Move left, I'm coming down."

He slid off the rock and into the leaves, disappearing from the face of the earth.

"Nash?" Her fingers touched him, as if assuring herself he was real. "I found something. Look here."

She guided him a few feet down the crevasse. "There's a little niche, see?"

He couldn't see a damn thing, but she guided his fingers.

"How big?" he asked.

"I'm not sure."

He felt around and discovered the ledge went back only three feet or so. It was long and tapered away at one end to nothing.

"We could clear some of the leaves away in here," she said.

Soon they were pushing leaves aside. New ones fell in from above. He rummaged about and gathered some sticks and logs that had fallen into the cleft. These he used to hold back the wall of debris. Then they crawled into the niche. The rock was relatively flat.

He pulled her close, letting her use his arm as a pillow. He grasped his water skin.

"Have some water, Delia."

She took the bag.

"It's nearly gone."

"Have a drink. I'll get more soon."

He heard the water pass her throat. She handed back the skin and he drank the last.

"What did you see?"

"There's a mess of them. I couldn't risk searching for the horses."

She was silent. Was she disappointed at his failure? At last she spoke.

"Thank you."

"What?"

"Thank you for not risking it, for not dying and for coming back to me."

He patted her shoulder.

"I always come back." He heard her yawn. "Best sleep now. We're staying here until them fellers find something more interesting to do than look for us."

He knew the moment she fell asleep. Her body startled, as if falling, and then relaxed. Her breathing changed to a slow, steady draw. He sighed and smelled the sweet musty odor of dry leaves. He closed his eyes and drifted away as well.

The sound of the warrior's voices brought him awake. He sat up and slammed his head on the rocky ledge above him. He muttered a curse. Delia startled beside him. He gripped his hand tight over her mouth and waited until she nodded. She was awake now and had time to remember. He swept his fingers over his brow and felt a lump rising there.

His fingers slid away. He pressed his lips to her ear.

"Quiet now, they're back."

The voices receded. He stretched a bit. His body was stiff as the barrel of his rifle. The muscles of his back ached to bend. The rustling would give them away. He had to stay put.

Her breath fanned his cheek. Again he vowed to get her out of here. *I'll see her safe, so help me.*

Suddenly he realized something. He'd told her to stay and she'd done it.

"They're gone," she whispered.

"Not for long."

All morning they heard the men calling above them. They crossed near many times. Finally it seemed they gave up.

He waited.

No sound reached him.

"I'm going to have a look," he said.

"Me, too."

"Delia—"

"Thomas, you can't leave me down here again, not again."

"Me first, then," he said.

She slid off the ledge. He heard her stifle a groan, but not one word of complaint escaped her lips. He crawled forward.

"Damnation," he said. Every muscle seemed to have shortened. Climbing up was difficult now. His body was weak from lack of food and water.

His head popped up from the leaves like a chip-munk emerging in springtime.

His head swiveled about. He saw no sign of them. He climbed up and he could see the trail below. There was no one about.

He lay on his belly and reached into the pit.

"Delia, grab hold." Instantly her fingers coiled tight about his wrists. When had she grown so strong?

He lifted her easily to the surface and held her as she steadied against him.

"Are they gone?"

"Maybe."

Together they crossed to the high rocks overlook-ing the valley. Far below, on the wide-open ground by the river, he saw them.

"Bastards!" he said.

She shook her head, but did not chastise him. Her fingers plucked dry leaves from his hair.

They had his horse and were racing the animal against their horses. Apparently this was better sport than climbing about searching for them. Why not—they had everything but his Hawkins.

Dear God, there was a hundred and fifty miles to go, without horse or supplies. He looked at Delia to find her whiskey eyes gazing up at him. She was frightened; he could see it there in the depths of her eyes.

"Don't go, Nash. There are too many. They'll kill you."

"They have my horses and beaver. I got nothing left."

"You have your gun, your possibles bag and me."

Chapter Seventeen

"Delia, it's well over a hundred miles to the Rendezvous."

"We'll make it."

He threw his hat down.

"How do you know?"

"Because you are the most talented woodsman I have ever seen, and I am the most stubborn woman you will ever meet."

He couldn't keep from smiling at the determined tilt of her chin. Pride swelled with each steady beat of his heart. His scrawny cub had grown into a lioness.

"You are that."

They crossed the rocky top of the hill and traveled south behind the cover of the low ridge. Late in the day they were miles downriver.

He checked her foot before the light faded. The skin was swollen and the scab oozed in places. Considering what she'd been through, it looked damn good. He knew she'd never be able to walk the distance.

"What do you think?" she asked, peering at her wound.

"It's healing up." He released her ankle with a nod of approval, then bandaged her again.

Game was plentiful. Bighorn sheep covered the hills and buffalo coated the river basin.

When a pronghorn crossed their path, Nash raised his rifle then lowered it again.

"I don't dare risk a shot."

She picked juniper berries at sunset and he set his hook in a stream that flowed into the river.

"I got one!" He pulled a lovely big trout from the water.

"Can we cook it?"

He looked about, fixing his eye on a rocky grove.

"When it's full dark, we'll have a little fire."

She gathered wood. He struck his steel on the flint until the sparks caught the tinder. Carefully he blew the ember to flame. Here behind the rocks, no light would be seen. He watched the smoke curl to the night sky.

"Pray God, they ain't close enough to smell it," he said.

"Thomas, was that a prayer?" she asked.

"Naw, I wanted *you* to pray for me. God won't listen to me."

She smiled and shook her head.

He wouldn't have risked a fire, himself. He'd have eaten the thing raw. But she deserved hot, fresh fish and much more.

Delia dropped the logs from her arms and came to rest beside the fire with a grateful sigh. He watched her reach into her bag and draw forth her journal.

She opened the battered leather cover and flipped to an open page. Next she rummaged about until she found the stub of a pencil.

"You writing about them Indians?"

"Mmm-hmm." She nodded, already lost in thought.

He didn't know where she found the energy. They had walked all afternoon with little food. But always she found time to scribble in that book. He had not touched it again, not since the time she caught him. That was hers. He understood now. Everyone has a right to secrets. He just wondered why you'd want to write what no one was meant to see?

The small fire lit her face and the ringlets of blond hair seemed gilded. She held the book to catch the scant light. Little twigs still clung to her head and her hair smelled like a leaf pile. Lord, she was magnificent!

And what was he? A defeated man. He'd lost all he had in the world. Eight dollars a pelt, gone, all gone.

He looked at her pink cheeks.

There would be no farm.

She turned the page.

There would be no livestock or business.

She raised her yellow cat eyes and smiled.

He had nothing to offer.

"You look dour," she said.

"Speak English." His voice sounded hostile.

Her eyebrows lifted. She stared at him for a time. "I wonder why you look so downcast."

"My shoe is pinching me."

She smiled. "You aren't wearing shoes." Her fingers moved and the journal snapped closed. "We have lost everything, haven't we?"

Everything, even his dreams.

There were no words to express it. He nodded.

"Then we'll have to start again."

"It ain't so simple."

"No, not simple." He wondered about her sad, knowing smile. "I left my friends to come here, to start over. I lost my husband, and started over again. I came to you. We'll start over together."

"I'm not you, Delia."

"Thomas—"

"Please, Delia, let me be."

He needed time to mourn. Delia understood that. Having lost more than possessions, she knew the time necessary to grieve over all the work and struggle the Blackfoot had stolen.

She twisted the cotton rag in the icy water. Her fingers tingled from the cold. She lowered her body to the bank, pulled off her moccasin and plunged her foot into the river. She sighed as the cool water soothed the relentless ache.

Finally her foot was numb. She retrieved a comb from her possibles bag and worked the fine tortoise-shell teeth through her mane, removing the bits of leaf and twig before braiding her hair by feel in the dark.

Thomas waited until she returned to douse the fire. The coals hissed in protest then died in the watery grave.

"Things will be better tomorrow," she promised.

He grunted and lay beside her on the ground. She rolled to face him, wrapping her arms about his neck, and lifted her head to kiss him. He stayed still as stone, allowing her only his cheek. He did not dip his head to touch her lips. She could see his eyes staring up at the night sky. She rested beside him, looking at the heavens.

"It's so lovely," she whispered.

"That it is."

She smiled and let sleep take her weary body.

A gentle shake of her shoulder brought her instantly awake. Her gaze locked with his and the smile told her there was no danger. She sat up and stretched.

They left the shelter of rock and began their journey without breakfast. Her stomach rumbled as they crossed the soggy bank.

By midday the river cut through narrow canyons and they were forced to climb up the yellow cliffs to follow its course. He stood on the high rocky ledge looking at the wide river in silence. She waited at his side.

"We'll never make it," he said.

"What?"

"The Rendezvous. We've only come a few miles. It will take us near a month and that's too long."

"Can we head for a fort?"

"Too far—too damn far." He held the barrel of his gun with both hands and leaned upon it as if it were a walking stick. She felt a tugging fear nibbling at her insides. Thomas was worried. They had no horses. She understood now—their survival was in serious doubt.

"What will we do?"

"We'll build a raft."

She'd lost her ax. Below them, gentle waters rolled lazily along.

"Do you know this river?"

"No—but I heard that Bridger made it once. If he could do it, so can we."

"Who is Bridger?"

"A trapper—one of the best. With luck, you'll meet him in a couple weeks."

"Well then, let's make a raft."

Bridger had made it all right, barely. Afterward, he had told the group not to bring the furs by river. He'd nearly drowned in a narrow canyon. The Indians wouldn't even try it. They called it "Bad Pass." Still the river was their one way out of this area and back to safety. Bridger's raft had been made of wood. The timbers had splintered but had held.

The craft hadn't been maneuverable. Bridger had been at the river's mercy. Nash knew a lighter craft would steer better; it would also swamp in rough water.

As they descended from the rocks he spotted buffalo five hundred yards away. She stared in at the herd. There must be seven hundred animals, all quietly grazing in the tall grass.

"I need a stick." He held his hand up before his chest. "Yea high, with a fork in the top."

Delia scrambled off the rock to look as he studied the animals. He needed a big one. She returned dragging a thick branch.

He stuck the end in a crack in the rock face and rested his rifle barrel in the notch. Closing one eye, he aimed below the shoulder for the lung and squeezed the trigger. A blast of acrid smoke belched from the end of the gun.

Delia faced the herd. The buffalo grazed as before. "You missed."

He smiled. A large bull bent his knees, going slowly down on his front feet as he lowered himself to the ground. About him the herd continued to graze. Finally the bull laid his head gently on the earth.

"Got him."

Delia looked at him in puzzlement, then turned to the field again.

"Who?"

Several of the buffalo lay in the sun chewing their cud. Only one lay with his head on the ground.

He fired two more shots at the feet of another big bull. He bellowed and ran, leading the herd away from the river, leaving the one lone animal lying in the field.

"Oh, Thomas, that is truly amazing."

The afternoon was spent skinning and cleaning the hide. Delia sliced the meat in thin strips to dry for jerky.

They gathered buffalo chips to smoke the meat and speed the drying.

"We'll wait until dark and start a fire over there in those rocks and dry as much as we can. You stay and slice her up and I'll go see about the raft."

He returned to the river and cut sandbar willow. He chose green wood at least two inches thick. Usually an inch was more than enough, but not for this trip.

He cut and staked the pieces in the ground, forming arching wickets. Then he ran one long branch across the others, forming the boat's bottom. He used green rawhide from the buffalo's legs to lash the wood together.

He glanced at the sky. The light was nearly gone. He found Delia laying the fire, adding dry grass beneath the chips.

"We can start her now," he said.

She knelt beside the grass and struck the steel to flint until a spark jumped to the grass. She blew and the spark blazed to life. He smiled with pride. He'd taught her that.

Above the coals she'd fashioned green-wood racks of buffalo meat. He looked at the sky and watched the first stars cut through the darkening heavens.

He pulled the frame up by the fire. He added a thick three-inch gunwale, lashing it to the frame. Delia helped drag the wet skin to his craft, where he upended the boat frame onto the furry hide.

Delia held the leather as he fixed it in place over the gunwale. He stood back to survey his work.

"The skin looks a bit baggy," she said.

"It'll shrink tight. That's why we have to tie it before it's dry."

"Oh." She nodded, looking at the shaggy boat.

He decided to tie some beams across the gunwales to add strength.

"Will it hold?"

"Delia, I've seen these boats carry three men, sixty steel traps and five hundred furs, plus guns and ammunition. She'll hold." *Until they hit the rapids. If she takes water, she'll flounder.*

"Then why are you frowning?" she asked.

Tell her. "I'm worried about rough water. She might swamp."

Delia studied the boat. "Why not cover the top as well. Then the water will roll off the hide and back into the river."

His jaw dropped open. He grabbed her in his arms and hugged her. "Delia, that's it!"

He kissed her soundly. Instantly his joy galvanized. Her mouth was soft and yielding. Her fingers grazed his back. He pulled her closer and let his tongue delve into her sweet mouth.

She sank to the ground and he followed her. Her fingers tugged at him, insistent, wanting. This was all that mattered, just Delia and nothing else.

Chapter Eighteen

Delia smiled remembering the night. Everything between them was all right. Her worries were just that. His touch was sure and his passions rose with her own.

She reached for him and found his place empty. He'd gone hunting. She remembered him telling her. Had he kissed her cheek? She didn't recall.

Somehow his touch washed away all her fatigue and uncertainty. In his arms, she was powerful and unafraid. How lucky they were.

She rose and washed, before returning to cut more strips from the buffalo. A rustling alerted her. She glanced up from the carcass to see the wolves trotting low to the ground and fast. They formed a semicircle about her. As she focused on the pack, they rose to full height and charged forward like seasoned soldiers.

She lifted the shotgun and fired one barrel at the closest animal. She missed.

The second barrel of shot took down the lead wolf. The others halted at the body of their twitching comrade. She darted toward the willows fifty yards away. Her legs pumped madly at the ground, matching the wild beat of her heart. Any moment she expected a wolf to take her heel and bring her to the ground. They'd tear her apart.

She jumped for the low branches and scrambled up the tree. Only then did she look back and see the wolves. None had pursued her. From her perch on the tree limb she saw them surrounding the buffalo carcass. She could hear the noisy growl and yip as they fought for the best pieces. The animal she shot lay beside the pack, licking his bleeding shoulder. She hoped they did not find the strips of meat drying beyond the rocks.

"Delia!"

"I'm here," she called.

"Stay in the trees. I'm coming."

She could see him now, trotting along the riverbank to the north. He stopped below her and climbed up the tree.

"You hurt?" She shook her head. He turned toward the pack. "Did they get our stores?"

"Not yet, only the carcass."

"They're welcome to that. If they take one step toward the jerky, I'll kill them."

They waited in the trees as the animals ate their fill. Finally the last lumbered off behind the others, his belly swollen with meat.

He helped her down.

"I heard your shot and came running. I got our elk, but I left it back in the woods."

"You better go get it, or they'll have that, too."

"Not that bunch. You be all right?"

"Oh, fine." She waited until he was out of sight

to sink to the earth. Her legs now turned to water and her hands shook like an old woman's.

He returned as she packed the dried meat. He skinned the elk and the process began again. By afternoon he had covered the boat in two overlapping hides that could be rolled forward and lashed together. They could sit between the two flaps, covered from the waist down.

"It might work."

She gathered huckleberries along the stream as he carved two paddles from green cottonwood.

"We're ready," he said.

After their meal of elk steaks and berries, he mixed the ash from the fire with elk tallow making a gray paste. This he spread thickly on all the places the rawhide pierced the bull boat and where the elk was sewn to the buffalo.

"We'll start tomorrow."

"Why not now?" She'd prefer not staying so close to the buffalo and elk remains, not with the wolves about.

"Not even Indians travel the river at night. You can't see the dangers. We'll sleep back on the knoll. Best to be away from the carcasses."

The wolves' howls split the still air that night. Their voices came from a long way off.

In the morning, they saw a grizzly with two nearly grown cubs feasting on the buffalo. Delia shuddered as she remembered the power in those thick arms.

It only took a moment to load the provisions and their two bags. Thomas extended his hand and guided her into the craft.

"Sit there." He indicated the bow. She lowered

herself to the buffalo skin, expecting it to sag beneath her. It felt as if it were a hardwood floor instead of a dried hide.

She looked back to see him push off the sandy shore and hop in behind her. He steered out to the middle of the water and soon the current pulled them slowly toward their destination.

The sun rose above them. All around was the smell of leather. She handed him some jerky and he passed her the water skin. She chewed slowly as she watched the riverbank roll by. She tried paddling a while and then rested. Trying to keep up with Nash was impossible. Her best guess was that they had already come twenty miles. That was more than they could make in the entire day. The narrow riverbed gave way to rising hills with high mountains beyond. Nash said they were the Bighorns.

In the afternoon, the river ran swiftly along and Nash needed only to steer, keeping them in the center, away from the rocks that occasionally cropped up. The wind rushed by cooling her skin. She smiled and turned toward the pleasant breeze.

"Isn't this lucky?" she asked. "You don't even have to paddle."

"Delia, start unrolling the top piece and tie it down."

"Why? The river looks clear."

"Not for long."

She followed his gaze. The banks of the river rose to sheer cliffs. Between the cleft in the rocks the river narrowed. Suddenly she was aware of the sound of rushing water. Ahead, white water pounded against the rock.

Her fingers tugged the first elk skin into position

and she cinched the laces, covering the right half of the boat. He stopped steering and helped her roll the second skin into place and tied the rawhide up the center about his waist.

"Lie down, Delia, stay down."

She shook her head and tied the laces tight about her body, down the center of the boat. Then she grabbed the paddle and turned to face the river.

"When I say right, you paddle for all you're worth on that side."

"Yes," she called. Already the river roared, tearing her words away as she spoke.

Ahead, the water frothed and foamed, spraying up, rolling off her buckskin and across the top of their little boat.

"It's getting dark!" she yelled.

"We're in a canyon." He sounded so far behind her.

She looked up. Above her, like light through a tunnel, she spied blue sky. Here on the river the steep walls of rock cast them in perpetual twilight. The world around turned an eerie greenish-gray.

"Left!"

She dug her paddle into the water. The river nearly pulled the handle from her. She wrestled free and stabbed again and again at the living wave.

"Hold!"

She held the paddle before her like a shield and gasped to breathe as the spray rolled in droplets off her face and hair. Her body jerked in surprise as she saw the large group of rocks shoot by her left side. She glanced forward. The river turned sharply left.

The boat was caught in rolling whitewater. She

watched the waves before her crash against the rocky wall before turning.

"Left!" His voice bellowed.

Again she stabbed at the water, pulling with all her might against the awesome force of the river. Were they turning? She could not tell. Yes, they were. The wall loomed ahead. Not enough, they were going to hit.

A scream tore from her lips as the wave threw their boat up against the cliff. She raised her paddle to push free. The wood cracked in two. Then they hit. The right side of the bull boat collapsed as it turned in the air. The bottom scraped against the rock and they rode high along the canyon wall for an instant. Then they fell, back to the raging current. She was sucked beneath the surface and tried clawing at the water. She could not free herself from the lashings. Cold black water swirled about her. Helpless, she was dragged along with the buffalo skin and shattered willow. Her lungs burned for air too long denied.

The boat popped to the surface like a cork released from the river's hand. Delia sputtered and threw the sodden hair from her face. Was he there or had he succeeded in tearing himself free of the boat? She turned. Nash howled at their near miss. He called something, but his words were stolen by the river's roar.

They shot down the canyon at speeds she could not even imagine.

"Right!"

She looked at her hand and was surprised to see it still held the remains of her paddle. She gripped the slick wood and tried to catch hold of the rolling waves.

She glanced at the side of the boat she had seen collapse. Somehow it had sprung back into place. The green wood, she thought, flexible as a bow.

Before her, the river disappeared as the boat sailed over the falls. *God, protect us.* The river tumbled down a watery staircase jarring her bones. Rocks scraped along the hide beneath her. The skin now sagged from the frame as the water soaked the buffalo hide.

Suddenly she was turning about. She looked at the falls they had just descended as they spun in a whirlpool.

''Left!''

She gripped the air. Her paddle was gone. She leaned to the left and pulled with both hands.

As suddenly as the whirlpool had grabbed them, it spit them out, throwing their sodden craft loose again. She faced downstream once more. The huge rocks loomed in the center of the water, parting the river like the fin of a great fish.

Giant logs rolled in the tumbling water before the mighty rock. She watched them split in two like matchsticks. She turned to say goodbye to Thomas and found him pulling his paddle through the water with all his might.

Looking forward, she saw he had managed to send them toward the right channel. The boat shot past the net of fallen logs before the giant rock. They bounced off the stones like a rubber ball and back into the tumbling water.

Up and down the rapids they fell, as they rode straight in the center of the gap. Gradually the roaring diminished. They bobbed along, but the spray did not blind her. She looked up and watched as the canyon eased back to the river.

The gap widened and instantly the water slowed. She looked back at the hellish canyon in wonder. How had they survived?

Then she focused on Nash. He still pulled his paddle swiftly through the water, as though he had not noticed the danger was behind them.

"We made it!" she called. Her joy tumbled into her words. "Nash, we did it!"

He did not answer or pause, focusing all his energy on his frantic strokes.

Her skin relayed a desperate message. There was water in the boat. The icy river had found a gap and now poured over her legs. She glanced frantically about. He steered toward the shore. But the river ran swift and the shore was a nest of jagged rocks. Ahead lay a sandbank as the river took a turn. She could tell that was his target, their only hope. She tried to judge the distance and their speed. It would be close, very close.

Sand scraped the bottom and she released the breath she held. They had made it.

He drew his knife and slashed at the binding holding him to the boat. He cut and pulled her free as well, then threw her toward the bank and turned to wrestle the boat from the river.

She landed in two feet of water and still the current dragged at her legs, trying to sweep her feet from beneath her.

Delia reached back and grasped his shirt, then dug her heels into the sand and pulled with all her might. Before her lay a fallen tree, cast upon the sandbar. Her fingers closed about the bare branch and held.

That boat had his rifle, their supplies and her journal. She groaned as her shoulder joint tore. He gained a step toward her, then another. He fell beside her, the boat upon him. She grasped the willow frame and pulled again. Together they dragged the skins up onto the bank and fell heavily on the sand beside it.

Her chest heaved as they lay still against the warm sand. Above her, the sun shone gaily down, denying the horror she had just experienced. Her shoulder throbbed. Her teeth chattered together like wild applause. She turned her head to see Nash lying on his side. His shirt was torn and his shoulder bled from many abrasions. Water ran from ropes of dark hair and disappeared into the sand.

His eyelids fluttered open and she stared into his eyes.

"We made it," he whispered. A half smile played upon his lips.

She groaned. Every muscle hurt. Her body had been rattled to the bone. She must have swallowed half the river. She lay on the warm sand and let the sunshine dry her face. Only a minute, she thought as she closed her eyes.

"Delia!" The frantic call and rough shake sent her rearing up to a seated position.

"What?"

She saw his shoulders sag. He slowly shook his head.

"I thought you passed out."

Had she? Perhaps. She looked about at the sandy shore covered with brush, then back to meet his gaze.

"You're bleeding," she said. Her fingers peeled back the wet buckskin and probed his wounds. The muscle of his shoulder looked as if a wildcat attacked him. The abrasions were not deep, thank heavens. Still, open wounds would fester.

"I hit that big rock back there," he said.

She laughed. "Which one?"

"Damned if I know." He took her hand. "Delia, you're a wonder. If you hadn't thought of covering the bull boat, we'd have swamped for sure."

Her cheeks felt hot. She lowered her gaze from the admiration in his eyes.

"Well, you're the one who steered us through. I never could have done that."

They had made it together.

"You hurt?"

"I wrenched my shoulder." She tried to lift it, but could not bring her hand above her head. "It's all right. What about you?"

"Just this scratch. I'm one lucky dog."

"Thomas, I thought we'd drown when the river took us under. I tried to pull loose, but the lashing held me."

"Good thing. We only came up because the boat is full of air. If you'd come out, the river would've had you."

His blue eyes held her. There were so many ways to die here.

"Woo-waugh!" he hollered, and hit his hand on his knee. "That was some ride!"

She looked at him, astonished. "Thomas, you enjoyed that?"

"I always enjoy living over dying, Delia." He ran a hand through his long wet hair. "Damn, I lost my hat. Come on, we got to get this gear dried or my guns will rust."

"My journal!" She pulled the waterlogged skins

aside to retrieve her bags. Reaching inside, she pulled the journal free. It was still tied tightly in the mink-oiled buckskin. Frantically she pulled at the binding cord. It fell away and the package came open. Not a drop of water fell from within.

"Oh, look! It's dry." She stopped herself from cradling the book against her wet bosom.

"That's more than I can say for us. Come on."

Together they dragged the remains of their boat up the bank. They stopped at a grassy knoll surrounded by more cliffs, rising ten feet above them. Judging from the amount of driftwood, she decided this area was prone to flood. There was no way out except up the sheer cliff or down the river.

"I'll get the wood," she said.

When she had finished stacking the logs and branches, she helped Thomas unpack the last of the supplies. The jerky bag was filled with water. His guns were wet, but his powder had stayed dry. She laid the jerky out on a stone and Thomas cleaned and oiled the guns.

She went to the riverbank and dug a hole in the sand, then waited as the water seeped in from below. In a few minutes she filled the water skin with clear liquid.

Back at the fire she stared at Thomas, sitting barefoot and shirtless, examining the boat. His battered shoulder was already beginning to scab. All their reserve clothing was draped over rocks and bushes.

He shrugged. "They dry faster off than on."

She sat on the ground and pulled off her sodden moccasins, setting them by the fire.

"How is the boat?" she asked.

He ran a hand over the bottom. "Some of the frame

is busted, small wonder. I don't see any cuts, except for this one.'' He popped a finger through a six-inch gash on the side.

They'd have to walk. Delia looked up at the cliffs for a moment. They towered above them.

He smiled. ''Don't worry, Delia. I can patch her.''

''That's what I was *worried* about.''

He snorted and smiled up at her.

''Don't. The rest should be smooth sailing.''

She sighed. ''You said you had never run this river.''

''Nobody has, but Bridger—well now, Bridger and us. The cliffs kept me from seeing the bad water, though I knew the rapids was there. Most of the rest of this river I've seen. I followed it up to the Yellowstone and crossed to the Musselshell. We'll be all right.''

''Really?''

''I won't lie to you, Delia.''

No, he wouldn't.

''Let's patch it then.''

He drew out his awl and a horn cup holding the remains of the gray patch. While he punctured holes in the leather, she cut a piece to fit. The skin was so wet the work was easy and soon finished.

He propped the frame on two stout branches so it sat nearly upright at the edge of the fire. She watched the smoke curl about the hide.

''Will it shrink again?''

''Sure will.''

''How far do you think we came today?''

He rubbed his chin and looked skyward as he considered. She took the opportunity to admire his phy-

sique. It was a mistake. Her blood began rushing, beginning a dull throbbing.

"I reckon we been over fifty miles. That's a third
the distance. We won't be going that fast from here
out, though."

"Thank goodness."

He nodded. His eyes stared fixedly upon her. His
eyes burned as they passed over the wet leather that
molded to her like a second skin. Her body pulsed
with anticipation. She smiled in welcome.

He pulled his gaze away. She watched him squeeze
his hands into fists.

"Best have something to eat. We have a long day,
tomorrow."

Suddenly her wet buckskin was cold as the river.
She shivered. He brought her to a boil with a glance
and then threw ice water on her. Why?

She looked at his shoulder. Was it his injury? She
hoped that was the reason. Needles of doubt pricked
at her.

She stumbled toward her clothing drying over
brush. Checking them was an excuse to leave his side.
He was battered and her shoulder throbbed. They
needed rest and nourishment, of course they did. Her
fingers tested the blue dress. Rivulets of water ran
from the sodden cotton fabric. When had she worn
this last? It seemed like a hundred long years ago.

She moved to the second doeskin dress. This one
he'd made for her, showing her how. At the time she
had thought it indecent, showing far too much leg.
She had made britches, now discarded in the warm
days of summer. He'd been right about its practical-
ity. But if he had wanted her in utilitarian clothing,
why had he sewn elk teeth across the bodice? She

smiled. This was dryer than the one she wore. She pulled it from the shrubs and stepped behind them, quickly exchanging the garments.

He was smoking his pipe when she returned. Somehow his tobacco, too, had stayed dry. She noticed the clay stem was broken. This didn't stop him from puffing on the ragged edge. She drew out her journal and began to record their latest adventures.

When she had finished, she flipped back through the pages, but only as far as the day she met Nash. Oh, what a rascal she'd thought him then, a scoundrel with a black heart. How had she ever thought it? She read the angry words she'd written after he'd read her journal and smiled. It did not seem so important now. Here was the bear attack. She'd been sure he'd die that day. Her heart sped up at the vivid memories. He had saved her life so many times. When she reached the writings about the Crow village, she stopped. Lifting her eyes from the page, she found him studying her silently across the fire. She held his gaze.

"Would you like to hear some of our adventures?"

His eyebrows lifted and he puffed upon his pipe a moment longer then lowered his hand and nodded.

Chapter Nineteen

Nash loved the sound of her voice. Her words were almost a song, the way she ran them all together. He'd never heard such a tale. This was different than the lies told by men around the camp, each trying to outdo the other.

Her words were real. He could see the Crow camp through her eyes. And by the way she described their escape from the Blackfoot warriors, he could feel her terror. He would never have thought of calling that little crack in the rock the outer circle of hell. But she was right. Falling into their hiding place did seem like descending into hell. She told of her feelings, too. All the raw fear and heart-pounding adventure of that wild river ride was there.

This was the next best thing to holding her in his arms. He was thankful she shared her words with him. After what he'd done, he couldn't see why she would.

She closed the book. He lifted his gaze from the firelight. The sun had set and the stars were out. He hadn't seen it turn, so caught up he'd been in her tale.

"That was something," he said. "I never heard

anyone tell a story like you just done. That was really something.''

Her smile raised a dull ache in his chest as if there was an empty spot there.

He resisted the urge to move to her. He had nothing to offer now. Somehow he had let that detail slip his mind and he'd bedded her, right there on the river-bank, next to the bull boat. He would not forget again. He had no right now.

''Why? You were there, you know exactly what happened,'' she said.

''But I never could tell it like you done. I could hear the river roar again. You got a gift.''

He gripped the log with both hands holding him in place as if to keep in an imaginary boat.

''Is that your stomach?'' she asked.

The growling from within came again.

''Guess so.''

''Well, we'd better have some of that jerky, before you starve to death.''

That night they lay under the stars. She nestled against his side. He allowed himself the luxury of holding her in his arms. If only there was a way for them. But he knew the world was very cruel to those without money or property. He had neither.

In the morning Nash lashed more green willow over the cracked pieces. The dry skin now fit tightly over the frame. He tested the boat in shallow water. The patch held.

''All aboard,'' he called.

Together they loaded their packs and the guns, now

wrapped in oilskin. He held her small hand until she sat, and then passed her a new paddle.

"Try and hold on to that one."

She grinned. "Aye, aye, Captain." Her mock salute brought a smile.

One quick push and they were river-bound once more. The current grabbed them immediately. His blood surged in rhythm with the rushing water. He cut his paddle behind the boat, making a rudder to guide their course.

Delia clutched both sides of the bow until her knuckles turned white. After the ride they'd had yesterday, he was amazed she got in the boat at all.

The morning sped by with the swift river. By midday he reckoned that they'd gone another thirty miles. The water flowed calmly and so he paddled steadily. Delia stroked along with him for much of the afternoon, finally giving up and having a long drink from the water skin. She was strong now and a better paddler than many men he'd seen.

"How is your shoulder?" he asked.

"It burns a bit."

He nodded, giving his own shoulder a tentative shrug.

They passed many tributaries leading from the mountains. Soon he'd have to pick one and they'd be on their feet once more. They had only fifty miles or so to travel, as the crow flies. He looked at the Wind River Range to the right. For them it would be straight up and straight down before they saw the Green River. Fifty miles would seem like a hundred.

"Don't you ever get tired?" Her voice sounded irritated.

He smiled. Her hair curled in small ringlets all about her face. Her nose was pink.

"You need a hat."

"I'm not an English gentleman. I don't want to wear a beaver on my head."

"Then I'll make you one of elk."

Her fingers felt the part in her hair. She frowned.

He confirmed her suspicions. "It's burned."

She rummaged in her bag and pulled a sad scrap of white cotton from within. This she folded into a triangle and tied it over her head pulling the peak out enough to shade her nose.

"I haven't burned before," she said.

"We've been under cover most days."

The smell of wood smoke alerted him. He looked about for the source. Up ahead on the left bank across from a large tributary, he saw a grouping of tepees. He swung their boat toward the opposite shore.

"What's wrong?" she asked, and then turned forward. He watched her lower her profile and reach for the guns.

"They're Nez Percé. I don't reckon we'll need the guns."

He paddled along until the woman at the river noticed their approach and sounded the alarm. Minutes later the warriors lined the bank.

He held the boat across from the village, waiting.

"Take off your kerchief, Delia, let them see your hair." She dragged the cloth away and knelt in the bow. He listened to a murmur run through the men. "Wave the cloth."

She waved the white cloth above her head. He

raised his open hand in greeting. One man came down to the bank and raised his hand in salute.

Nash paddled toward them.

A warrior helped Delia out of the boat. He lifted her braid then let it fall back to her shoulder. Her blond hair always caused a stir. Who could blame them? Hair the color of cornsilk was rare anywhere he'd been, as well.

A wild cry slit the air, followed by the answering calls of many women. Delia turned a worried eye to him.

"That's a kind of welcome," Nash assured.

Men led them up the bank. Nash passed by the Indians' horses, guarded by young boys. Damn, he wished he had something to trade. An awl and a few beads would get them a horse. But that all had gone with the Blackfoot, damn them.

Delia graciously accepted a platter of food. Nash explained in sign they were heading over the mountains. He was led to believe through sign that many broad hats, their sign for trappers, passed over recently.

They confirmed to him that he should follow the North Fork and cross the flatland to the Green River where the broad hats gathered.

"How far?" asked Delia, between bits of the fat cow she ate.

"Less than fifty miles, over those." He pointed to the Wind River Range far beyond the bank.

"That looks like a tough trail to walk."

He nodded. "Walking and hunting, it will take us over ten days."

"Will they still be there?"

"I think so." Someone would. The fur companies would remain along with a few trappers who stayed until the whiskey or money ran out, then they'd leave in debt for another season.

"Will these people trade for horses?" she asked.

"I got nothing to trade, except my revolver and shotgun and I'll be damned first."

She reached into her personal bag and pulled out a tortoiseshell case, inlaid with mother-of-pearl.

He'd forgotten that. She'd told him once that it was a sewing case from her great-aunt. It had great value in both worlds. He wouldn't let her give it up. It was a precious reminder of her life in America.

"Put it away," he said.

But already the Indians gathered around. She held up the case. The men leaned in to look.

"Delia."

She set her teeth like a horse with the bit. "Thomas, I don't want to walk to the Rendezvous."

"That's yours, Delia, and no one else's."

She looked him straight in the eye and said, "Things aren't important, Thomas, people are."

"And horses," he added.

She smiled and flipped open the case, revealing the silver-handled embroidery scissors, which she demonstrated on a bit of cloth. Next she displayed a crochet hook, tortoiseshell comb, ivory needle case and red velvet pincushion.

The men gasped in amazement. She withdrew the comb and began to brush out her braid for the last time. The realization made him clench his jaw as impotent anger seethed in his blood.

Next, she trimmed her fingernails and opened the

needle case, withdrawing one slim needle. She used the black thread and created a chain stitch in the shape of a flower on the kerchief and then ran a blanket stitch along the edge.

A man stepped forward with an armful of beaver skins and lay them at her feet. She shook her head and pointed to the horses. She held up two slim fingers. Within minutes two horses were led before them.

"Are these sound?" she asked him.

"Delia, you don't have to give up your case. We'll make it." They might. Being on foot placed them at a serious disadvantage. Wildcats, Indians, grizzlies— they needed the horses. She stared at him. He rose and inspected the Appaloosa and then the bay. "They'll do."

She took the contents out of the case and laid it on the cloth. There was a rumble through the group. The man before her frowned and shook his head. He held up one finger. She shook her head as well and pointed to the furs. There was a long, silent moment as the two faced off. The brave nodded, scooping up the case and contents before Delia could change her mind.

"There now." She brushed the remains of a dried chokecherry from her skirt. "We have our horses."

He felt a cloud settle over him. This was worse than having nothing. Now he was in debt.

Nash managed to get some traveling provisions in exchange for their boat. The dried ground buffalo mixed with pounded dried fruit and fat made a meal the size of a currant bun.

The new owner of the boat rode across the river

with them as the horses swam behind on long leads. Their boat mate untied the wet animals and handed the lead to Nash. They watched the man climb back into the boat and push off, the currents pulling him farther downstream.

They rode along the river flats for much of the afternoon. He noticed the days were shorter. Soon there would be frost. With each hoofbeat on the grass, he drifted further into despair. How would he ever live without her? *That's not what matters, focus on seeing her safe and headed back East.* He'd been a damned fool to think he'd ever have her. Hadn't he learned the last time that love and life are temporary?

"Thomas?"

He swiveled about to look back at her. She sat astride the Appaloosa, her tan legs dangling on either side of the creature's chest.

His eyebrows rose in a silent question.

"I was just thinking—we need to make some plans." He had hoped to get her to the Rendezvous before telling her. "We don't have enough furs to make much money. What will we do?"

She still had hope. His had died when he cut loose the packhorse.

"I'm going to sign on with a trapping outfit."

"You are?"

The confusion in her expression ripped into him like the steel jaws of a trap. He swung back to face the trail. She rode up alongside him as if seeing his face would explain everything.

"Thomas, you said those contracts are for over a year."

"It's a three-year stint."

"But—but what about us?"

He stopped his horse and met her gaze. Her eyes looked huge in her pale face.

"There is no us."

Chapter Twenty

He would leave her.

Delia stared into his cold eyes. Certainty filled her as swiftly as the river water swamped a boat. He had his way with her and now he was leaving. Why buy the cow, when you can get the milk for free?

No—not Thomas, she wouldn't believe it. There was more.

"But you love me," she said.

"That's why I'm sending you East."

Abandoned again, yet he was right before her. No—not again. She'd fight this time.

"You are not walking out on me."

"Delia, I got nothing for you. I got no furs, no land, nothing. You are going back to America. God knows this is no place for you."

"But we have horses and guns. We can start again."

"No."

"But why?" She reached out. Her fingers clung to his fringe of his sleeve.

He shook his head. "A million reasons. We got no

traps, no scent, no ammunition. I need an outfit, not just a half-wild horse and a rifle.''

''We'll get them.''

''With what, my good looks? Delia, I ain't paid for last year's traps yet. The only way I get more traps is to sign on with a fur company. Everything I catch will be theirs. If I'm lucky and live, I could wind up in debt to them. It's easy enough when they charge a dollar and a half for a pound of coffee.''

''I'll go with you.''

''You can't. The outfit is up to thirty men, living wild, trapping one valley to the next.''

''What will I do, without you?'' Her voice was tiny, as small as she felt.

''You've been saying it since the beginning. You don't belong here.''

She thought her heart had died, dried, withered and fallen to dust long ago. But it was not so, for it bled again.

''You want me to go?''

''You won't last another winter in these mountains, Delia. Winter's hard and you know it better than most.''

She shuddered as she remembered the wolves at the door, the bone-chilling wind.

''So you send me away.''

He looked her in the eye and nodded.

''Yes.''

They plodded on and her heart kept beating. She glanced about, dazed. A bird flitted overhead. Far above an eagle soared, even as her life fell to ruins once more.

''I thought you loved me.''

"That's why I'm sending you East. You deserve a husband who can take care of you proper. You deserve a home and pretty things."

"I don't want pretty things. I want you." She heard her voice turn to the whine of a small child. Tears blurred her vision. "You offered to marry me."

"Not no more. Not with my head down in shame, I won't."

"There must be a way."

"There ain't. Don't you think I've gone over this again and again? There ain't no other way. We lost everything back there. It's finished."

"But what will I do without you?"

"You're a survivor—you said so yourself."

"Not this time." She dug her heels into the horse's ribs. The animal gave a surprised lurch forward then sprang ahead of his mare.

She rode along before him, allowing the horse to find her own way. A rush of tears blurred her vision. She sniffed, wishing for the handkerchief she had traded to the Nez Percé. Buckskin had its uses, but the smoked, tanned leather was not absorbent.

Twelve months ago her husband walked over a hill and out of her life. Now Thomas meant to do the same thing. How could she stop him? She had opened her heart once more and this was her reward. Her throat burned. He hadn't even asked her to wait. A needling awareness bristled in her belly. He did not ask because he knew he might not come back.

She had survived the mountains. That was better than many, but it wasn't enough.

She was weary. Her body felt decades older than when she had come to this new territory, only a year ago. It took all her strength to merely stay her seat on the horse as she climbed the mountain trail. She didn't realize her horse had stopped and was busy grabbing hanks of grass until Thomas rode past and grasped the single rein from her hand.

They crossed through the first gap late in the day. She could see that higher peaks lay beyond. Thomas stopped the horses. She heard the sound a moment after he did. The low huffing of a bear reached her ears.

Instantly, the ennui dissolved as her blood rushed through her veins. She glanced to the left to see low berry bushes covering the rocky flat. The mother grizzly fed ravenously on the berries beside a large cub. The bears had not seen them yet.

Thomas passed her the reins and motioned to the sharply descending trail. She nodded. Then he silently spurred his horse and she followed, charging down the hill. Behind her, she heard a roar of protest. She glanced back to see the grizzly charging after them.

She forced her eyes forward. The rocky trail slashed downward. If her horse fell, the bear would have them. The sound of panting came from immediately behind. Her horse flattened her ears and kicked.

Her mount lurched. She turned to see the great bear's claws tangled in her mare's tail. The horse screamed and raced forward, dragging the bear along for several feet. Sliding gravel skidded past her, hissing like a thousand snakes.

A well-placed hoof met the bear's shoulder with a solid thud and they were free. Her heart beat in her throat as they careened down the mountain. She glanced back again and saw the bear retreating. Before her, Thomas sat motionless, his rifle aimed and ready.

He lowered the weapon now.

"I've never seen anything like it. That bear looked like a sleigh behind your horse."

Her breathing came in frantic blasts. It took several minutes before she could speak.

"Without these horses, we'd be dead now, wouldn't we?"

He nodded.

"Hello the camp!"

Delia startled at the unexpected call.

"Hello," Nash replied.

Out of the darkness stepped two trappers, leading their horses.

"I told you, Jacob. That's a white woman." She looked at the man, noticing his tobacco-stained beard, hooked nose and wide-brimmed hat. She could see little else. She reached for the shotgun, closing her finger around the cold metal trigger. "Howdy, I'm Gabe Laster. This here's Jacob Black. Mind if we join you?"

She looked at Nash. He sat relaxed beside the fire with his Hawkins across his lap.

"We got coffee," Jacob said. She noted the man's girth. He looked like a bear with his big barrel chest and rounded belly. His hair and wiry beard were dark.

Nash nodded. She released the trigger and smiled.

"Of course, you're welcome," Delia said.

"Did you hear that, we're welcome?" Jacob

pushed back his hat and leaned forward, peering at her.

Cordelia glanced at Nash but he remained silent and watchful so she made introductions. "This is Mr. Thomas Nash and I am Mrs. Cordelia Channing."

Jacob gaped. "I can't believe my eyes. I ain't see a woman, a white woman that is, for three years."

"Is there anything we can do for you? Would you like coffee?" Gabe stepped between her and Jacob, momentarily gaining the upper hand. He was thin by comparison to his partner, all muscle and tendon. "We got sugar."

She laughed and slid the shotgun back into its sheath. These two acted as if she were some kind of royalty.

"Coffee would be lovely."

"Did you hear that, Jacob? Lovely. Get the pot."

"You get it!"

The men faced off silently for a moment. Gabe backed down, disappearing into the night. He returned in record time carrying a tin coffeepot, sack of coffee and brown cone of sugar.

Jacob ground the beans on a flat rock with the butt of his butcher knife.

"I'm afraid we don't have any cups," she said.

Gabe disappeared again and returned with two tin and two horn cups.

"Do you like sugar?" he asked.

"I hardly remember, it's been so long." She laughed.

Jacob threw the ground coffee into the pot already warming on the coals. Carefully Gabe shaved off slivers of sugar into each cup.

The aroma of coffee filled her with memories of civilization. Soon she would have coffee and tea, but she would lose Nash.

"Are you headed to the Rendezvous?" Jacob seemed to have just remembered that Nash was there and took his eyes off her for a moment to ask the question.

"Yup," said Nash.

What was wrong with him? He was more talkative with the Indians than his own people.

"I told you, we shoulda stayed." Gabe's voice came out as a whine.

"Any longer and we'd have lost everything we made," Jacob said.

"Oh, but a woman. Isn't she fine?"

Jacob turned to Nash again. "Most men wouldn't bring a wife into such country. You two missionaries?"

"She is," he said. "But she ain't my wife."

The trappers stared at each other. Jacob's mouth made a silent little O. Gabe stroked his beard for a moment.

"We got to go back," Gabe said.

Nash waved his tin cup at the fire.

"Coffee's burning," he said.

Jacob grabbed at the handle and scorched his hand. Gabe used the hem of his long shirt to pull the pot to safety, then poured her a cup, stirring in the sugar with a battered horn spoon.

He held out the cup with both hands like an offering. "Is your husband waiting at the Rendezvous?"

"My husband passed away last fall." She saw him

trying to keep the glee from his expression. A smile quirked his thick mustache.

"That's a real shame."

"A woman shouldn't be without a man out here."

"She ain't without a man," Nash said. "I just ain't married her."

Delia felt her face burn with shame. He made her sound like his mistress. She dropped her eyes to the fire as she realized she was just that. Now these men knew she was a fallen woman. She couldn't face them.

"Of course she is. But maybe she might like to have a change."

Delia lifted the coffee to her lips. The brew tasted like sweetened ash. How appropriate, she thought.

"She don't," growled Nash.

"Mind your manners, Gabriel," Jacob said.

Gabe had the decency to look contrite. "I'm sorry, ma'am. It's just such a wonder to see you here. You remind me of home."

"It's good to meet you, as well. I thank you for the coffee."

Her words seemed to remind him of the pot he clutched, and he poured three more cups, offering them to Nash and his partner. He took a long drink and spit the liquid on the fire.

"It's burned! God, awful! Don't drink that, Miss Delia. We'll make some more."

"How far to the Rendezvous?" asked Nash.

"Took us two days to get here. That's mostly uphill. I'd say you could make her in one."

* ** *

The next morning, they left the trappers arguing by the fire about whether to return to the Rendezvous.

By full light, they were over the mountain and on the final downhill climb. The trail was well-worn by the coming of many men and horses. Nash saw evidence of their camps all around.

He expected Delia to cause a stir at the Rendezvous. He just hadn't anticipated his response. His gut felt as if someone pumped him full of buckshot. *I wonder if I can get through this without killing somebody?*

Well, he'd have to find someone to take her East, wouldn't he? He needed a reliable man, well equipped and honorable. He shook his head. This was going to be hard.

Delia spent the morning wearing an unchanging somber expression. Only her amber eyes flashed the fire his words ignited within her. She answered him in a clipped tone he found irritating as grit in cornmeal.

From this slope, he could see the Green River coiling through the grassy plains like a sleeping serpent. Far off, the smoke of many fires rose from the trees. They'd make camp by dark.

He passed her a leg from the rabbit he had roasted last night. She refused it. He hated the cold shoulder she showed him.

Insects buzzed as they crossed the river flats, following the winding curves. As the afternoon wore on the bullfrogs along the banks began to croak. At one time he would have enjoyed their song. Now it only reminded him they were near the Rendezvous, nearer to the end of his time with her. He didn't want to spend his last moments with her solemn silence.

"Delia, I'm only doing what's best for you."

"You have no idea what is best for me."

"Then why don't you tell me?"

"What's best is for a man and woman who love each other to marry and live together, in good times and bad."

"I can't marry you."

"So you've said."

He got off his horse and stood beside her, resisting the urge to cling to her long leg.

"I can't ask you to wait. You know the dangers. I'll do all I can, but it wouldn't be fair."

"Thomas, if you love me, you'll find another way."

He met her level gaze, feeling the heat from her amber eyes. She was magnificent, tanned and strong. She looked like a savage queen.

"I'm sorry, Delia."

"I'm sorry as well."

He mounted up and they set off again. Several miles downriver, he caught wind of the campfires. Next he spotted the smoke again, and finally the low buzz of many men reached his ears.

"That you, Tuck?"

Nash turned toward the familiar voice. He couldn't believe his eyes.

"Milt?" There was his old trapping partner, sitting astride the prettiest dappled gray he'd ever seen. He noticed the fat deer tied to the animal's rump. Both men dismounted. Nash frowned to see Milt still favoring his leg, as if it pained him.

"Well, I'd about given you up for dead." Milt laughed, hugging him fiercely for a moment. Nash thumped his back several times. "Where's your plew?"

Nash glanced at his moccasins.

"Lost."

"Oh, sorry to hear it, Tuck, real sorry. But look here. This looks much more interesting." He regarded Delia intently.

"Milton Sublette, this is Delia Channing."

"It's a pleasure." He removed his greasy hat, showing matted hair. Then he turned to Nash. "Your wife?"

"No. I'm just getting her back to her people."

"Then you're a fool." Now he faced Delia. "It just so happens, Miss Channing, I'm headed back East at the end of the Rendezvous. I got to see a doctor about this damn foot. Oh, sorry, ma'am. I'm going to St. Louis. You're welcome along."

"Thank you, Mr. Sublette. I may take you up on that. But it's Mrs. Channing."

"Oh, I see. Where is your husband then?"

Nash spoke up. "He died last fall. Flathead brought Delia to me in June. She survived the winter alone in the foothills of the Bull Mountains."

Sublette's jaw dropped open. He stared at her for a long moment. "I've heard of you."

"Have you any word of the wagon train?"

"Can't say I do. We'll ask in camp. There's over three hundred men. Someone must know something."

Nash watched him struggle to mount and offered him a leg up. He accepted it with a gruff word of thanks.

"Why do you call him Tuck, Mr. Sublette?" asked Delia.

"Oh that's a story in itself. Best wait until you're settled and I'll be glad to swap a tale or two with you."

"Most of which will be lies," Nash said.

"Just the same, I'd like to hear," Delia said.

"Well, ride beside me, I'll tell you now," said Sublette.

The trail was only wide enough for two horses. Delia glanced at Nash. He didn't try to stop her, though he wanted to. Realization gnawed at him like a beaver at green wood. Soon he'd send her away. The thought made him want to reach out and drag her onto his horse.

He waited for her to decide.

She gave Sublette an apologetic smile. "I think I'll ride with my partner."

Chapter Twenty-One

A few hundred yards upriver they met Mr. Sublette's current partner, a man named Joseph Meeker. Delia liked him immediately. He had an honest face and a gift with words.

Nash gave up his place beside her on the trail, riding next to Mr. Sublette and allowing Mr. Meeker to accompany her to the Rendezvous.

"Old Tuck's been hiding you all summer, the dog. Can't say as I blame him. Where you been trapping?"

"North along the Musselshell and the Three Forks," she said.

"Three Forks! Damn fool." He pivoted to face Nash. "You idiot, what are you doing bringing a woman trapping in Blackfoot country?"

"I didn't bring her. I found her there."

"She was wintering in the Bull Mountains," Sublette added.

Meeker rested a hand on his horse's rump and leaned farther out over the back of his saddle.

"Wintering there? In Blackfoot territory?" He spun to face her again. "Why?"

"Our wheel broke and we were separated from the wagon train."

"Where bound?"

"Oregon. We were missionaries. John thought we'd catch up."

"But you didn't," Meeker said.

"No. My husband went hunting one fall day and did not return. I found his remains two weeks later." She glanced away from his piercing brown eyes. "Then the snows came. Well, that's all, really."

"That's all? You survived a winter *alone* in Blackfoot country and that's all? You must be the luckiest woman alive, or the smartest. What did you eat? You hunt for game?"

"I had no gun. So I butchered the oxen."

"See any wolves?"

"Many." She couldn't quite repress the shudder.

"Stay in the wagon?"

"No, I built a shelter from cottonwood, mud and straw."

He whistled. "Nash find you, did he?"

"No. In the spring, two Indians appeared in the meadow."

He turned back to Nash.

"Blackfoot?" he asked.

"Flathead," Nash said.

Meeker faced her again. "Damn lucky. Blackfoot would have lifted your scalp. You should have shot them, just to be safe. Oh, you had no gun. Lucky again."

"Yes, well, they brought me to Mr. Nash."

"When?"

"I recorded the date as May fourteenth."

"Recorded? You write?"

"Yes, I kept a journal."

Meeker nodded. "I'd like to see that."

"Some other time."

Meeker leaned forward. "When?"

Nash's voice came from behind them. "Some other time is polite talk for no, you old buzzard."

Meeker glanced at Delia for confirmation and she nodded.

"Now, Mrs. Channing—"

"Mr. Meeker, I have answered a great many questions. Perhaps, you would answer a few of mine."

"It'd be an honor." He swept off the ridiculous wolf turban that he wore as a hat. His hair was brown and curly beneath the monstrosity.

"Have you any word of a wagon train lead by Reverend Harcort?" She waited, her breath catching in her throat.

"Don't reckon I do. I'll ask Bridger. If anybody knows, he will."

"Thank you."

They rode in silence through the woods. Delia watched the golden splashes of sunlight dance across the green leaves above them.

"Anything else I can do for you?" Meeker asked.

She thought for a moment.

"Why do you call Mr. Nash, Tuck?"

"Wagh! That's a tale. Milt and I were running from Mexicans and met up with Tuck on the Gila River. Navajo country, very tough. Tuck was there when old Tom took a ball in the leg. Shattered the bone, it did. We still outrun them. Poor Tom's leg was flopping, plum ruined, it was. We stopped awhile and decided that he'd lose the leg to gangrene, sure. Nobody wanted to take her off, though. Finally Milt done it. Nash gave Tom some whiskey and stitched her up.''

She looked from one man to the other in disbelief. "Did he live?"

"Sure! You'll meet him upriver. Peg-leg Smith they calls him now."

"But why Tuck?"

"Well, I'm getting 'round to that. Tuck was riding point along the river. Brush was kind of thick, you know and so he never sees the grizzly until he's on her. The bear rears up and he hollers. We come running. I seen the bear tear into his leg. The horse throws him and there he is with his gun facing an eight-foot bear rearing up to make him lunch.''

He paused there to scratch his beard. She couldn't resist asking, "What happened?"

"He fires his rifle and the bear doesn't flinch. So he drops his gun and jumps into the air. Then he curls into a ball and rolls down the bank and into the river. Tucks up, you know?''

She nodded.

"So Smith shoots the bear in the mouth and then he tells us, 'It gave her a terrible cough.''' He slapped his leg and laughed hardy. "Damn big bear."

She thought of the puckering scar on his thigh—another grizzly. "When was that?"

"Oh, 1829, I think. That reminds me of another bear." And so the new tale unfolded and then another until she could hear the shouts of men.

She saw more than a hundred campfires ahead glowing against the approaching night. There were

tepees, lean-tos and several blankets thrown over a
rope. Men sat about drinking in groups. Near the
river, a wrestling match drew a rowdy crowd. The
clang and rattle of pots and pans added to the ruckus.

"Wagh!" called Meeker. "Looky what I got?"

Several men came running. She found herself surrounded by many white men and several Indians.
They stared up at her in wonder, some remembering
to remove their fur caps.

Meeker raised his voice to make his announcement.

"This here is Mrs. Delia Channing, a missionary's
wife who survived the winter all alone in the Rockies
and was asked to be an Indian queen. She be the only
white woman this side of the divide. No doubt you
heard of her. This be the Winter Woman."

"Winter Woman?" cried an Indian.

"That's her."

"I thought she was a legend," said the tall man,
doffing his hat.

"She killed a grizzly with a shotgun," Meeker continued.

A cheer rose from the men.

Delia looked over the shouting throng and saw
more men running to see what the commotion was
about. Her heart skipped in a nervous rhythm.

She turned back to Nash.

"Thomas?"

"You're all right, Delia. Just smile and wave. They
won't hurt you."

She waved and a second cheer rose. One man did
a little jig.

"Mrs. Channing," said a trapper with a wide black
beard, "will you say something to us?"

"What shall I say?" Another cheer sounded. They were easy to please. She cleared her throat. "Gentlemen, I am pleased to see you all here and touched at your warm reception."

"She talks like a real lady."

"Look at her hair. Yeller as sunshine."

"All right, boys." Meeker lifted both his wide hands and the crowd instantly silenced. "You all can come by tonight. Mrs. Delia will be telling us how she survived the winter. Give her time to eat, is all."

The men parted, allowing the horses to pass. Joe led her to his camp and he helped her dismount.

She saw Thomas and Milton attending to the deer. That poor man really should have a cane. She wondered what was wrong with his foot.

She turned to her escort.

"Mr. Meeker—"

"Please call me Joe."

"All right then, Joe. I—"

"May I call you Delia?"

She looked to Thomas for his reaction. He nodded.

"That will be fine. Now, about this story I am supposed to tell. I really would rather not. I am not much of a yarn spinner. I don't know where I would begin."

Meeker rubbed his neck.

"In an hour you'll have every man who isn't drunk sitting around this fire. You'll have to tell them something."

She turned to Thomas for rescue. "What will I do?"

"You could read to them," he said.

"I don't have a book." She glanced frantically

about the camp looking for some rescue or escape. However could she entertain so many men?

"You do." Thomas lifted up her bag. "You have your journal."

She inhaled sharply. "I couldn't. That is personal ramblings. It's not fit for reading aloud."

"You read it to me." He reminded her.

"That was different. I mean, these men are strangers."

"Only until you get to know us," Meeker said. She drew reassurance from Milton's smile. "They're mostly young boys far from home. They miss their sweethearts and mothers. You being here is a real treat. They won't let you lift a finger. I do assure you."

Joe had a fire lit in record time. When the flames died to leave mostly coals, Milton set a rack of venison to cook above them.

Before the juices hit the fire, the first of the men arrived.

A young man with downy fuzz upon his cheeks laid a bundle beside her.

"For you, missus," he said.

She smiled and thanked him as her fingers untied the red trade cloth.

"Oh, potatoes! And look, turnips! Oh, thank you. You can't imagine how much I've missed them."

Several men jumped up and darted into the darkness. Within the hour she sat beside a stack of potatoes as tall as she was. There was also dried corn, coffee and sugar. They brought enough food to host a wedding feast.

"Nash, I can't accept all this," she said.

"We'll cook it and feed it back to them. It'll be fine."

Succotash in a large kettle was distributed to many empty bowls and cups. She tried to make biscuits, but two men took the flour from her hands and began to mix the batter.

"This is better than Christmas dinner." She laughed. Joe was right, she did not have to lift a finger. The crisp apple cider washed away the dust from the trail. She held a hot potato in her lap, waiting for it to cool enough to eat. When she broke it open, two men were there to offer her salt. She noticed several trappers passing jugs around. The smell of liquor seeped through the night air.

Joe Meeker entertained the boys with a tale about how he and his partner had rescued Milton's wife, Mountain Lamb, from the clutches of the Crow.

Nash settled beside her for the story. She found herself drawn into the tale, leaning forward to catch Joe's next word.

When he finished, she whispered in Thomas's ear. "Is it true?"

"Only the part about her name being Mountain Lamb, though Milt calls her Isabel. You'll be expected to tell a story next."

"What should I do?"

"Look through your journal and find something you can read." He handed her the book, safely wrapped in buckskin.

Joe Meeker held the crowd in rapture. "So we swoop down, guns flashing fire. Three of the warriors hit the ground. The others run off, leaving Mountain Lamb alone on the trail."

As if summoned by the story, a beautiful Indian woman stepped into the circle of light. Her buckskin dress was stained bright green. Twin braids of black hair hung over the swell of her bosom. Her smile made her high cheekbones look even more exotic.

"There she be!" said Meeker. Mountain Lamb sat beside Milton Sublette.

"This is my wife, Isabel. Isabel, this is Mrs. Delia Channing."

"I am pleased to meet you." Isabel's words were correct, but her accent made it difficult for Delia to understand. She extended her hand to the woman.

"It's my pleasure."

Isabel took her hand firmly and shook it once before releasing.

"You will tell a story now?" Isabel asked.

The gathering grew very quiet. She felt the weight of many gazes upon her. Men sat breathless, waiting. Suddenly she could hear the logs on the fire crackle and pop.

"Yes, I think I will read to you from my journal." She glanced at Thomas. "Mr. Nash and I were guests of the Mountain tribe of the Crow Indians, while I recovered from an infection in my foot." A whoop of approval rose from a group of Indians to her left. She opened her journal to the place she had marked with a blade of grass.

Thomas was unusually nervous, jumping at every sound. I could not understand his mood, until I heard the bloodthirsty cry and saw the Blackfoot Indians swarming down the hill toward the village.

She read on, raising her voice to nearly a shout so the men sitting quietly in the dark might hear her. She read about their daring escape up the mountain to the place where Thomas cut the packhorse loose. A groan rose from the crowd. She continued reading about their hiding place in a crack in the earth, how their enemy crawled over the rock above searching for them.

She marked her place and snapped the book shut.

"I will read from here tomorrow night."

There were many groans and complaints that she could not stop there.

"We don't know if you live or died," one man complained.

A fellow slapped him over the head with his hat.

"Course she lived, idiot. There she is, ain't she?"

Meeker rose and lifted his hands. "Miss Delia had a long ride and she done read over an hour to you. How about some gratitude, you stump heads?" Wild applause and whistles mingled with raucous cries. "Now get and don't be bothering the lady tonight."

The group departed calling farewells.

"That was a wonderful tale, Mrs. Channing," Milton said. "I look forward to tomorrow night."

Isabel helped him to his feet, then followed her husband into the darkness.

"You can have my lean-to tonight. Tomorrow, I'll have the boys build you a cabin," said Meeker, and then he, too, departed. She found herself with Thomas.

He stared at her, his eyes glowing with what looked like pride. Her heart accelerated at the warmth in his gaze. Surrounded by the bustle of camp, they were somehow alone. She wondered who would see if she kissed him?

"You did real fine, Delia. I told you that you have a gift. That journal is special."

She basked in the warmth of his praise.

"Thank you, Thomas. I never could have done it without your encouragement."

"What a place to leave them. Ha! They'll all be talking about it tonight and wondering how we got away. And tomorrow they'll hear about the river rapids. That was something."

He stared off at the stars now, remembering, she felt certain, the wild ride.

"Yes, quite a trip." She thought back on all their adventures, knowing that this was the most exciting occasion of her life. Never had she felt so alive as when she stood beside Thomas to face the wilderness. And now their time was finished. Soon she'd be out of the Rockies and never again see the pink snow on the high peaks as the sun set behind them. He was sending her back alone. Sublette had already offered her escort to St. Louis. Soon she'd be surrounded by buildings, starched collars and quilt circles. The images drowned her, flooding her mind with wave after wave of quiet desperation.

"Thomas, I don't want to go back East."

His gaze returned to her. His eyes no longer twinkled with happiness. Now they shone cold and clear.

"You have to." He tossed down a buffalo robe, probably a gift from one of her admirers. "I got to see to some business."

"Don't you sign that contract, Thomas. I'll never forgive you."

Chapter Twenty-Two

She likely wouldn't forgive him. But Nash would get her home and for that he must have money. He found Joe drinking with Peg-leg Smith.

He thumped Smith on the back in greeting.

"Joe says you lost your catch to Blackfoot."

Nash nodded and Smith passed him a jug. Nash tipped the heavy stoneware and fire burned down his throat. He passed it back.

"Well, that's behind you. What now?"

"I'm planning on signing on with you fellas." He believed the Rocky Mountain Fur Company would be glad to have him, having survived the test of nature, unlike the green recruits they brought in each year.

"Well," said Meeker. "You're welcome. You got traps?"

"Nope, only my horse and rifle."

Meeker scratched his bristly cheek.

"So you'd be a company man?" Smith asked.

"That's right."

"Why you want to do that? You could be running your own outfit." Joe slapped his hat on his knee.

"If I had traps. I need the signing money to send Delia East."

"You done enough for the woman." Meeker's voice reminded him of his father's during a lecture. "She'll find a way back. Sublette can take her or one of the supply wagons."

"She's my responsibility."

"How you figure that?" Smith returned his pipe to his mouth after speaking.

"I plan to marry her, if I can bring in a catch."

"Times is hard," said Smith. "Beaver is getting scarce. You had to go into Blackfoot country to get yourn. And look what that got you. You ought to head back with her, Tuck."

Nash scowled. "You going to sign me or not?"

He nodded. "We'll talk to Bridger tomorrow."

"Fine." He sat beside his friends and accepted the jug once more. Maybe if he drank enough he wouldn't see the tears he caused Delia or think of the years ahead without her.

Delia regarded the lanky man before her. His arms showed wiry muscle and tendon. His wide-brimmed hat was low over his eyes. The skin she could see above his beard was tanned, the color of a hazelnut.

"Nash about?" he asked.

"I'm afraid he went upriver with Mr. Meeker, searching for a friend."

All day the men had made excuses to see her. Looking for Nash was one of the most common ploys. You'd think Nash was the mayor, he was suddenly so popular. She smiled at the man. He looked differ-

ent than most, older, with a wisdom in his hazel eyes.
This man had seen what the mountains could do.

"I'm Jim Bridger." He extended his hand.

Her eyes opened wide in surprise. Yes, he would
be.

"How do you do, Mr. Bridger. Thomas has spoken
of you with high regard. It is you they went searching
for. I'll tell him you stopped by."

"We also came to see you."

She looked past him now and for the first time
noticed the well-dressed man standing just beyond
him. Unlike most men here, he wore a woolen jacket
and trousers rather than buckskin. His beard was
closely trimmed. Pale skin, leather boots, this man
was new to the mountains.

She was glad she'd changed into her faded blue
dress. She'd pulled her hair up into a bun and tied it
with a ribbon Isabel gave her. If not for her moccasins
and tanned cheeks, she might also look like a new-
comer.

He extended his hand. She felt the smooth palm of
a man who did not engage in physical work.

Bridger spoke again. "This here is a friend of mine,
Tyde Bonner."

"A pleasure." She turned her attention back to
Bridger. "I wonder if you have any word about a
wagon train led by Reverend Harcort?"

"They never made Three Forks," he said. She
stared at him, waiting. Her mouth dropped open in
surprise and he paused. "Are you sure you want to
hear?"

She needed to know. Slowly her head bobbed up
and down.

"Blackfoot took them. Beckwourth found what was left of them in July. I'm sorry."

His words hit like a blow to the chest. She had imagined them all safely in Oregon, farming and ministering to the Indians there. The illusion broke like a soap bubble. She sank to the log behind her. Nash was right. They never should have come west.

"Tyde, get some water." The man trotted off, leaving her with Bridger. He squatted before her. "I heard you was a brave woman. I know it's true, just looking at you. You'll get by this. It ain't your fault you lived and they didn't. Those men had no business here."

She stared up into his eyes. How could he know she felt those things?

"They didn't deserve it," she said.

"No one does. It happens. This here is wild country. You takes your chance or you stay home."

"They never knew about the Blackfoot. One tribe was the same as the next."

"Bad ideas to travel where you don't know the trail. Sounds like your preacher had no right leading you folks across the Rockies."

No, he didn't. She saw that now. He had known nothing about this land or the dangers. He'd filled their heads with nonsense and dreams, and they'd followed him like sheep. How could she have been so stupid? The arrogance of the man, to lead them blindly into danger. Her hands were balled into fists, ready to strike out at past wrongs.

"He was wrong to put us in such jeopardy," she said.

"Reckon so. Folks deserve an experienced guide."

Mr. Bonner returned red faced and panting. "Here's the water."

She shook her head. "No, thank you. I'm fine now."

He looked disappointed. She was about to reach for the cup when Bridger grasped it and drained the contents.

"Thank you kindly." He turned back to Delia and said, "Bonner be a writer of dime novels. He heard about your story last night."

"Yes," he said. "I'm very interested in your tale, Mrs. Channing. People back East are desperate for tales of the Wild West. I believe you've had the adventures of a lifetime. I work for a newspaper in Chicago. I'd like to buy your story for syndication."

"I'm afraid that's impossible." She didn't want everyone in the country knowing she had lived with a trapper for several months. Whatever was the man thinking?

"Have you sold it already?" He looked desperate. "I'll double the offer."

"Whatever offer? Mr. Bonner, I'm not interested in selling my journal. It is private."

"Not even for fifty dollars?"

She was shocked that he'd try to buy her. Then she considered what that money could do.

"Mr. Bridger, how much does a trapper make on his catch?"

"Depends on the trapper." He offered no more.

"How much would Nash have made?"

"Well, he's independent so he gets to keep all he brings. He don't owe nobody that I know, so maybe four hundred."

"How much to buy traps and an outfit for a trapper," she asked.

Bridger smiled. "I figure a hundred and fifty would get you supplies and traps."

She pointed at the horse she'd bought from the Nez Percé. "How much for that horse?"

Bridger walked to the spotted pony and ran a hand over her withers and down a front leg.

"Twenty dollars is a fair price. I'll give you that or trade in supplies."

Without her horse, she had no means of transportation back East. If she sold her journal, she'd expose her innermost thoughts to the world, but she might be able to stop Nash from signing on with an outfit. She didn't have to sell. She could keep her horse and her privacy and take them back to the States alone.

"My year's stories are worth more than a stack of beaver." She was quite sure they were not. Still, she had learned something about bluff and bluster from spending the summer with Nash. "I'll sell them for a hundred and fifty."

The man smiled, seeming to enjoy the prospect of bartering with her.

"Well now. I'd have to see that journal of yours to know what it's worth. Why don't you let me borrow it?"

He must think she was three times a fool. "Oh, no. The journal stays with me."

"Then how do I know what it's worth?"

"Mr. Bonner, I lived alone in the mountains from October to May. I was rescued and captured by Indians and traded to Nash. Two different chiefs asked for my hand in marriage. I shot a grizzly, escaped

Crow and Blackfoot and traveled the Bighorn rapids
in a bull boat. And I recorded it all in this journal.''
His eyes lit up at the worn leather book she held
tightly in her hands.

"You say the Bighorn?'' Bridger asked. "Anything particular you remember?''

"I'll read it to you gentleman.'' She sat on the log.
Bridger took out his pipe and smoked as she began
her tale. When she finished, she looked up at him to
find his wrinkled face creased with a lopsided grin.

"You sure did run her, didn't you?''

She nodded.

"Now there's three of us,'' he said.

She glanced at the reporter, afraid that her tale
would not meet his approval. He looked stunned. His
eyes focused at some place beyond her.

"I never dreamed a river could run like that. What
a story! It's better than gold. Mrs. Channing, I'll give
you a hundred twenty-five dollars.''

"Sold, Mr. Bonner.''

They didn't find Bridger upriver. Nash shifted on
the trade blanket he used for a saddle. Meeker had
talked for the past five miles without stopping for air.
He was about ready to tell the man to plug his hole.

"Missionaries wintered with the Nez Percé up a
ways.''

"Missionaries?'' It couldn't be Delia's group.
"Who's the boss?''

"Don't know.''

"I'm going.'' Nash kicked his horse to a gallop.

Meeker quickly caught up. "What's the hurry?''

"Joe, Delia was traveling with missionaries.''

"You think it's them?"

"How many missionaries you see this year?"

The horses raced side my side across the river meadow, startling several pronghorn.

"Not many."

When he finally saw the smoke rising, he slowed his lathering horse. Joe reined in beside him.

"Why don't they join the Rendezvous?" Nash asked.

"Too religious. They don't approve the drinking and gambling. Trappers prefer it, too. Their preaching is a damn nuisance, always yapping about damnation. Dampens a man's thirst, it does."

Within a loose circle of battered tents, Nash found seven men all dressed in neat black suits, as if ready for Sunday services. They looked so out of place, camped here by the river, he laughed aloud.

"Damn ridiculous clothing," Meeker muttered.

"Hello the camp," Nash called.

A portly man with florid cheeks stepped up.

"Greetings, brothers. I'm Reverend Ruxton. Are you here to be saved?"

"From what?" asked Meeker. Nash sighed. His friend was bruising for a fight. Nash dismounted and extended his hand.

"I'm Thomas Nash. I'm looking for a group led by a man named Harcort. He here?"

The man looked stunned for a moment then grasped his crisp lapels with both hands.

He blustered. "I know of him, rest his soul."

"What happened?"

"Our brothers met with hostile Indians. We are

men of peace not war. We are not prepared for fighting.''

Behind him he heard Meeker mutter, ''Dunderheads.''

''Did you know him or any in his party?'' asked Nash.

''No, brother. We only know of him. We share the same mission and are also bound for Oregon. God favored us. We found these lost souls along the way.'' He motioned to the Indians standing about. Nash noticed several men wore wooden crosses upon their bare chests. Their women were dressed in cotton skirts to their ankles. The ragged hems told of the impracticality of this latest innovation. ''We saved their souls and they kept us alive through the cruel winter.''

''Hallelujah!'' Meeker shouted.

The reverend frowned at Nash's companion.

''Would you gentleman care to join us for lunch?'' asked Ruxton.

Nash glanced at Meeker, whose sarcasm disappeared at the mention of food.

''We'd be obliged,'' Nash said.

Nash accepted their hospitality for lunch. During the meal, they exchanged information. Meeker put his resentment aside long enough to eat and tell a few stories that featured Nash's prowess as a mountain man.

''Perhaps you are an answer to a prayer,'' Ruxton said. ''We are in need of a guide to lead us to Oregon. Have you been there?''

''Been there,'' Meeker interrupted. ''Of course he

has. He found the Wenatchee pass. He even seen the Pacific Ocean. I ain't even seen that.''

Ruxton smiled. ''It sounds like you are our man, Mr. Nash. You wouldn't be a religious man, I suppose.''

''I spend some time on my knees, Reverend.''

''Splendid. Then you'll consider it? We could pay you, say, two hundred dollars. And of course you would be welcome to one hundred acres of whatever farmland you choose upon arrival.''

Meeker's elbow poked him in the ribs. ''Sounds like a fair offer, Tuck. And you'd be free by November to head back East.''

''Are you interested, Mr. Nash?''

''None of the other trappers are,'' said Meeker. ''We ain't farmers. And the idea of spending three months with this bunch gives me a headache.''

He'd have enough money to send Delia back East and follow her in the spring. A thought struck him, forming like a cloud bank in his mind. His heart beat faster. She had been heading for Oregon in the first place. Would she—would she go with him?

''I might have a wife,'' Nash said.

''Perhaps we can convert her. Is she Nez Percé?''

''She's white.''

''White? You have brought a Christian woman into this wilderness?''

''No. I ain't a fool. A group of missionaries brung her.''

The reverend harrumphed for a moment. ''This is a dangerous trip. I don't think a woman would be strong enough. She might jeopardize our mission.''

''Jeopardize? Reverend, you ever shot a grizzly?''

The man shook his head.

"Skinned an ox or other large critter?"

"Well, no."

"Escaped from Blackfoot raiders or run the rapids of the Bighorn Canyon?" Nash scowled at the man. "She done all that, and more."

"She sounds like a remarkable woman."

"That she is." He couldn't keep his pride for her from puffing up inside him.

"Well then, bring her along. If you are interested, that is."

"Yes, Mr. Ruxton, I'm interested. Have your people ready in two days. I'll be back."

Nash clenched the reins, resisting the urge to race back to her. They could marry. He could hold his head up and ask her to be his wife.

Chapter Twenty-Three

His horse skidded to a halt before her. Cordelia jumped to her feet at his frantic arrival. His lathered horse told of some catastrophe. He had signed the contract. Oh, please, God, no! She had sold her most precious possession for nothing.

He slid off the horse and she rushed to his arms.

"Delia, I got news."

"I do, too." Her mouth felt dry. She could barely get the words out. If he had signed, she could do nothing. When she had sold the journal she'd searched the camp for him but he was gone, so she had waited here. It was the longest day she could remember.

He kissed her quickly on the lips. She stared at him in wonder. His eyes twinkled and his face was flushed.

"What is it?"

He threw up his hands. "Well, I don't know how to tell you, so I'll just say it." He glanced quickly about the camp. "Where's your horse?"

"I sold her." She watched his eyes narrow as he

spotted the sixty steel traps lying on a red blanket by the fire. Her mouth went dry.

"What's that?"

"Traps. I bought them for you."

He didn't look happy. Didn't he want to be an independent trapper again? Those traps freed him from being a company man, unless he'd already signed. The thought froze her blood more surely than all the dark days of winter. He didn't look pleased. Rather, he looked furious.

When she spoke, the accusation was clear in her voice. "You signed."

"Your horse didn't bring enough for that. Where did you get the money?"

"I sold my journal."

He looked stunned. "You sold your—what do you mean?"

"A man from the newspapers offered to buy it, so I sold it to him."

He grasped her shoulders. She lifted her gaze to meet his.

"Your journal?"

She nodded. "I have enough to buy you ammunition and supplies. Whatever you need for your own outfit. Just tell me you didn't sign."

"Your journal was private, Delia. How could you do that?"

"I don't care about my privacy. I care about you. I love you."

He was grinning now.

"Delia? I didn't sign."

"Oh, thank God." She threw her arms about him,

hugging him so tight she heard a rib pop. "Where were you? I was so worried."

"Sit down, Delia." Something *was* wrong. She sank to the log, clasping her hands in her lap. Why didn't he tell her, instead of staring at her with that strange look on his face? Her hands were instantly slick with sweat. The sun suddenly seemed too warm as she sat on the log behind her.

"I heard some missionaries were living upriver with the Nez Percé."

John…Harcort. Were they alive? But Bridger said they were all dead. Her insides felt as if a thousand bees stung her all at once.

"Delia, it's not them. It's a different group."

The wind left her lungs and her body shrank, hunching down.

He was speaking again. "They're heading to Oregon. They asked me to guide them. Delia, they offered me two hundred dollars for the trip and acreage if I want it. If *we* want it."

"We?" A tiny prickle of hope tickled her belly.

He crouched before her. He grasped her hand in his.

"Delia, will you marry me?"

Her body trembled like a plucked banjo string. This was everything she wanted, he was all she needed in the world.

"There's no guarantee, Delia. I understand that now. I'm ready to take the time God will grant us and be grateful for it. Be my wife. Come with me to Oregon."

Tears streamed over the shallow dam of her lower lids. She tried to speak, but only a croak came from

her lips, so she clamped her teeth together and nodded
frantically.

"Is that yes?"

More nodding.

"Oh, Delia, that's fine!" He hugged her.

From behind her came the sound of one man clap-
ping. She turned to see Joe Meeker grinning from ear
to ear as his paddle-wheel hands slapped together in
a slow rhythm.

The following morning Delia stood in a new buckskin dress stained white with clay. She had bought it
from the Nez Percé. A porcupine quill design in green
and blue covered her from shoulder to shoulder.

The honorable Reverend Ruxton began the ceremony.

She glanced about the meadow. No drinking or
gambling today. There was a wedding to attend. The
rugged gathering of buckskin-clad men, Indians and
several missionaries spread over the sloping meadow.

Nash held her hand, looking as proud as a Tom
turkey.

He interrupted Reverend Ruxton's welcome.

"I got a ring."

"Oh, all right then, let's have it." He blessed the
circle of silver, then placed it on the Bible. Thomas
slipped it on her finger. She looked at the ring. It was
covered with small rosebuds. The circle shape was a
little rough, as was the seam where the ends joined.

He leaned close and whispered, "It was a silver
spoon. I shaped it for you. Does it fit?"

She clasped the band of silver to her chest. "It's
perfect."

The trappers groaned as the reverend began his reading from the Bible. Fur caps were drawn from many heads. His words droned on like the humming of a bee. Delia stifled a smile at the pained expressions of some of the trappers. Bridger stood stone-faced, and Meeker moaned as if he had a toothache. Somehow the reverend managed to get many of them to sing a hymn.

Finally Nash spoke his vows and she promised to be his wife. Before Reverend Ruxton could pronounce them man and wife, Nash scooped her into his arms for a fiery kiss. The flash of heat that always followed his touch ignited.

The sound of gunfire startled her back to her surroundings. The men cheered and others fired their rifles. Two trappers swung around and around, linked at the elbow.

Ruxton shouted above the cheer. "I now pronounce you man and wife."

Joe Meeker stepped forward. "Let me be the first to kiss the bride."

Several men scrambled forward to form a line. Old Bill pushed Peg-leg Smith, who turned around and punched Bill in the stomach.

Nash pulled Delia behind him. "No one kisses *this* bride. Go find your own." A groan of disappointment sounded. "No," he said. "Now back off, you old billy goats."

The men dispersed. She exhaled the breath she held. He was right to stop them.

"Thank you," she said.

"The only one you're kissing from now on is me." As if to emphasize the point, he bent her over his arm for a wild blending of tongues. When at last he righted her, she was dizzy from his kiss.

Reverend Ruxton cleared his throat. She turned to face him, feeling embarrassed heat burn her cheeks.

"We'll be heading back upriver," he said. "I'll expect you tomorrow morning. Enjoy your celebration."

"Thank you, Reverend." She extended her hand. "The service was lovely."

"I wish you had a fine church in which to be wed, my dear. After all you've been through, you deserve that much."

"What better church than God's blue sky?" she asked.

Thomas slipped his arm about her waist. She saw the approval in his eyes.

Mr. Ruxton looked as if he was about to take issue, then changed his mind.

"See you in the morning, Mr. Nash."

Delia turned to find Mr. Meeker still hovering about. "I think you're a bad influence on us," said Meeker.

"How's that?" asked Nash.

"Bridger's getting married tomorrow."

Delia smiled, thinking of the Indian woman she saw him with.

"Give them our congratulations," she said.

"Ain't you staying?"

"No, I'm afraid we'll be heading out tomorrow morning," she said.

"You're staying for the wedding feast, ain't you?"

Nash looked him in the eye and asked, "Would you?"

The trapper lifted his chin and scratched his throat, considering. His eyes were on her now. She felt her face heat under his gaze.

"Reckon not." He leaned forward and, quick as a striking rattler, kissed Delia on the cheek.

Nash stepped forward. "I ought to shoot you."

"But you won't, partner, you won't." Meeker slapped Nash's cheek playfully, turned and howled like a wolf, then danced away.

Nash stood glaring after him. Her laughter brought his attention back to her. His angry scowl melted and a smile brightened his face.

"I still think I should shoot him."

"He slipped that one by," she said. Her face was suddenly serious. "Did he take the traps?"

"Yes." Her shoulders slumped with relief. "For ten percent less than they cost."

Her eyes followed Meeker's retreating back. "I changed my mind. Shoot him."

Now it was Thomas's turn to laugh.

"Well, wife, I bought you a wedding gift."

"You did?" She didn't think she could possibly feel better than she already did. Her mind raced with excitement and she clapped her hands together. "What is it?"

He walked to his pack, strung across his squeaky new saddle upon his new horse, and took out a bundle wrapped in indigo fabric. She accepted the package, carefully collecting the precious white ribbon with which the cloth was tied. She felt something hard within. Around and around she turned the gift to unwind the yardage. There was enough to make a fine dress at least. Finally the cloth came away and beneath it was white linen tied with pink ribbon and lace.

"Thomas!" Her voice was a combination of irritation and pleasure. He laughed.

"Open it!"

"I'm trying." She carefully rolled the white fabric up as it uncoiled. "Is there anything in here?"

He shrugged and smiled.

The fabric was gift enough, plus ribbon and lace. What a wondrous bounty! At last the inner gift emerged. She turned the fine leather binding over in her hands. Her breath caught as she opened to see page after page of blank white paper with gilded edges.

"A journal!" she cried.

She threw her arms over his shoulders, clutching the journal in one hand. He pulled away and offered her a narrow box. She unfastened the metal clasp and opened the lid.

"Oh, my!" she said.

"It's pens and ink, pencils, too," he said. "And scissors and a comb."

"Oh, thank you!"

He kissed her lips. Drawing away at last, he said, "Somehow, I don't think our adventures are over just yet."

* * * * *

ITCHIN' FOR SOME ROLLICKING ROMANCES SET ON THE AMERICAN FRONTIER? THEN TAKE A GANDER AT THESE TANTALIZING TALES FROM HARLEQUIN HISTORICALS

On sale September 2003

WINTER WOMAN by Jenna Kernan
(Colorado, 1835)

After braving the winter alone in the Rockies, a defiant woman is entrusted to the care of a gruff trapper!

THE MATCHMAKER by Lisa Plumley
(Arizona territory, 1882)

Will a confirmed bachelor be bitten by the love bug when he woos a young woman in order to flush out the mysterious Morrow Creek matchmaker?

On sale October 2003

WYOMING WILDCAT by Elizabeth Lane
(Wyoming, 1866)

A blizzard ignites hot-blooded passions between a white medicine woman and an amnesiac man, but an ominous secret looms on the horizon....

THE OTHER GROOM by Lisa Bingham
(Boston and New York, 1870)

When a penniless woman masquerades as the daughter of a powerful marquis, her intended groom risks it all to protect her from harm!

Visit us at www.eHarlequin.com

HARLEQUIN HISTORICALS®

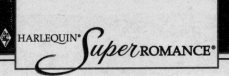

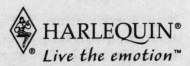

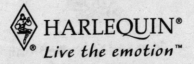